ANNA JACOBS is the author of fifty novels and is addicted to storytelling. She grew up in Lancashire, emigrated to Australia in the 1970s and writes stories set in both countries. She loves to return to England regularly to visit her family and soak up the history. She has two grown-up daughters and a grandson, and lives with her husband in a spacious waterfront home. Often as she writes, dolphins frolic outside the window of her study. Inside, the house is crammed with thousands of books.

www.annajacobs.com

By Anna Jacobs

Cherry Tree Lane
Elm Tree Road

a&b

Cherry Tree Lane

ANNA JACOBS

Allison & Busby Limited
12 Fitzroy Mews
London W1T 6DW
www.allisonandbusby.com

Hardback published in Great Britain in 2010.
This paperback edition published in 2011.

A CIP catalogue record for this book is available from
the British Library.

10 9 8 7 6 5

ISBN 978-0-7490-0907-6

Typeset in 10.5/14.5 pt Sabon by
Allison & Busby Ltd.

The paper used for this Allison & Busby publication
has been produced from trees that have been legally sourced
from well-managed and credibly certified forests.

Printed and bound in the UK by
CPI Group (UK) Ltd, Croydon, CR0 4YY

*This book is dedicated to
my wonderful friends:*

*Claire Boston
Leonie Knight
Lorraine Mauvais
Teena Raffa Mulligan
Susy Rogers*

Chapter One

Mattie Willitt started clearing away the pudding plates after tea, longing for the evening to end. Her stepfather was in a strange mood and when he was like that, she and her two half-sisters tried to keep away from him because it always meant trouble – always.

Bart jabbed one finger in her direction. 'Leave those for later. I've something to tell you.'

She put the dishes down and came back to the table, clasping her hands in her lap and waiting, her nerves on edge.

He leant back, thumbs hooked in his wide leather belt, enjoying keeping them all waiting. Just as she thought she could bear the suspense no longer, he leant forward.

'Our Mattie's getting married,' he announced.

All three of them goggled at him.

'First I've heard of it,' she said, trying to keep her voice steady.

'Because I've only just agreed to it. Stan Telfor's been on at me about it for weeks, though.'

'Stan Telfor!' The words were out before Mattie could stop herself. The man was a younger version of Bart, better looking but just as strong – and equally frightening, as far as a small woman like herself was concerned. She'd never marry a man like him. But she managed to bite back an angry refusal and say casually, 'Why would I want to marry him or anyone? I'm happy here looking after you three.' But she was only staying until her sisters were old enough to escape her stepfather's clutches. She'd promised herself that.

'You'll marry him because it suits me, and because for some reason he's got it into his head that he fancies you.' Bart studied her, head on one side. 'He thinks you're pretty. Me, I like women with more meat on their bones, and I'm not fond of foxy-coloured hair, neither. There's no accounting for taste.'

'I'm surprised you agreed to it.'

He grinned and rubbed his forefinger and thumb together. 'Money's a great persuader.'

'You sold me.' Anger seethed behind her quiet words. She hoped it didn't show.

'Aye. I've give you a home all these years, for your mother's sake, but you're no kin of mine.

About time I got some payment for it. Nell's old enough now to take over the housekeeping. It's a daughter's duty to look after her father. So me and Stan have arranged to have the first banns called next Sunday.'

She closed her eyes to hide the fury. Bart had not even considered whether she wanted to marry Stan, just seen a chance to make some money and taken it. He'd do anything for money, her stepfather would.

If she refused, he'd beat her senseless to force her to obey him. He'd done it once before when she fell in love and wanted to get married. She'd held out against him till he'd threatened to beat her sisters next and sent Renie, the littlest, flying across the room with one backhander. She'd known it was hopeless then.

He heaved himself to his feet. 'I'll go and tell Stan you've accepted him.' He chuckled, a wheezing, chesty sound, then spat into the fire.

Filthy devil! she thought. *I hate you, Bart Fuller.*

When he'd left for the pub, her other sister Nell asked in a whisper, as if afraid he might still overhear, 'You're not going to marry that Stan, are you?'

Mattie shook her head.

'What *are* you going to do?'

'I've not worked it out yet.' She hesitated. 'I

saw you talking to Cliff Greenhill today, Nell. You love him, don't you?'

Her stepsister looked at her warily then nodded.

'Has he asked you to marry him?'

Nell smiled, such a soft, happy smile that Mattie felt a pang of jealousy. 'Yes.'

'Your father won't let you.'

'I know. Me and Cliff have talked about that. He's got a good job at the railway works, been there since he was fifteen, did his apprenticeship as a carriage upholsterer. He doesn't want to leave. He's set for life if he stays.'

'If he stays, you can't marry him. Dad would beat him senseless if he tried, maybe cripple him.'

Nell flushed and said in a low voice, 'We have to marry. I'm expecting. It's just – we don't know how to manage it.'

'I'd guessed already about the baby. I've been waiting for you to tell me.'

'Cliff says we could have Renie to live with us after we're married, because he knows what Dad's like, but not both of you.'

Mattie stared at her thoughtfully. 'Did he really mean it?' She didn't need to ask why he didn't want her, because she knew. Soft-hearted Nell would let her take charge. Mattie wouldn't mean to, but she was the oldest, as much a mother as a sister, used to telling the others what to do.

And Cliff would want to be master in his own home, with his wife as mistress, a woman bound to do as he told her. Well, most men wanted that, didn't they?

Renie stared at them both, open-mouthed.

'You'll have to run away. You've no choice now because I'm leaving, and the sooner the better. Go and see Cliff tonight. Your father won't be back from the pub for an hour at least.' She rubbed her head, which was aching. 'I'm going upstairs. I'm tired today. You keep the fire going, Renie.'

As she got into bed, enjoying a rare moment or two of privacy in the room she shared with her sisters, Mattie thought again of the way her stepfather had sold her like a dumb beast. How much was she worth? Five pounds? Ten? Twenty even?

She didn't cry. She was a long way beyond tears now.

Could she do it? Dare she help her sisters to run away from him, then run away herself?

She had to, and do it carefully, whatever it took. She'd only get one chance of freedom, she was quite sure of that. So would they.

The next morning Mattie woke up with a heavy cold, one of the worst she'd ever had. It wasn't flu, mustn't be flu. Nothing must stop her getting away. When the others had gone to work she struggled to do the housework, but had to sit down for a rest. Later she went to the corner shop, where she helped out for a couple of hours in the middle of the day, but had to come home again and lie down because she was simply too dizzy to stand up.

She fell into a heavy sleep and didn't wake until the door banged as her stepfather got home from work. When he found nothing ready for tea, he yelled up the stairs for her. She tried to sit up but her head spun. She tried to answer him but only a croak came out.

He came pounding up the stairs, took one look at her and backed away, whipping out his handkerchief and pressing it to his nose.

'Got a cold,' she whispered. 'Feel dizzy.'

'Yer as white as them sheets. You'll have to sleep down in the front room or you'll be giving it to your sisters. Of all the stupid times to get sick! What's Stan going to say?'

'Sorry about . . . tea.'

'We'll buy some fish and chips.'

'Not . . . for me. I'm not hungry.'

He shrugged and went back downstairs. After a few moments, she got up and took some bedding downstairs to the front room, huddling on the sofa. He didn't offer to bring her a hot drink or light a fire in here, and she didn't ask, though she was shivering now and desperately thirsty. She huddled down, dreaming of escaping, of never seeing *him* again.

What sort of life was this? Her mother would have been horrified. Jane Willitt had married Bart because she was lonely. He'd been a fine figure of a man in those days before he'd run to fat. And give him his due, he'd treated her mother nicely when they were courting and first married, been fond of her in his own way. But it had been a big step down in the world for the widow of a schoolteacher, daughter of a clergyman, to marry a man like him, as they'd found out.

He'd deceived them about his prospects at the railway works in Swindon. No one was going to make Bart Fuller a foreman, because he was too aggressive, couldn't manage men, only bully them. That lack of success at work had soured him. As for his fancy wife, she'd given him only daughters, then up and died on him, leaving him to raise them with the help of a fourteen-year-old girl.

Mattie sighed and snuggled down, trying to get warm. What use was it to go over the past? It was the future which mattered now. Much as she loved her sisters, she wasn't going to tie herself to a man like Stan Telfor to keep the peace. And anyway, Nell needed to get away now as well.

No, it was definitely time to leave. The freedom she'd dreamt of for so long was close.

It was a relief when her sisters came home from work. Nell brought her a cup of tea while Renie got permission from her father to light a fire in the front room.

'How did you persuade him to let me have a fire?' Mattie whispered.

'Told him you might die of pneumonia if we didn't keep you warm, then he'd lose his money.'

'Have you seen Cliff?'

Nell nodded and moved closer, speaking in a low voice and keeping an eye on the door. 'We were going to leave on Friday, after he gets paid, but we'll have to put off our escape till next week. You're not fit to go anywhere.'

'No! We have to leave this week.' Mattie began coughing but when the bout was over she grasped Nell's arm. 'We'll talk after he's gone to the pub.'

It seemed at first as if her stepfather was going to stay in, because it was raining heavily. But after fidgeting round the kitchen for a while, he went to peer out of the back door, then came back and got his coat and hat. 'It's not raining so hard now. I'm off to wet my whistle. Don't let anyone in while I'm away.'

He said this every time he went out. Who did he think would want to come and visit his house? Mattie often wondered. He never invited anyone, or made neighbours welcome if they popped in, had no relatives he bothered with and preferred to spend most evenings in the bright warmth of the Fettler's Arms.

After he'd left, the three of them gathered in the front room and Mattie pulled herself into a sitting position, ignoring the way her head spun.

'You'll not be fit to go anywhere,' Nell said again.

'We have to do it this week. I don't want to go round to Stan's house after church on Sunday. You know what he'll expect.' Her stepfather had winked, as he made it plain that she was to 'be nice to' Stan.

No, whether she was better or not, she was leaving as planned. Stan Telfor wasn't going to have his way with her. They'd only get one chance to escape. She wasn't losing it.

Jacob Kemble knelt to plant some seedlings, a task he loved because you could think as you worked. He looked round in satisfaction. Turning the small farm his father had left him into a market garden had made all the difference and he wasn't short of a penny now, even though this bit of land would never make him rich.

What he was short of was . . . oh, he didn't know. Companionship was the nearest he could come to it, someone to work alongside him and raise his children, someone to talk to in the evenings. And a wife to look after his house. Even with the help of a woman from the village, he was making a poor fist of it, he knew.

But he wasn't going to make another marriage of convenience. Alice had been a decent soul, a hard-working wife, especially in the early years, because she too loved being out of doors. It hadn't been enough, though. She hadn't been a good companion for a thinking man, because she'd not been interested in anything beyond her home and family. In fact, she'd bored him, though he felt guilty every time he admitted that to himself.

He hadn't realised how much Alice had helped him around the place, though, until he had to manage without her. Images flashed through his mind as they did every time he thought of the accident. A horse had unseated its rider during a hunt a few fields away. He'd learnt later that the man had been whipping it and caught it in one eye. It had run away and leapt a hedge, crashing into their little cart and sending Alice flying like a rag doll.

They'd had to put the horse down, it'd been screaming in agony. His wife hadn't screamed. She'd died before he could even pull himself out of the wreckage and across to her. He'd broken his leg, which had left him with a permanent limp. It wasn't a bad limp, but it did slow him down a bit and ached sometimes if he overdid things.

As he stood up to ease his back, he saw Miss

Newington leaving the big house. She came to the gates, stood staring down the hill and when she saw him, waved and set off towards him.

He hurried across to the bucket to wash the worst of the dirt off his hands and dried them on his trousers for lack of a towel. Miss Newington was quite elderly, so couldn't walk fast, but she liked to get out and about and he always enjoyed a chat with her. He suspected that she was even lonelier than he was.

She waited for him to open the gate for her, then said in her abrupt way, 'I want to talk to you, Kemble.'

'Would you like to come inside and sit down, miss?'

'No. I'd rather sit on that bench of yours. They say there's rain on the way, so we don't want to waste this beautiful sunshine, do we?'

He waited till she'd sat down, then obeyed a wave of her hand and joined her on the bench.

'Now that Hillman's dead, I'm going to need someone to collect my rents from the village and oversee the small repairs. Are you interested in the job?'

He didn't hesitate. 'I certainly am.'

'Think you can handle it? They do try to get out of paying. And then there are the accounts to keep.'

'I'm good at figures, take after my mother

there, and I'll know who can pay and who can't.'

'The job's yours, then. Five per cent, you'll keep, like Hillman did. Come up to the house this evening and I'll pass on the paperwork.' She stared across his main field. 'Your crops look to be doing well.'

'They are, but they'll be better still for a drop of rain.' He looked up at the sky. No clouds yet, but he could sense the rain coming.

'My rheumatism tells me they'll get more than a drop.' She eased herself to her feet.

He didn't try to help her, because she was fiercely independent. She'd had to be to take over a run-down house at her age. No one had expected her to inherit. The estate had been sold off piece by piece by the last owner, who hadn't cared about it after his only child, the son and heir, had been killed in the Boer War.

Every house in the village had tied a black bow to their front door when that happened and kept their curtains drawn as a sign of respect. The landowner hadn't been seen for months after the funeral, then he'd emerged from his drinking bouts a changed man, bitter and uncaring about his tenants' welfare.

He'd not left the house to his nephew, a sharp man who lived in the next village, but to his niece, who had moved away with the rest of his youngest brother's family when she was in her teens. Her inheriting had surprised everyone. They'd been even more surprised when she didn't sell the place to her cousin, because everyone knew Arthur Newington had expected to inherit and was eager to set himself up at the hall.

You never knew what life would bring you, Jacob mused.

He and Alice had had such plans for improving this land and making it into a thriving market garden, selling quality produce at higher prices to the best greengrocers' shops in nearby towns. In that, at least, they'd been compatible. But he couldn't seem to think straight since the accident, had just carried on as best he could with the one field under cultivation and the others rented out for the grazing.

He really should take one of the fields back and put it to better use. But it was all he could do at the moment to tend this one and look after his children. His eyes lifted to the cherry trees that bordered the lane. They were just coming into bloom, the mass of pale-pink blossom so beautiful he looked forward to seeing it every spring.

He really must pull himself together now that he'd got the rent-collecting job. The money would make a big difference, allow him to put something by for the future, and hire better help in the house.

Collecting village rents was only part of the

work Hillman had done, because Miss Newington had a few properties in nearby Wootton Bassett. He wondered who was looking after them for her. A shrewd lady, Miss Newington, and well liked in the village, for all her outspoken ways.

It was willpower that got Mattie up and moving round the house on the Thursday morning, but she didn't go to work. She kept telling herself it was the third day of this cold and everyone knew you were past the worst after three days, so tomorrow she'd be all right to leave – she had to be.

That evening her stepfather plonked the housekeeping money down on the table, as usual, hesitated, then added another shiny florin. 'Here's two bob extra. Better get yourself a lemon and some honey. You need to be well for Stan on Sunday. We're not letting him down.'

'Thanks.' Mattie scooped up the money and put it in her purse.

The following morning Bart went off to work as usual when the hooter sounded at the Works. It was so loud they said you could hear it from ten miles away, and it sounded not only to start the day, but to end it, too. Most able-bodied men in Swindon and the nearby villages hurried off to the Railway Works on its command; most housewives planned their days around it.

Nell and Renie got ready for their jobs in the

local laundry, both looking slightly plumper than usual because they were wearing as many clothes as they could.

Nell came running back to give Mattie a final hug. 'Are you sure you'll be all right?'

'Of course I will.' But Mattie's voice rasped and she could feel the phlegm rattling in her chest as she fought the urge to cough. 'We've got no choice, you know that.'

'I'm going to miss you.'

Mattie saw tears welling in both her sisters' eyes. 'None of that! Do you want to make people guess something's up?' she demanded sharply. 'We'll see one another again.'

'We won't even know where you are, or you us,' Nell said, sniffing and wiping away a tear. 'And you're still not well. I don't know how you're going to manage.'

'Cliff can write to his family in a year or two. I'll find out where you are from them.' She reached out to hold on to the table.

'You're still dizzy,' Renie protested. 'How can you possibly manage on your own?'

'I'll manage because I have to. I want to get away as much as you do. More. This is my only chance to escape marrying Stan.' She not only feared her stepfather's violence, but the way he might use her sisters again to persuade her to do what he wanted.

She packed as much as she could in a bundle and dressed in some old clothes she'd been keeping to tear up for cleaning rags, covering her head with a shawl they used to run out to the backyard privy. Today she wanted to look old and poor. But her red hair showed clearly still, so she got out the flour and rubbed it into the front. That was better.

Pulling the shawl low over her forehead, she practised hobbling along with a stoop and thought she was doing quite well. But she didn't try to leave the town. Not yet. She knew she was taking a big risk, but she couldn't, she just couldn't leave till she'd made sure her sisters had got away safely.

As the fingers on the big station clock twitched their way towards nine o'clock, she stood across from the station, leaning against the wall in a little alley. She watched as Nell and Renie arrived, hurrying into the station by the side entrance. Nell had been going to pretend they had a dying relative and needed to visit her.

Where was Cliff, though?

The station clock ticked the minutes off and Mattie waited, getting more and more anxious. What were the others going to do if Cliff changed his mind at the last minute? They hadn't even got the money for fares, because their father took everything they earned.

With only three minutes to go till the train

left, Cliff came running down the street, carrying an old suitcase. She closed her eyes for a minute in shuddering relief and when she opened them, she saw him at the ticket window, pushing some money across. He ran towards the platform and out of her sight.

She waited in the alley till the train left in a cloud of steam and even then she had to go across and check that her sisters weren't still standing on the platform.

To her horror she met a neighbour coming out of the station, but the woman didn't seem to recognise her and simply walked past. Had she seen Renie and Nell?

Feeling faint with relief that they'd got away safely, Mattie turned and went across to the tram stop. She spent some of her precious coins to go to the end of the line, heading south-eastwards. Then she began walking towards Wootton Bassett, thinking of making her way to Bath eventually. She couldn't afford to spend any more on fares, not if she wanted to eat. She wasn't sure how she would earn a living, but surely something would turn up? She was a hard worker, and wouldn't mind what she did.

If only it would stop raining! She was soaked already and it was hard moving against the driving rain coming in from the west. She felt to be burning up with fever one minute and shivering with cold the next. Every now and then she was forced to stop and rest, because she felt so weak, but fear of what would happen if Bart caught her made her summon up the strength to trudge on.

As she was taking a rest on a stone by the side of the road, a man in a trap stopped to ask, 'Are you all right?'

'Just a bit tired, thank you, sir.'

'Are you going far?'

'Bath,' she said. 'To my brother's. But I've not got the money to go by train.'

'That's a long way to walk.'

She nodded.

'I can give you a ride for a few miles, if you want.'

Unable to believe her luck, for a minute she couldn't speak, then she gasped. 'Thank you. Oh, bless you for that, sir.'

'Hop up.'

The struggle to haul herself up left her breathless.

He eyed her pityingly. 'You're not well. You shouldn't be out in weather like this.'

'I don't have any choice. I'm really grateful for your help.'

It seemed only a few minutes before he set her down again, but she felt it was an omen, because it had moved her on more than she could possibly have managed on foot, even if she wasn't ill, which would surely put them off the scent if they came after her.

She was going to get away, just like her sisters, she told herself, her spirits lifting. She was going to do it. Why, even the rain had stopped. She looked up at the sky and her heart sank. More dark clouds were massing in the west. It'd not be fine for long.

She lost all sense of time, but later it started to pelt down and she stood under a tree for a while, shivering as she sheltered. But the rain had clearly set in and she couldn't stand here all day. She was still much too close to Swindon, so had to keep moving.

She was soaked to the skin and her shoes squelched as she walked, which made her smile grimly. If she died of pneumonia, she'd definitely get away from him.

After a while she found herself talking aloud and stopped in dismay, trying to pull herself together. But soon she found herself muttering again. 'Just a few more steps, just a few more steps.' It helped to walk to the rhythm of those words, so she gave up trying to keep quiet. There was no one to hear her because no one else was mad enough to be out in such a storm.

Time passed in a blur and she found herself sitting on a bench under a tree without the faintest idea of how long she'd been there, then resting in the lee of a wall overhung by a tall bush. Her clothes were dripping water, her bundle too.

She wasn't sure where she was when night started to fall. She seemed to have left the main road and taken a side road, but that was probably a good thing, because *he* wouldn't know where she'd turned off the main road, even if he traced her this far.

'Find a barn,' she muttered. 'Got to . . . find a barn. Got to . . . stop for the night.' Darkness had fallen now and she was shivering continuously, her hands and feet feeling like blocks of ice. She had some bread and cheese in her bundle. It'd be soggy, but you could still eat it if you were hungry, only she wasn't. She had the housekeeping money to buy more food with and water was free in any stream. She was managing. Just. But oh, she felt so weary and so cold.

Surely there should be houses nearby? She looked ahead for lights but saw none. She'd slowed right down now, could only stagger a few steps, stop, stagger on again.

Then, just as she was thinking she couldn't force herself to take one more step, she saw it – a light shining in the distance, slightly to the right, and a lane that turned in that direction. A few steps more and she could see what looked like the lights of a village down a lane to the left, but they were further away than the first light, so she headed for that.

A few steps, then stop. A few more steps. She stumbled and fell, lay for a minute or two with rain beating down on her in the darkness. Dragging herself up on her knees, she summoned up the strength to get to her feet and staggered on.

When she fell again, she couldn't get up or even find the breath to call for help. Darkness wrapped itself around her, sucking her down into a big hole.

I'm dying, she thought, and was too exhausted to care.

Chapter Two

Rain beat against the windows and pounded down on the roof. Jacob sighed and looked at the clock. Half past eight. Time seemed to be dragging tonight. He tossed another lump of wood on the dying fire and picked up his book. But he was so tired he couldn't settle to it, though normally he relished a good read in this last half-hour of the day. His little lass was asleep, but his son wasn't home yet.

Luke had been to the Friday night choir practice at the village church and should have been back an hour ago. He couldn't come to much harm when he left the other lads, because he only had to walk up the hill from the village, then along their lane, so the practice must have gone on for longer than usual. A boy his age shouldn't have been out so late on a stormy night like this, but Mr Henty didn't think of other people when it came to his beloved church choir.

As another squall made the window panes rattle and an icy draft whistle under the door, Jacob scowled round at the big room that was both kitchen and living area. Oh, it was tidy, he made sure of that, however tired he was. But it wasn't home-like any more. Mrs Grey from the village hadn't been able to come in and clean for the past week, because her husband was ill. Little Sarah had done her best to help him in the house, but there was only so much an eight-year-old child could manage and it was the busy time of year for him in the gardens.

The evenings could be very quiet after the kids went to bed. Recently one of his friends in the village had told him he should look around for another wife to be a mother to the children and look after his house, but Jacob had told him to mind his own damned business and that had been the end of that. If he ever married again, it'd be because he loved the woman and wanted to spend his life with her. His mother and father had been like that, loving and kind to one another. They'd had him late in life and he'd lost them before he was twenty, his mother simply fading away after his father died.

He'd spoken a bit sharply to his friend, maybe,

but Ben hadn't taken offence and most likely wouldn't mention the matter again.

Jacob had been more than a bit sharp with the new curate, too, who had said the same thing to him last Sunday for the third time, probably at his wife's urging. Mrs Henty liked to poke her nose in everyone's affairs, but it was Ernest Henty's job to see to the welfare of his flock. The suggestion that Jacob marry Essie Jupe from the village had been the final straw, though. She'd lost her husband six months ago and desperately needed a father for her three unruly sons, but it wasn't going to be Jacob. He'd been at school with Essie, hadn't liked her then and she'd not got any kinder over the years. He wasn't having a shrew like her bringing up Luke and Sarah.

The door burst open and Luke nearly fell into the room. 'Dad! Dad! Come quick! There's a dead body in our lane!'

'What?' Jacob went to grasp his ten-year-old son's shoulders and look him in the eye. 'If you're making this up—'

Luke gulped for breath. 'I'm not! When I was running up the lane, I fell over something. I thought it was a pile of old rags, but it wasn't! It was a body, a woman's body. Dead! In our lane!' He spoke with some relish.

'You're sure?' Luke had a vivid imagination, which often got him into trouble.

'Dad, there is a body!'

Sighing at the thought of going out into such a wild storm, Jacob reached for his oilskin jacket, which was hanging on the wooden pegs near the back door. He lit the old lantern, clicking his tongue in exasperation at the cracked glass panel he'd been meaning to replace for some time, then led the way outside. 'Show me!'

Luke splashed through puddles beside him, seeming oblivious to the cold and rain. He was still talking excitedly, but the sense of his words was snatched away by the howling wind. Within seconds Jacob was shivering, but he hunched his shoulders and carried on. You couldn't leave a body lying there. If it *was* a body.

'Here, Dad.'

Jacob held the lantern up and blinked away raindrops from his eyes. To him, too, it looked like a bundle of wet rags. There was a smaller bundle beside it. Together father and son bent over, but as Jacob tried to check whether the woman was indeed dead, the wind at last succeeded in blowing out the lantern. Muttering in annoyance, he felt for her face, touching damp flesh. She didn't move or respond to him in any way, but it seemed to him there was still some warmth in the cheeks, and when he felt carefully, he could feel a faint pulse in her throat.

Thrusting the useless lamp into his son's hands,

he bent to pick up the body and felt a shiver rack her. Definitely alive, then. But whether she'd stay alive was anyone's guess. How long had she been lying here unconscious? 'You bring that bundle, Luke. It must belong to her.'

By the time they reached the house, Jacob had lost his cap, was as wet as his burden and almost as cold. He kicked the rag rug away from the floor in front of the big kitchen range and set the body in its sodden clothes down gently on the stone-paved floor, gesturing to his son. 'What are you standin' gawpin' for, Luke? Shut that door quick, then light the other lamp!'

He had to smooth the tangle of hair back from the woman's face before he could see what she looked like. The intimacy of this action made him feel strangely tender towards her. He unwound the shawl from her head and shoulders. It was so wet it made a flopping sound as he dropped it on the floor. What was a woman doing out on her own on a night like this? She was a stranger in the district, to add to the mystery. He knew everyone in the village of Shallerton Bassett, because he'd lived there all his life, knew their relatives too.

As he sat back on his heels, wondering what to do next, a sigh escaped the blue-tinged lips.

'She's alive.' Luke's voice was flat with disappointment.

Jacob would have smiled if the matter hadn't

been so serious. To a lad of that age, finding a dead body was much more exciting than finding a live one, something to boast about to one's friends. 'I wonder who she is. Never seen her before.'

Another sigh, then the young woman's teeth began to chatter and she moved her head from side to side with a moan.

'We'd better get her out of them wet clothes. Go an' throw down a towel, Luke, then pull the blankets off my bed and throw them down the stairs. Change out of those wet things into your pyjamas and don't come down till I call. This poor creature won't want a lad of your age gawpin' at her.'

She wouldn't want a strange man gawping at her, either, but Jacob had no choice. He had to get her out of the sodden garments if he was to save her life. They were beginning to steam gently at the side nearer the fire and were so wet, tiny runnels of moisture were still escaping from them.

When he began to investigate the mysteries of her clothing, he found she was wearing several layers. To keep her dry? Well, they hadn't succeeded, had they? Or perhaps they were all she owned.

As his work-roughened fingers fumbled with the tiny buttons of her final blouse, he couldn't help noticing that she had a trim, gently curved body. He turned her over and paused, frowning. The white skin of her back was marred by some old scars. He'd seen the like before on the back of a lad he'd played with many years ago, scars left by a belt buckle. Someone must have given her a vicious leathering when she was younger, poor thing, to mark her like that.

Within minutes he had her dried and wrapped in a blanket. Holding her body in his arms again, he kicked the rug back into position close to the fire and laid her gently down on it. The only thing he could do now was keep her warm and hope she survived the night.

'Who is she, Dad? Luke says he found her lyin' in the lane.'

He swung round to see Sarah standing in the doorway, in nightdress and bare feet, long blonde hair streaming over her shoulders. 'We don't know. She's a stranger.'

'She's caught a chill, poor thing. Look at her shiver!'

'And you'll catch a chill if you don't put something else on. Just a minute.' The pitiful state of the stranger and his own embarrassment at her nudity forced Jacob to a momentous decision. 'Go up and put a shawl round yourself, then . . .' he had to take a deep breath to nerve himself to utter the next words '. . . fetch me one of your mum's nightdresses from the bottom drawer in my bedroom.'

Sarah stared at him open-mouthed and he

knew why. No one except himself had been allowed to touch Alice's things since she died. He still remembered how Poll Titcombe had come and asked him what he was going to do with Alice's clothes. The day after he buried his wife! He'd been still on crutches from the accident. He'd slammed the door on his neighbour and then cried like a baby, leaning his head against the wall. He pushed that memory away.

'While you're upstairs, Sarah, tell our Luke to get himself off to bed. There's nothing more he can do down here.'

Within two minutes, Sarah was back, proffering the faded nightdress. 'It smells of mothballs.' She wrinkled her nose in disgust.

'This poor soul's in no state to worry about how it smells.' Jacob forced himself to ignore the memories the nightdress roused. It was only a piece of flannel, that was all, he told himself firmly. And Alice would be the last to begrudge the loan of it to someone in such dire need. 'Right then, Sarah. I'll hold her up an' you slip the nightdress over her head.'

Eyes screwed up with concentration, breathing deeply, Sarah managed the difficult feat of dressing a grown woman who was as helpless as the Titcombes' new baby. As they laid the sick woman down again, she moaned, as if in pain, then jerked her head from side to side.

'Mustn't let him catch me,' she said in a hoarse voice.

That explained why she was trudging across the countryside on such a stormy night dressed in several layers of clothes, in spite of being ill. Who was she running away from? Jacob wondered. A husband? He glanced quickly down at her left hand. No sign of a wedding ring, nor was the skin on that finger marked to show a ring had ever been there.

She groaned again and muttered, 'Mustn't stop . . . walking. Mustn't . . . stop!'

He guessed she'd forced herself on till she dropped and had likely come from Swindon way, a tiring journey on foot in a storm like that.

'Dad! Dad!'

He realised Sarah was shaking him.

'You need to get out of your wet clothes, too.'

'I never catch cold.'

'Me an' Luke have to change when we get wet. An' you'll need these clothes dryin' out for tomorrow.'

'All right, then, my little love.' He hugged his daughter. 'I'll nip upstairs and change into my old things. You keep an eye on her. I won't be long.'

Sarah sat and stared at the stranger. Mum's nightdress was far too big for her, and now that her hair was drying out, you could see it was a lightish red in colour, not brown.

When Jacob came down again and knelt to check the stranger, she opened her eyes and stared round in panic, trying to raise herself and failing. 'Who are you? Where am I?'

'My son found you lyin' in the lane unconscious, so I carried you back to our house.'

The stranger searched his face and something she saw there seemed to reassure her. 'Thank you!'

A cough racked her, going on and on. He held her upright until she'd stopped spluttering, but he could still hear the rattling in her chest.

'Can't . . . breathe properly.'

'I reckon you've got a touch of lung congestion. You'll feel better if you stay warm.' He remembered how worried she'd been so added, 'And don't worry, we'll keep you safe.'

'Safe?'

Her eyes lingered for a moment on Sarah's face, then she looked at Jacob, stretching out one hand to touch him, as if to reassure herself he really was there. He took hold of the hand, warming the slender fingers between his own.

'You won't tell anyone . . . I'm here?'

She looked so desperate he said, 'I promise I won't.'

'Thank you.' Another sigh and her eyes closed. But her breath was still rasping and rattling, and he was afraid she had more than a bad chill. If he wasn't mistaken, she'd got the dreaded pneumonia that killed so many people, rich and poor alike, because there was nothing anyone, even doctors, could do to make it better.

Sarah spoke in a whisper.

'She's asleep again, Dad. And she didn't tell us her name.'

'We can ask her in the morning. It won't have changed by then.' He looked round. 'I'm going to light a fire in the parlour. She can lie on the sofa there. It's as good as a bed and there are fewer draughts in there. Fetch my winter sheets, love. The flannel will be warmer than cotton. Quick as you can.'

When the stranger was settled, he sent Sarah back to bed but stayed up to keep an eye on the sick woman. And it was a good thing he had done. He spent the night alternately pulling the blankets off as she grew hot and feverish, then piling them back on when she began to shiver.

Morning took him by surprise. He looked out of the window and saw the nearby fields clearly in the misty grey light. It was still raining, but more gently now. The force had gone out of the storm.

There were sounds from upstairs and a short time later the two children peered into the room.

'Is she still alive?' Luke asked.

'Yes, but she's not well. I fear she's got pneumonia.'

'Like old Mr Benness?'

'Yes.'

'He died.'

'She's much younger. She's got a better chance.' Jacob looked at the clock and yawned. His eyes felt gritty from lack of sleep, but the work on his market garden waited for no man. 'You keep an eye on her while I feed the hens.' He sold eggs to a couple of the neighbours, or swapped them for things, and they made good quick meals for his children, though he had fewer hens these days than when he'd had Alice to look after them.

'Shall I go and fetch Mrs Henty?' Luke asked. 'She helps sometimes when folk are sick.'

Jacob had a quick think. It would be good to have a woman's help, but the curate's wife was an inveterate gossip and if she came here, the whole village would soon know about the stranger. 'No. I promised this woman I'd not tell anyone she was here and you mustn't, either.'

Luke's face crumpled in disappointment. 'Aw, Dad.'

'If I hear that you've said a word about her to anyone – anyone at all, even a hint – you'll be in serious trouble, my lad. Give me your word as a Kemble that you'll keep quiet about her.'

Both children promised and he felt reasonably certain they'd keep the information to themselves. They were good children, the best.

Bart went home from a hard day's work, cold and wet from his walk, to find the house dark and cold. No fire was burning in the grate, the dirty breakfast plates were still on the table and there was no sign of the three girls.

'What the hell—?' He stood in the kitchen, amazed and outraged, then clumped upstairs, his heavy work boots making dull thuds on the wooden steps. He didn't believe in stair runners. Carpet stopped you knowing if someone was going up or down.

The back bedroom was empty. He looked round carefully. The top drawer was slightly open. He flung it open and frowned to see it only half full of clothes. He tugged the others open, pulling the last one right out and hurling it across the room, scattering its contents. Usually these drawers were full to bursting, because he checked them every now and then. He liked to keep his eye on everything that went on in his own house, every single thing.

Where were the girls? Anger still burning through him, he sat on the bed, thumping it with his fist, trying to work out what was happening. He scowled at the upturned drawer and kicked it across the room as a dreadful suspicion crept into his mind.

Could they have run away?

Why would they do that? He gave them a good

home, didn't he? This was one of the railway houses, well built and maintained.

But they'd never been late home before, not all three of them, and some of their clothes were missing. What else could they be doing but running away?

Then he realised why. It was Mattie's doing. She didn't want to marry Stan, the ungrateful bitch, and she'd have persuaded the others to leave with her. They were too soft, his two, always did as she said. Well, he wasn't having it. He damned well wasn't!

Where could they have gone? And how had they got the money to run away?

On that thought he heaved himself to his feet and clattered back down the stairs, reaching up for the money pot, which always stood on the mantelpiece. Empty. He'd half-expected that, but still sucked in his breath in shock. Letting out a growl of anger, he threw the pot across the room to smash against the far wall.

He began to pace up and down, wondering what to do, but his stomach rumbled. First things first. He opened the bread crock to find only half a loaf. Pulling it out, he thumped it down on the table, cut a slice and slathered on some butter and jam. He took great snapping bites, because he was always ravenous when he got home from work. This would hold him for a while, then he'd go out for some fish and chips.

It was hard going at the Railway Works. He was a strong man still, though he wasn't as young or strong as he had been, which was why he was saving hard for his old age, as any man of sense would. He needed those girls and the wages they brought in to keep him in comfort when the company sacked him, or offered him low-paid work, as they always did. He'd seen it happen to other men once their strength failed and had no doubt the same fate was in store for him.

The girls were not going to cheat him out of that security. It was a child's duty to look after its parents. Other folk might be stupid enough to let their girls go off and marry, but he wasn't. He was going to keep his two at home, and with the money he'd saved, nicely added to by what Stan was going to pay him for marrying his stepdaughter, he'd manage all right. He had planned it all out years ago.

'Damn you, Mattie Willitt!' he muttered. 'I'll be glad to be rid of you. Stan's damned well welcome to you.'

He saw the shards of broken crockery from the money pot and frowned. They couldn't have gone far on the housekeeping money. There wasn't enough for train fares for the three of them, or only to go a stop or two down the line. So how did they think they'd get away from him?

He'd find them, whatever it took. No woman had ever got the better of him and no one ever would.

On the Saturday Jacob kept the children at home, even though the weather had cleared up. He didn't want them to have any opportunity to mention the stranger, not till he'd heard the full story.

She was very ill, alternating between sleeping and tossing around muttering incoherently, poor woman. He kept her in a half-sitting position to make breathing easier but the coughing kept waking her up before she'd been asleep for too long.

From time to time he left Sarah to keep an eye on her while he nipped outside to do odd jobs.

In the afternoon, since the weather had cleared a little, he set Luke, who hated to be penned up indoors, to cleaning out the henhouse. They had only six layers at the moment, but the henhouse was a sturdy construction and could house more, if Jacob could only find more time in the day to care for them.

He passed another disturbed night on an armchair in the front room and it seemed to him that the woman he'd rescued was getting worse. How sad if she died without them even finding out her name. As it was a Sunday, the whole family should be going to the morning service at the little village church. Luke had to go anyway because he sang in the choir, but Jacob couldn't leave the stranger. He decided to keep Sarah at home, pretending she wasn't well as an excuse for his own lack of attendance, and made sure Luke knew what to say if anyone asked.

He wondered how long they'd be able to keep her presence a secret. His home was just outside the village, had been a keeper's cottage on the big estate once. His father had bought it and the few nearby fields, using up his life savings to achieve his greatest ambition of owning his own land.

The stranger stirred and Jacob abandoned his thoughts to make sure she was all right and persuade her to drink some water.

He wondered what Miss Newington would say if she knew about his unexpected guest. She was his father's generation and would perhaps be shocked at a man caring for a grown woman who was not a relative.

No, it was Mrs Henty he had to fear. She'd kick up a right old fuss if she knew and try to send the stranger to the poorhouse instead. He'd not send a dog there.

Miss Newington would see he'd had no choice. He rather liked the old lady, but he could also see that she hadn't really settled down here. Folk said she was rich, but she didn't live or dress rich. She didn't go out much either, though she did attend the village church most weeks. Sometimes she talked wistfully of her old friends and Whitley Bay, where she'd lived by the sea.

Money didn't make you happy. Was anyone truly content with their life? He wasn't. The stranger was running away from someone.

Ah, he was being stupid. He had a lot to be thankful for. A lot.

Emily Newington waited until the maid had closed the door, then gestured to the chair on the opposite side of the hearth. 'Do sit down, Mr Parker.'

Her lawyer took the seat opposite, clearing his throat and tugging at his tie. 'Mr Arthur Newington has asked me to tell you that he would be happy to buy the house and miscellaneous properties from you.'

She nodded. It wasn't the first time Arthur had made this offer but she didn't want to do this to the people in the village, who were decent sorts on the whole. Her cousin had a reputation as a poor landlord who rarely repaired his properties. If she sold she could move back to Whitley Bay, where she had friends still.

But the will had said she must live here for ten years as a condition of inheritance and during that time she could only sell to her cousin Arthur. She wasn't stupid enough to turn down a bequest like this, so she'd come to live here. She sighed. She missed the sea, missed her friends too.

'What is my cousin offering this time?'

Mr Parker named a figure which made her frown, only slightly higher than the previous offer. She'd made careful enquiries and had a fair idea of the worth of her various properties. The offer was only two-thirds of that. 'I've told him before that I'd never accept such a low offer. I'll stay here for the whole ten years if I have to and leave everything to . . .' Her voice trailed away and she thought furiously because she had no other relatives. 'I'll leave it to charity.'

'Your cousin was very firm in his refusal to increase his price, I'm afraid. And surely, if you're not happy living here, it might be for the best? It's still a handsome sum. You could live on it in comfort.'

'I shan't sell so cheaply, so we'll let the matter drop.'

'I would advise you to accept. It's a generous offer, given the circumstances.'

'Whose side are you on?'

He avoided her eyes. 'I'm on both your sides, of course.'

'I think not. It seems to me you're on my cousin's side.' She saw a dull flush stain his cheeks and knew what she'd suspected was right. 'I shall dispense with your services. I'll go into Swindon this very day and find myself a new lawyer. Please hold yourself ready to send him all the necessary papers.'

'My dear Miss Newington, I must protest. I've only been advising you for your own good and—'

She stood up. 'Goodbye, Mr Parker. Please send me the bill for your services. I'll see that it's settled promptly – as long as it's a fair one.'

She rang the bell. 'Please show Mr Parker out, Agnes.'

She went to the window to watch him go and was surprised at how long it took him to get out of the house so went out into the hall to investigate. He was still standing just outside the front door, talking to her housemaid, Agnes. They were both whispering and then she saw him slip some coins into Agnes's outstretched hand.

Without hesitation, she walked out into the hall and flung back the front door. They turned towards her, guilt on both their faces.

'I was . . . um . . . just asking Agnes how her father is,' Mr Parker said. With a nod, he went down the steps and tossed a coin to the elderly groom, who had been tending his horse and trap.

Horace tucked the coin in his pocket and picked up the bucket, tipping the water over the flower bed and walking stiffly back to the stables.

Emily stared at the maid. 'Come into my sitting room, Agnes.' She went to stand in front of the fireplace.

'Tell me what Mr Parker really wanted with you.'

Agnes's face went pale. 'Like he said, miss, he was asking after my father.'

'We both know that's not true.'

'It is, miss.'

'Mr Parker is a pompous ass and would never stop to gossip with a maid. What was he saying and why did he give you those coins?'

Agnes burst into tears.

'He's been paying you for information about me, hasn't he?'

Agnes sobbed even more loudly.

'I think you'd better find yourself other employment since you clearly bear no loyalty towards me. Pack your things and leave at once. Horace will drive you to wherever you need to go. I shall pay you until today.'

Emily refused to change her mind and watched with feigned calmness as the weeping maid went up to pack her things. She couldn't stand disloyalty.

When she went to inform Cook about Agnes leaving, the woman hesitated, then said, 'Her father works for Mr Arthur. But it's not right to tell folk about what goes on here.'

'Can you manage with just Lyddie for a while? I shan't expect you to do anything more than you do now and I'll find help with the heavy scrubbing.'

'Yes, miss.' Cook smiled. 'You're not a big eater

and you don't expect miracles. I'm happy to stay. And you won't find me passing on information, I promise you.'

'Thank you. I appreciate that.'

'Lyddie's all right, too. She comes from the village. She's one of us.'

Emily walked out, satisfied. Cook was getting on in years but was good at her job and not wasteful. She saw no reason to overwork servants or make their lives miserable, and had closed down a lot of the rooms because one woman didn't need all this space.

She went out to ask Horace to harness up their one elderly horse to the equally old dog cart. She then drove Agnes into Wootton Bassett herself, left her at the railway station, took the horse and cart to the livery stable and caught the next train into Swindon.

There she went to visit a new lawyer who had opened up rooms a year or so ago. She'd passed them last time she was in town. She was hoping desperately that he might have some ideas about what she could do with her house, how she could get back home. She had just turned seventy and didn't want to spend the few years she had left in Shallerton Bassett, however pretty the countryside.

Chapter Three

Bart didn't go to the pub on Friday evening, was still trying to come to terms with what had happened. The house felt empty without the girls, and he hadn't enjoyed the fish and chips half as much as Mattie's cooking. Too greasy. Gave you indigestion. He fumbled through the cupboard for the bicarbonate of soda, but it didn't help him much.

He slept badly, kept waking, thinking he heard the front door. But it was only the wind, which was hurling rain at the windows. Damned weather. Nothing spring-like about it today.

On the Saturday morning, Bart went to work without his usual box of sandwiches. He felt outraged that he'd have to send the lad out for something to eat. Waste of money, that was, but he'd run out of bread. He'd have to buy a loaf on his way home, and there wasn't much butter left, either. He wasn't used to managing on his own, doing women's work.

In the afternoon, once his half day had ended, he called in at the laundry to pick up his daughters' wages, only to find they'd taken this week's money early, pleading a dying relative they needed to visit.

'They weren't in this morning,' the manager said. 'I'll have to fine them for that. I presume they'll be back on Monday.'

'I'm . . . er . . . not sure. Their old aunt is very ill and she's got money to leave them. We can't afford to upset her.'

'Then I'd better strike them from the rosters this coming week.'

'Yes. Yes, that'd be best. I'll let you know when they're back.'

Still furious, Bart went round to the shop, only to find that Mattie had no wages owing, either. He made the same excuse about an old auntie to cover the coming week and, he hoped, keep the job safe. He softened up the man by doing his own shopping there, seething with resentment at having to pay out more money when he'd already given the housekeeping money to Mattie.

If he went on at this rate, he'd not have enough left for his week's ale money and would have to dip into his savings. He hated to do that.

He dumped the shopping on the kitchen table, surprised at how untidy everything was. He wasn't used to living in a mess.

But he didn't have time to stop and deal with that now. He gobbled down some bread and ham, then went out again.

As he walked along the street, he bumped into one of their neighbours.

'I saw your girls at the station yesterday,' she said. 'Where were they going?'

He stopped dead. 'You saw the three of them?'

'No. Only Nell and Renie. Yesterday morning.' Her face was full of curiosity. 'Didn't you know they were leaving?'

'Not till I got home from work. Sudden bad news. Old auntie ill. Which train did they catch?'

She frowned. 'Was it the nine o'clock or was it the next one? No, it was the nine o'clock. They nearly missed it, anyway. The young man who went with them came racing down the street at the last minute.'

'Young man? Which young man?'

'Don't know his name. You'll know him by sight. He's at the Works – does upholstery, I think. Nice-looking young fellow.'

No stopping her gossiping, he thought, but what did he care about that? The only thing he cared about was getting his girls back. The first thing was to find out about this fellow.

At the railway station he found out who had been on duty on Friday and was relieved to find it was the brother of a fellow he knew slightly at work. He went round to the man's house to ask if he'd seen three lasses catch a train on Friday morning.

'No, not three. There were two hanging around the station. I remember them clearly because they looked so anxious. Pretty pair, they were, dark-haired, tall. A man came rushing in at the last minute and bought three tickets, then they all ran for the train. He had a suitcase. They didn't have any luggage.'

'Where did the train go to?'

'Bristol. But they only booked as far as Wootton Bassett.'

'Did you recognise the man?'

He frowned for a moment, then shook his head. 'I've seen him before. He's at the Works but I don't know which section he's in.'

'Thanks.' Bart walked slowly home, trying to work out what the hell was going on. He'd ask around, find out if any of the upholsterers were missing. He hated that lot, thinking they were better than men like him, dressing fancy, not getting their damned hands dirty. If Nell had taken up with one of them, he'd make the bugger regret it.

But where had Mattie gone if she hadn't been with the others? You'd have thought the three of them would have stuck together. They usually did.

Where the hell *could* she have gone? She didn't have any relatives that he knew of and her closest friends were her sisters.

He'd find her and marry her off to Stan, and do it in the registry office, pay whatever was needed to marry the next day, like someone at work had done. He wasn't taking her back into his house, that was sure. But he still intended to get his money for her from Stan. He was owed. He'd taken her in, hadn't he?

Well, Wootton Bassett wasn't that far away. He'd go and find out where they'd got to and by hell, he'd bring Nell and Renie back.

At the pub Bart bought himself a pint and waited for his friend to join him. Stan was half an hour late, by which time Bart was finishing his second beer. He waved the empty glass to show he wanted another and pointed to the seat next to his, which he'd kept in the face of several attempts to commandeer it.

'Get that down you, lad.' Stan dumped a foaming pint in front of Bart, sat down and took a long pull of his own beer. 'How's your Mattie? Is that cold of hers better yet?'

Bart hesitated, but it had to be done. 'When I

got home today, I found she'd run off.'

Stan blinked as this sank in. 'What do you mean, run off?'

'What do you think I bloody well mean? She's run away. They all have, all three of 'em.'

'But . . . Mattie and me are going to be wed. They're calling the banns on Sunday.'

'Yes. You'll have to stop 'em.'

'Where has she gone?'

'Don't know. But she didn't go with the others. I'm telling everyone there's an old auntie sick. I'm going to find my two and bring 'em back. You can go after Mattie and wed her like we agreed. Better do it quick at the registry office.' He explained what he'd discovered so far.

'If she didn't catch the train to Wootton Bassett, where did she go?'

Bart shook his head, then a thought came to him. 'She was allus going on about Bath, had a book about it, used to look at pictures of buildings. Maybe she's gone there.'

Stan looked at him sharply. 'But she was going to get wed. Why would she do that?'

Bart moved uneasily. 'Mebbe I didn't tell her as tactful as I should have.'

'What did you say to her?'

'I just . . . told her she was going to wed you.'

'You damn fool. Didn't I tell you to say I cared about her, wanted to wed her?'

'I'm not good with words. Anyway, she's allus done as she was told before.'

'I've got to find her and put things right.' Stan drained his beer. 'Bath, you said?'

Bart nodded.

'We'll try there, then.'

'She'd not have the money to get there by train. She must have set off walking. Maybe she was following the others. They went to Wootton Bassett. I'm going there tomorrow to find my girls.'

That made Stan stop and think. 'I'll go there with you. They must have some idea where she was going.'

Bart smiled. 'Yes, someone will have seen them and then we'll ask them about Mattie.'

Of course, his girls might not be there. But it didn't matter how far Nell and Renie went, or how often they changed trains, they'd not escape him. He'd find them in the end.

The other one could go to hell, for all he cared, but it might be useful to have Stan with him, in case he had to force them to come home.

The curate's wife noticed that Jacob Kemble and his daughter weren't at the service on Sunday morning so stopped Luke as he was walking down the side of the church after changing out of his choir smock. 'Is your father not well? It's not like him to miss church.'

'He's . . . er . . . looking after Sarah. She's not feeling well.'

Frowning, Jane watched him go. Luke had such a fresh open face, you could tell in a minute when he was lying. He had squirmed uneasily today, avoiding her eyes. He hadn't stayed to chat to the other boys from the choir, either, but had run off through the village.

His clothes were looking as uncared for as ever, washed but never ironed, and his hair was chopped off roughly, as if someone had taken the shears to it. Such a pity his father was being obstinate! A man simply couldn't manage on his own. Jacob Kemble needed a wife. And if the rumours were right and Miss Newington was about to sell the cottages in the village, then Jacob's rent-collecting job would vanish and he'd be in even more trouble. She hadn't been living here long, but Jane had made it her business to find out all about the villagers, every detail of their lives. It was her job to help her husband keep an eye on them.

She didn't wait for Ernest, who was talking to some of the parishioners. She hadn't been able to break him of the habit of gossiping with the poorer folk. As she walked slowly back to their house behind the church, she looked at it thoughtfully. It wasn't a large house though comfortable enough. Jacob Kemble wouldn't be the only one in trouble if the estate was sold. Miss Newington owned the house and let the curate have it for a very low rent, as the previous owners had done.

Would a new owner be as kind? Curates' stipends were not generous.

You couldn't rely on anything. People cared more about money these days than about doing their duty and living decent lives. She blamed the Boer War for that. Men from the village had gone away and come back changed, dissatisfied with life. They didn't know their place any more.

Jacob Kemble, who now collected her rent every week, never had known his place. She didn't like such independence in the lower classes and mistrusted men who read as widely as he did. The other villagers treated him as if he was someone special, but she couldn't see why. She'd been saying to Miss Newington only the other day how badly he needed a wife, and the landowner had agreed.

Why hadn't he followed her advice and found himself another wife? Those children needed a mother. She'd have another word with Miss Newington about him.

Jacob stood beside the sick woman, very worried. Should he be seeking help? Perhaps call in Mrs Henty? No, the curate's wife would never keep the news of the stranger's presence to herself, and he'd promised to keep the poor lass safe from whoever she was afraid of.

Her cheeks were hectic with fever and the startlingly blue eyes were one minute hidden, the next staring round without really seeing anything. Sweat was pouring off her. He wiped her face gently. In a few minutes, she'd be shivering, poor soul.

For the rest of Sunday and the whole of Monday, fever burnt through the stranger's body. Jacob sponged her again and again, feeling embarrassed about seeing her helpless body. But it was the only way to cool her down. He tried to get her to drink but couldn't get much down her and slowly began to despair of saving her life.

He did only the necessary work outside and wondered several times about calling in the doctor, because he was pretty sure she had pneumonia. But what could a doctor do about that? Nothing. Not even for a rich man. Besides, Dr Blair didn't like coming out to visit patients at weekends. He'd only tell Jacob to keep the sick person propped up, as he'd told Mr Benness's family last year, and try to get her to drink as much water as possible. Jacob was doing that already.

He kept seeing those scars on her back as he sponged her down and that only strengthened his resolve to keep her hidden. He wasn't going to hand her over to someone who beat people like that.

During the next forty-eight hours, her fate

would be resolved one way or another. It was in God's hands now.

And Jacob's.

Sunday morning saw a bleary-eyed Bart waiting at the station. Stan arrived at the last minute, having gone to church to hear the banns read first.

'I don't know why you still wanted them banns read today,' Bart grumbled.

'Because we'll get her back and then she's going to wed me. I'll ask her properly this time and persuade her that I'll look after her, make her happy.'

Bart looked at him sourly. Stan didn't seem at all affected by their heavy night's drinking, and looked fit and well. Bart felt like death warmed up. The train was on time but jolting along the track jarred his head and made him feel even angrier at his stepdaughter. He wouldn't have had to waste time and money like this if Mattie hadn't run mad.

'I think you should belt the living daylights out of Mattie when we find her,' he said to Stan. 'Start as you mean to go on.'

'I don't believe in beating women. They can't fight back. Besides, she must have had some reason to run off other than the marriage. She could always have said no to me, couldn't she? What did you do to her?'

'Me? I did nothing.'

They got out and stood there until the train had chugged slowly off into the distance. As they looked round, Bart saw the man at the ticket window start to slide down the wooden panel. 'Hoy!' He hurried across and put his hand out to stop him.

'There isn't another train for two hours,' the clerk said. 'I usually take my lunch early today, so look sharp. Where do you need tickets to?'

'We've already got returns to Swindon. What we need is some information.' Bart tried to speak calmly, to hide his anger, but it must have shown anyway, because he saw a wary look come into the clerk's eyes. 'We're looking for my daughters. They came through here on Friday morning with a young man. Two of them, tall with dark hair, pretty.'

The man smirked. 'Run away, have they?'

Bart thumped his fist down on the surface. 'None of your business.'

He stopped smirking. 'What did the man look like?'

'I don't know.'

'Which train did they come in on?'

'The one that left Swindon at nine o'clock.' Bart waited, tapping his fingers on the small counter outside the window, itching to grab the fellow by the collar and shake the information out of him. Only you couldn't get away with that sort of thing these days like he had in his youth, because the damned police were always interfering. So he forced himself to wait.

The man had his head on one side and was eyeing them slyly. 'It's hard to remember. We get a lot of people through on Fridays.'

Stan slid a half-crown piece into the hollow in the counter but kept his forefinger on it. 'Just a little something for your trouble.'

The man screwed up his eyes, looking into the distance and saying nothing for a minute or two, then shook his head. 'I wish I could help you, but I can't remember anyone like that. There were some women, just odd ones, and some men, both young and old. There was a young married couple, all lovey-dovey they were, couldn't have been married long. But there definitely weren't two pretty young women together. I'd have remembered that. There are usually older folk at that time of day, because the younger ones are at work.'

'Could they have left the station without you seeing them?' Bart asked.

'Might have if they went singly. I'm sorry. I'm sure I'd have remembered them if they'd been together.'

Stan leant forward. 'Could they have crossed to the other platform and taken a train back to Swindon?'

'I'm sure I'd have seen them if they'd been waiting.'

'What about buses?'

'Well, there is one stops outside the station.'

'Do you know the driver?'

'No. They come from Swindon or Chippenham, them buses do, not driv' by a local chap.'

When the coin was pushed towards him, the clerk snatched it up and pocketed it quickly.

'Thanks for your trouble.' Stan yanked Bart's arm and pulled him along to the station entrance. 'Let's have a look round.'

'I think he knew somethin' else.'

'He didn't.'

But though they walked round the outside of the small station carefully, looking for other ways out, Bart couldn't see how anyone could have left it without being seen.

They went back inside, crossing to the other platform to wait for the next train back. They were the only people there.

Stan stretched out his legs and thrust his hands into his jacket pockets. 'They must have doubled back. Clear as the nose on your face. Only thing they could have done.'

'Why would they do that?'

'To make sure no one in Swindon knew where they were really going.'

'But that ticket fellow says he'd have seen

them if they'd waited on the other platform.'

'They could have gone into the Ladies' till the train came in, couldn't they? He'd not have noticed them nip out at the last minute.'

Bart clenched his fists and glared round. '*She* must have put them up to it, worked out a way for them to escape.'

'Mattie, you mean?'

'Yes. Too smart for her own good, that one.'

'I like a woman who's got some sense.'

'You're mad. They cause trouble if you let them think for themselves.'

Stan threw him a dirty look. 'It's you who's caused this trouble. She doesn't know why I want to marry her or she'd not have run off. She didn't get on the train with them. Do you really think she was making for Bath?'

'How the hell do I know? It was just a thought.'

'What exactly did she take with her?'

'Clothes. They all did. Must have worn extra, because we don't have any suitcases. Why would we? I don't like going away from home, wasting money on summer holidays. Mattie might have made a bundle up, though, because she left after me.' Bart thought hard and added, 'She took an old shawl that used to hang by the back door. We all used it for going down the back when it rained. I got bloody soaked yesterday without it.'

'Old shawl, eh? Trying to hide what she looked like, do you think? Fine-looking woman, your Mattie. Her hair's real pretty when the sun shines on it. People would remember her.'

'She didn't look pretty on Friday. Had a stinking cold, nose was red, wasn't at all well.'

Stan continued to think aloud. 'It was raining on and off, so it'd not look out of place if she wrapped a shawl round her head and kept her face hidden. My cousin's a tram driver. I'll get him to ask among the other drivers. Someone must have seen her and I bet there weren't many people out on a day like that.'

Bart brightened. 'You're right. And when we find her she can tell us where the others went. She's bound to know. She probably put them up to playing tricks and getting on and off trains.'

On the Monday, the weather being pleasant again, Jacob saw Miss Newington walking down the lane from the big house. She stopped by the gate, reaching up one hand to caress the blossoms on the lower branches of the flowering cherry trees. They were just beginning to flower, so the heavy rain hadn't done much damage. In a week or two they'd be beautiful. They might not produce anything he could sell, but he'd taken a cutting and his own young tree was also in bloom lower down the slope just inside his gate. He was thinking of taking other cuttings and putting more trees along the lane.

His eyes went back to Miss Newington. She wasn't striding along as she usually did, but walking slowly, and she looked tired. She must be coming to see him, because if she went into the village she usually took the dog cart. What did she want with him again? The rents weren't due yet.

He walked across to join her as she reached the other side of the perimeter wall and walked along the inside as they headed towards the gate. 'Good afternoon, Miss Newington. Bit brighter today, isn't it?'

She glanced up at the sky and nodded agreement, then put her head on one side and studied his house. 'Your family have lived here for a while, haven't they, Kemble?'

'Yes, miss. My father and grandfather leased this smallholding before Dad bought it. I grew up here.'

'Do you have any money saved?'

He shook his head, puzzled by the question. 'Not much. I save every summer to see me and the kids through the winter, when there's less money coming in. But last year's money's nearly used up now.'

'But you do at least have the sense to save for the winter.'

He looked at her in surprise. 'How else would we manage if I didn't?'

'Not all the villagers are as thrifty. I wonder, would you offer me a cup of tea, Mr Kemble? I wish to discuss something with you.'

He thought of the stranger, still feverish, the kitchen in a proper old mess. 'The place isn't fit to entertain a lady in. Not having a wife, and Mr Grey being ill, I've had no help and . . . Well, I've not had time to clear up today. I had to come out and get these seedlings in, you see. Perhaps I could come up to your house later?'

Miss Newington gave him one of her piercing glances. 'I need to talk to you and I wish to do so now. If the house is untidy, it won't worry me.'

Somehow he couldn't argue with her. She had such an upright spine, such a piercing gaze – and anyway, she was his employer now. He didn't want to upset her and lose the extra money.

As he opened the back door for his visitor, he heard the stranger moaning and talking in disjointed snatches. His heart sank. No hiding the presence of the sick woman now.

His companion stopped to listen. 'Who's that? It's not a child's voice.'

Sarah came to the hall door. 'She's worse, Dad.'

Miss Newington didn't wait for an invitation to enter, but moved forward, following the sound of the voice. She stood by the sofa in the front room, staring down at the sick woman. 'Who is this?'

'A stranger. Luke found her lying unconscious in the lane on Friday night. She's feverish, not making sense, so I don't know who she is.'

'Why haven't you sent for the doctor?'

'He can't do much for pneumonia. No one can.'

'You should have sent for Mrs Henty, then. It's not fitting for a man to care for a sick woman, especially one who's a stranger.'

'Mrs Henty would have sent her to the poorhouse. They wouldn't look after her as well as I do.'

'I'm helping Dad,' Sarah volunteered. 'That's why I've not gone to school today.'

'You're a good lass,' Jacob said. 'Go and get the best cups out, then make sure the kettle's on the boil. We'll offer our visitor a cup of tea when she and I have finished talking.'

When Sarah had gone, he shut the door and looked at his landlady, trying to gauge her feelings. But the stranger moaned and tossed off the covers, so he went over to sponge the burning brow yet again. 'She's running away from someone and . . . she's been badly beaten in the past, bears the scars from it.'

'Show me.'

Flushing slightly, trying not to show more of the woman's body than needed, he undid the neck of the nightgown, and pulled it away at the back to reveal the scars. 'She was half-conscious when we found her and I . . . well, I promised her I'd keep her safe, not let whoever it is catch her. She was upset but my promise calmed her down straight away. If I called in Mrs Henty . . .' He didn't know how to say it delicately.

Miss Newington surprised him by grinning and finishing his sentence. 'The whole village would soon know about it, if not the whole county.'

'Yes.'

'I nursed my father when he came down with pneumonia and he survived. We need to prop her in an even more upright position and that fire is too hot. Let it die down a little. Do you have another pillow?'

'Yes. Shall I fetch it?'

'Indeed.'

When he came downstairs with the pillow, which he'd put into a clean if unironed pillowcase, his visitor was sponging the stranger again. After that, they made her more comfortable and she fell into a doze.

'She's not wearing a wedding ring,' Miss Newington said thoughtfully. 'And apart from that shawl and those ragged things, the rest of her clothes are those of a respectable young woman, well cared for – darned and mended, though. She's decent, I'm sure. I wonder why she's running away. Or from whom?'

He'd wondered that quite a few times over the past two days. 'She calls out sometimes, words like "Don't let him catch me" and tries to get up.'

'Well, she'll be able to tell us her troubles when she recovers.' Miss Newington pointed to the two armchairs. 'The cup of tea can wait. Sit down. I still need to talk to you. We can do it here as well as anywhere.'

He could only obey, but he felt anxious. What did she want of him? Had she changed her mind about him collecting the rents? Or . . . she wasn't going to sell the big house, was she? He'd heard that Arthur Newington wanted it and knew the village would be in bad hands if that man came here.

And although Jacob owned his own land, a rich man had ways of making life difficult if he took against you.

Bart got ready for work on the Monday, angry that he'd not bought enough bread for his sandwiches, or anything to put in them, either. He'd had to get up earlier than usual to get his own breakfast and he was furious that he'd not really found out anything about where his daughters had gone. The anger made his chest feel as if it was about to burst, it was so hot and strong inside him.

He was amazed that Stan still wanted to marry Mattie. He wouldn't. There were plenty of single women or widows who'd snap up a husband earning a decent wage, without a man marrying one who'd taken the bit between her teeth and run off like that, the ungrateful bitch.

That thought made him stop, butter knife in hand. Should he find himself another wife? He could do it easily enough and it'd solve one problem, at least – looking after the house. Then he shook his head. He'd had two wives and buried them both. The second one hadn't even given him a son. He didn't want any more daughters, or worse, a house full of brats, which might happen if he married someone younger than himself.

And wives were harder to manage than daughters, always wanting money for this and that, complaining if you went out for a drink. He'd vowed when Mattie's mother died that he'd not go through that again. After all, you could get your pleasures elsewhere for the cost of a few drinks.

He got on with his work. He was a good worker, took a pride in what he did and in his strength too. But he was getting on, nearly fifty now, starting to weaken just a little, though he hoped he'd hidden that. It only showed that he'd done the right thing, saving hard for his old age, and it meant it was even more important that he got his daughters back to look after him as he got older.

The foreman came round but didn't say anything, just letting them know he was there. Bart spat as he watched the sod walk away. They both knew where they stood. The foreman didn't pick on him and he did his work well.

Chapter Four

Emily studied Jacob as she spoke, hoping she'd not mistaken her man. 'I have some plans which you may be able to help me with and I'd be grateful if you'd not mention what I'm going to tell you to anyone.'

'I can keep my mouth closed.'

'Yes, I've noticed. The fact is, I'm not getting any younger and wish to move back to Northumberland. It's home to me, as Wiltshire never will be, and I love living by the sea. I had a job there, an easy one as companion to a wealthy lady, but someone else has taken that now.' She paused, staring into the fire. 'However, though I was left the big house and some land and cottages, I wasn't left any money, that went to my cousin. And the rents aren't enough to pay for the upkeep of such a large house as well as the rent of another place in the north.'

As she paused for breath, Jacob made a noise to show he was listening, then she continued without looking at him, almost talking to herself.

'I think my uncle wanted to cause trouble, the way he left things. He was a bitter man after his son died. Cook tells me his wife simply faded away, died a couple of years later, because she'd lost heart. I hadn't expected to inherit anything. The cousin who lives near here seemed the likely choice, but he only inherited the money and I doubt there was as much of it as people thought, anyway.'

'Mr Arthur Newington, that'd be.'

'Yes. He'd set my housemaid to spy on me and report to the lawyer who handled the estate. I've dismissed them both and found myself a new lawyer.' She saw Jacob's look of surprise. 'You're wondering why I'm bothering to tell you all this?'

'Yes, miss.'

'Because you're honest and intelligent. I trust you, as I do not trust my cousin, and I think we can help one another. Anyway, let me finish my tale. To further complicate matters, I'm only allowed to sell the house to my cousin, not to anyone else, for ten years after I inherit. I can sell off some of the smaller pieces of land and one or two cottages, the ones that weren't in the original estate. I've done that now, sold all I can, and had to use most of the money to repair the roof. So there still isn't enough money to support me in any comfort if I move back to Northumberland.'

She sighed and stared into the fire for a few moments, then continued. 'My new lawyer says there's nothing to prevent me from letting Newington House, however. It's large enough to bring in a decent rent. The money from that and from the other rents would be enough to manage on and to maintain the big house till the ten years are past, which is only another three years to go. But I'll have to be careful with my money, very careful indeed.'

He frowned at her, clearly still puzzled.

'That's where you come in. I want to appoint you my rent agent for the big house as well as for the remaining cottages. There's no one else suitable in the village and the lawyer in Swindon is too far away to keep an eye on things, though he'll supervise renting the property. You could deal with small maintenance matters there, I'm sure. I'll be watching my pennies carefully and I think you'll do the same for me. It'd best for me to have someone on the spot to look after things.' She waited for him to comment.

He was staring at her in amazement.

'Well?' she prompted.

'I don't know what to say, Miss Newington.'

'Say yes. After all, you've done repair work before.'

'Only on my own house.'

'I've seen what you've done and you've done it well.'

'That's not the same as dealing with the sort of folk who'd live at the big house, or repairing such a big place.'

'It's close enough for my needs. To be frank, I only wish the house to be in a fit state to be sold at the end of the ten years. It need not be perfect.' She was surprised Kemble hadn't accepted at once, and a little annoyed at having to persuade him. 'It'd mean more money, regular money even in winter. I'd pay you a set amount per week plus extra if there were repairs to be done or workmen brought in to oversee.'

He nodded a few times, very slowly, then took a deep breath. 'I'll do it.'

'Good. But I have one condition. You must find yourself a wife. You'll need to be better dressed if you're dealing with the tenants at the big house. You're better spoken than most. I gather your mother was a schoolteacher before her marriage?'

He nodded, taken aback by this condition.

'I know others have said it, but you really do need a woman to look after such things, Kemble, so I must insist you find yourself a wife. But unlike other people, I'm not making any suggestions as to who that should be.' She didn't say anything, just let the suggestion sink in. He'd see the need to smarten himself up, she was sure, and anyway, men as young as him were not meant to live celibately. 'Now, I'm quite thirsty and would like the cup of tea you promised me, after which Sarah and I will give this poor woman a sponge bath before I leave.'

'You'd do that?'

'She needs our help.'

Later he saw his visitor out and walked with her to the lane. Emily had noticed before that he was a courteous man and she liked that in him. She stopped for a moment. 'Do you think you can find yourself a wife, Mr Kemble?'

'I'll promise to give it serious thought, Miss Newington, nothing more.'

She smiled. 'Well, if you have trouble finding one, let me know. I'll be happy to help.'

Jacob watched her go, not sure how he felt about her or what she'd offered. She was a strange lady, prone to barking out orders to her tenants – though usually sensible orders. And yet she'd not been too high and mighty to give the stranger a sponge bath. What's more, he'd listened to her chatting away to Sarah as they worked, and the child clearly felt at ease with her.

To his relief, Miss Newington had promised

to return the following day to perform the same intimate services for the stranger.

The villagers marvelled that she managed that big house with so few servants when it had taken three times as many to run it before. But she'd shut up a lot of the rooms, the maid said. In fact, now Jacob came to think of it, that Agnes had been a right old gossip. You shouldn't gossip about your employers. He wouldn't.

He stopped on that thought. The wages she was offering would be a step up in the world for him. But why the hell had she taken it into her head that he needed to marry to do the job properly? She knew who lived in the village, must realise no man of sense would fancy any of the unattached women there, and more to the point, none of them would make the sort of efficient wife a rising man needed. Because if he did take the job, he'd definitely rise in the world. It would be just the impetus he needed to bring his ambitions back to life again. Didn't every man want to make a better life for his children?

His mother would have liked that. She'd been well educated for a woman, had come to the village as schoolteacher and stayed on to marry his father. She had given her son her own love of reading, but his father had never touched a book that Jacob had seen. Plants, now, his father had had a gift for growing things. Jacob would never be as good at that as him, even though he did quite well.

As the day passed, Jacob couldn't get the thought of what this job would mean out of his mind. He wanted to accept it for the children's sake, but where was he supposed to find a suitable wife? You couldn't just go out and ask some stranger to marry you.

No, he'd have to find a way to change Miss Newington's mind about that. She'd realise it was impossible once she really thought about it, he was sure she would. He'd discuss it with her next time, pointing out the lack of suitable candidates round here.

For the moment, he had a market garden to plant and stock, two children to look after, an invalid to care for – and not enough hours in the day.

A wife would change that, a little voice said in his head, but he didn't let himself dwell on the thought. But he couldn't help remembering the restless nights where his body reminded him of its needs. And looking after the stranger had made that worse.

That night someone tried to break into Newington House. Cook and the young girl who helped out were the only servants left, apart from a scrubbing woman who came in three times a week from the village, and Horace who looked after the horse and trap, and also did a bit of gardening. The old man slept above the stables, the female servants in the attics and Emily had a bedroom on the second floor which had excellent views of the nearby countryside. She preferred it to the old master's bedroom.

She was lying wakeful, something which often afflicted her, worrying about her future, when she heard the sound of glass smashing. It sounded to come from the rear of the house. She slid out of bed at once, because that sort of noise couldn't happen by mistake. Heart pounding, she crept onto the landing which overlooked the stairwell and looked down.

In the moonlight she saw two figures emerge from the kitchen area and start creeping up the stairs. They seemed to know their way and on the first-floor landing made straight for what had been the master bedroom previously.

Not an ordinary burglary, then, she thought. She picked up her bedroom poker before creeping up the stairs to the attics to rouse Cook and the girl. She put a hand over Cook's mouth as the woman tried to scream and whispered a quick explanation. 'Get something to hit them with.'

'They'll murder us, miss,' Cook said at once.

'No, they won't. There are three of us to two

of them and we'll arm ourselves. Hurry up.' She went and roused the maid, who slept next door.

'I'll help you, miss.' Lyddie shrugged on her dressing gown and snatched up her water ewer, hefting it in her hand.

'Good girl.'

Cook joined them on the landing brandishing a poker and wearing a voluminous dressing gown, with her hair hanging down her back in its customary straggly plait.

Emily stepped forward. 'I shall go first. Don't let me down, now.'

'No, miss.'

They crept down from the attic and pressed themselves out of sight against the landing wall while Emily peeped over the second-floor banisters. She was in time to see the men start creeping up the second flight of stairs towards them.

She stood behind a chest of drawers, waiting till the men had almost reached the top of the stairs before rushing out at them, screaming at the top of her voice and waving the poker.

One yelled out in shock and stumbled, falling a few steps before he could grab the wooden rails and save himself.

The other moved towards her, but jerked to a stop as the young maid sprang out of hiding and struck out at him with the metal ewer, screeching even more loudly than her mistress.

Cook was yelling, 'Help! Police! Murder!' over and over again and waving her poker wildly.

The man who'd fallen down a few stairs turned and fled.

Cursing loudly, the man next to Emily tried to punch her but missed. She managed to hit his shoulder a glancing blow with the poker and raised it for another. But with a yell of pain, he turned and ran after his companion.

Emily didn't make the mistake of pursuing him. 'Well done!' she told her two helpers and had to lean against the chest of drawers for a few moments till her heart stopped fluttering unevenly in her chest.

Cook plumped down on the top step, patting her massive bosom. 'Oh, my. Oh, my! I never thought to see the day.'

'Let's go and make sure they've left the house.' Emily led the way down the stairs, followed closely by the young maid, with Cook trailing reluctantly behind them.

They found a broken window in the scullery but no sign of the intruders. Then a man's shadow wavered across the backyard area, coming towards them.

Emily tensed.

'Miss Newington?' a voice quavered. 'Be you all right?'

She took a deep breath and refused to give in

to a slight dizziness. 'Come in, Horace. We've had burglars, but we chased them away.'

She had to make the cups of tea herself, because Cook decided to 'throw a spasm' and sat weeping loudly into a tea towel. Lyddie was still so excited she broke a cup and looked like breaking another until Emily took them out of her hands. 'Sit down and pull yourself together this minute!'

'Sorry, miss.'

'We'll send for the police first thing in the morning,' Emily said. 'In the meantime, I'd be grateful if you'd sleep in the house tonight, Horace. I'm going to load one of my uncle's shotguns and if they dare to come back, I shall have no hesitation in shooting them.'

'Better load one for me, too,' he said. 'I'm too old to fight anyone, but I can still pull a trigger, yes and hit a target.'

'You know how to use a gun?'

He chuckled. 'Oh, yes, miss. In fact, I'll come and help you load them.'

Emily slept rather badly for the rest of the night, but she felt they'd all acquitted themselves very well, considering, and told her little band of helpers so in the morning.

Cook had provided a more substantial breakfast than usual, 'to build up our strength'.

The woman wasn't too upset to clear her plate, Emily noticed, hiding a smile, but she didn't grudge them the ham and eggs. They'd stood by her at some risk to their own safety and that was what counted.

As soon as it was light she sent young Lyddie into Wootton Bassett on the bus that passed occasionally along the main road, with a note to let the police know what had happened. Then she waited for someone to come out to investigate. She had had a quick look round herself and found boot marks in the damp soil at the edges of the lane.

She was quite sure this was part of an attempt to drive her away and force her to sell the house to her cousin. Well, Arthur didn't know her very well if he thought she'd give in to this sort of bullying.

She would go and see her new lawyer again as soon as she could get into Swindon. She intended to make a new will. He'd told her she was free to leave her property to someone other than her cousin, because the conditions of inheritance would be broken by her death if she died before the ten years were up. Her former lawyer had told her she was obliged to leave it to her cousin. Malpractice, that, but it was no use challenging a lawyer. The other lawyers and judges would only close ranks on her. And Parker had only ever said that to her, not put it in writing.

Anyone would do as a legatee for the will, just

temporarily. She'd get it signed and leave it safely in her lawyer's hands, then let her cousin know he'd not be inheriting. That should protect her from misadventure.

And she'd sleep with a gun beside her bed from now on, with the bedroom door locked.

Once she got away from here, she'd redo the will and leave her money to charity, or maybe some of her old friends. She sighed. It must make life very easy if you had children to leave everything to and relatives you could turn to. The only thing she was sure of was that she wasn't letting this house fall into Arthur Newington's hands, or those of his children. Bad blood on that side of the family.

They'd come here fussing around her when she first arrived, but she'd seen them eyeing the house, estimating values, and had soon sent them packing.

The police didn't turn up until midday, then a plump young fellow puffed his way up the lane on an elderly bicycle. By that time Emily was very annoyed at being kept waiting.

He was so young, looking more like a boy than a man to her, and confessed that he'd only been in the area for a few months. He bounded around the house like an eager puppy that wasn't quite sure what was expected of it. She answered his questions patiently and suggested he report everything to his sergeant.

She didn't mention her suspicions that this incident had been caused by her cousin, because she didn't intend to give Arthur cause to sue her for slander. But who else could it have been? There was little of value in the house to tempt burglars. Everyone in the neighbourhood knew how run-down it was.

When the young policeman had left, she walked down the lane to help care for the stranger, as she'd promised, taking with her a jar of chicken broth made by Cook.

'I'm sorry I couldn't get here sooner, Mr Kemble. We had burglars last night.' She explained briefly what had happened.

He didn't say anything, but she could see faint frown lines on his forehead as he thought about it.

'You should take care, Miss Newington.'

'I am. I now have a loaded shotgun by my bedside and anyone else breaking into my house will get well peppered. I don't suppose they'll come back, though, not now they've seen we're prepared to fight.'

He smiled. 'No, probably not. But the gun is a good idea.'

'How did your visitor go last night?'

'She slept a bit better, thank goodness. And I

think she's breathing easier today. I've managed to get a little water into her every now and then, but she didn't really wake up, just drank a few mouthfuls as if she was thirsty.'

'That's good. But you look exhausted. Did you get any sleep at all?'

He shrugged. 'I can manage without. I've done it before.'

She looked at the little fob watch pinned to her prim grey jacket. 'I can give you a break for a couple of hours. Go and lie down. I'll wake you when it's time for me to leave.'

He hesitated.

'Do as I say!'

She went into the kitchen and tidied it up, because she wasn't too proud to do her own housework if necessary, or help her neighbours. She kept an ear open for the stranger, and when the two hours were nearly up, went and washed her. The woman's breathing might have improved slightly, but it was still rasping in her chest, and it was still touch-and-go whether she'd recover.

Such a pity if she didn't. She had a pretty face and couldn't have been more than thirty.

Chapter Five

On the Wednesday morning Jacob sent both children to school, repeating his warning to tell no one about their guest. He was feeling deep-down tired for lack of sleep, so took his cup of tea into the front room and sat with it by the fire, watching her. He'd done that a lot over the past few days. She'd been quite slender to start with, but flesh had been stripped off her, leaving a frail, ethereal-looking creature. He'd seen that word in books and looked it up in his dictionary, but had never been able to use it before. Now he knew exactly what it meant.

He wondered what she was really like. She had hard-working hands, reddened, marked with needle pricks from sewing. His wife's hands had been like that.

As if she could feel him staring at her, the

stranger began to stir. Her head moved from side to side, then her eyes slowly opened. She closed them again, blinked, then opened them fully. Once again, he was struck by how blue they were, like the periwinkles that grew down one end of his garden. He'd always liked those flowers and spared a clump or two when weeding, for the pleasure they gave him.

This time, she was aware of her surrounding and gasped in fear at the sight of Jacob, her eyes darting to and fro as she tried to work out where she was. He sat perfectly still and asked calmly, 'How are you feeling now?'

She tried to speak, but her voice came out as a croak.

'You're probably thirsty,' he said. 'Shall I get you a drink? My son brought in some fresh water from the well before he went to school.'

'I remember . . . a child. A girl?'

'Yes. My daughter Sarah. She's been helping me look after you. My son found you lying unconscious in the lane during the storm.'

'Storm?' She repeated the word, with a dubious glance towards the sun streaming in through the window.

'A really bad one, too. Trees uprooted, roofs damaged, and some of my seedlings battered into the ground.' He brought the water and helped her drink, then asked, 'Would you like a cup of chicken soup? Miss Newington brought some yesterday. I can soon warm it up. They say it's very nourishing and you've been quite ill.' She still was, but he didn't say that, wanted her to think she was recovering.

She nodded.

It didn't take long to warm up a cupful. When he brought it back, he thought for a minute she was asleep, but she opened her eyes again, looking at him warily. He felt as if he was dealing with a wild bird that would rather fly away than stay – and for some strange reason he didn't want her to leave. He set the mug on the hearth. 'We'll have to leave that to cool for a minute or two, else you'll burn your tongue.'

She tried to sit up, but couldn't. 'I feel . . . so weak.'

'You've had pneumonia.'

She began to cough, fighting for breath until the spasm passed.

'Let me help you sit a bit higher.'

She flinched back.

He stilled. 'I won't hurt you! What sort of fellow do you think I am?'

She took a deep, shuddering breath and this time allowed him to slip an arm round her shoulders and ease her into an even more upright position, propped against the pillows. When he held the mug to her lips, she drank eagerly.

Once she'd emptied it, he stepped back, not wanting to loom over her. 'From what you said when you were delirious, it was obvious you're running away from someone. I don't know who it is, but you're quite safe here with us, I promise you.'

The flush had faded from her face now, in spite of the warmth of the room, and she was looking chilled again, her cheeks devoid of colour. Even her lips seemed bloodless.

'My name's Jacob – Jacob Kemble,' he said by way of encouragement.

'Oh. Yes. My name's Mattie . . .' She broke off, not giving him her surname.

'Mattie, short for Matilda?'

She nodded.

'I had an aunt called Matilda. Auntie Tilda, we called her. Have you any family we should tell? Someone who'll be worrying about you?'

She shook her head. 'No. There's no one left.' Her eyes filled with tears and she swallowed convulsively.

'Then you'd better stay here with us till you're better, hadn't you?'

She regarded him even more warily.

He smiled. 'I dare do nothing else but keep you. My Sarah's decided to adopt you, like she does injured birds and other little creatures. She'll be fussing over you the minute she gets back from school.'

'I can't impose.'

She began coughing again and he gave her a clean handkerchief, holding her as the spasms racked her. 'You don't really have a choice. You can't even sit up on your own.'

She stopped coughing and he waited. When her breathing became deeper and she said nothing, he realised she'd fallen asleep, cradled against him. He looked down at her pale face and that pretty marigold-coloured hair, and felt tenderness suffuse him. 'I wonder who's hurt you so badly and where your family are,' he murmured. Perhaps they were all dead. She'd had a grieving look on her face when she said there was no one left now.

After he'd propped her against the pillows again, the impulse to stroke her cheek was irresistible, and the skin was indeed as soft as it looked. Then he drew the blanket up carefully and tiptoed out into the kitchen, with a feeling of certainty that she wasn't going to die. He was surprised at how pleased he felt about that.

A few hours later, Mattie woke again, to find the little girl sitting beside her.

The child's face brightened and she leant forward. 'Are you really awake?'

Mattie moistened her lips. 'Yes. Is there . . . ? I'm very thirsty.'

A small hand patted her shoulder and as the

father had said, the child seemed to regard her as a pet. 'I've got a glass of water here. Dad said not to fill it too full. Shall I help you drink?' Tongue sticking out of one corner of her mouth, so deep was her concentration, she did so, then set the nearly empty glass down.

Mattie felt like smiling at her young helper's earnestness, but didn't because it wouldn't be polite.

'Dad said I should warm up some porridge because you need something to eat. It won't take me long. We made extra this morning. I can put honey on it, if you like.'

'That'd be nice.'

'My name's Sarah.'

'And mine's Mattie.'

'Dad told us, but you didn't tell him your other name, an' me and Luke can't call you Mattie, can we?'

'Why not?'

The child's grey eyes widened in surprise. 'You're a grown-up! We have to call grown-ups Mrs or Miss something. It's not polite to call a grown-up by her first name.'

'Well, I don't mind. Just call me Mattie.'

A man's voice interrupted. 'Sarah, love, don't pester our visitor. It's not good manners.'

'But I was only—'

'Leave it, Sarah!'

'She wants something to eat.'

'Go and warm her porridge, then.'

Lips pressed together in a stubborn line, resentment of unjust treatment showing in every line of her body, Sarah marched out of the room.

Jacob came to stand in front of the fire, warming his hands, bringing a breath of cool, fresh air and a smell of the outdoors to the room. He must have left his boots at the door but hadn't waited to find his slippers. 'You look a bit better than you did this morning.'

Mattie nodded. 'Still weak, though.'

'Miss Newington will be here in a minute or two to help you have a wash. I saw her walking down the lane from the big house.'

'Miss Newington?'

'She lives in the big house, owns half the village.'

Shortly afterwards there was a knock on the back door and it opened almost immediately. Brisk footsteps came towards them. A thin older lady entered, clad in muddy-coloured tweeds that flapped around scrawny ankles poking out of sensible boots. A shapeless felt hat was pulled down over her grey hair, which was dragged back into a tight bun.

She studied Mattie. 'You're awake and have come to your sense. Good.' Then she took over.

Half an hour later, after she'd helped Mattie

to use the commode and washed her as if she was a baby, she hesitated, then said, 'Just so that you don't say anything that upsets him: Jacob's wife died over a year ago. There are only him and the children living here now. He's a good man, won't hurt you.' She called him back in and sat down on one of the armchairs. 'Now, my dear, tell us what brought you here.'

Mattie looked from one to the other, feeling trapped and helpless. She didn't want to tell anyone about the past, because it'd bring back memories of her sisters. She didn't even know where they were now, or if they were still safe, and wouldn't for a long time, if ever. Best if she made a new life for herself and kept her thoughts away from the past, surely?

'We can't help you if we don't know who you're running from,' Miss Newington prompted.

'Perhaps we should give her time to get to know and trust us,' Jacob said.

And it was that understanding and kindness in his face that made Mattie change her mind. She managed to explain exactly why she was there and what had happened to her sisters, by which time she felt exhausted and could hardly keep her eyes open.

'Let her sleep now,' Jacob said.

What a lovely man he was, Mattie thought. She smiled at him and let herself slide into sleep.

Miss Newington led the way into the kitchen. 'She's had a bad time with that stepfather if what she's telling us is true.'

'I'm sure it is. She hasn't got a liar's face.'

'I agree with you. Rather a nice-looking young woman, actually, even now, when she's not well. Not a beauty. Comely is the word I'd use to describe her. The pretty ones fade by her age, but comely stays with a woman.'

Jacob didn't comment on his guest's looks. He thought she was very pretty, with those lovely blue eyes. 'That stepfather sounds a nasty sort.' He waited for Miss Newington to reply, but she didn't and when he looked at her, she was staring blankly ahead, her expression bleak.

'Some fathers are like that, think they own their children, make their lives a misery,' she murmured.

He was suddenly sure that, lady or not, she'd had a domineering father, but he didn't say so, of course.

She shook her head quickly, like a dog shaking off raindrops. 'I'd like to go on helping her. It's not fitting for you to nurse her, a man on your own.'

'We can hardly move her to the big house. She needs to be kept quiet and warm until her congestion eases.'

'Yes. I'd send young Lyddie down to help you,

but I need to keep the girl with me in case we get more intruders. She's the only one nimble enough to run for help if necessary.' She looked round. 'You definitely need a woman's touch in this house.'

'We manage all right.'

She speared him with a glance. 'Not really, Mr Kemble. This room could do with a good bottoming. Mrs Grey hasn't been doing a very good job. And I daresay the rest of the house is as bad. Your clothes may be clean but they're torn and haven't been ironed.'

He couldn't help scowling. 'It's a small village. There isn't anyone I could hire to do my mending who wouldn't take advantage. Mrs Henty said I should marry Essie Jupe.'

'Good heavens! No man in his senses would marry that slovenly fool.'

'Exactly.'

'If you're to help me as I wish, I believe I must first help you sort out your life. I shall look for a wife for you, one who will be a helpmeet and a credit to you.'

Before he could refuse this offer she stood up and made for the door.

After it had closed behind her, he came back to sit in front of the kitchen range and have a think. The way Miss Newington had spoken made him feel uneasy, because he had a suspicion she was planning something. He didn't want to marry again, well, not unless he met someone he could love and respect. He had his children and that was enough for the moment.

But if he had the new job, he could perhaps afford to hire Lyddie's sister to be his housekeeper instead of marrying someone he didn't particularly like. Yes, that might be the thing to do. Surely Miss Newington would understand that? He'd put it to her next time he saw her.

That night intruders once again tried to attack Newington House, three of them this time. Horace greeted them with a blast of his shotgun from the room above the stables.

The shot and their howls of fury woke Emily and she picked up her own weapon and crept down to a bedroom overlooking the backyard, whose window she'd left open deliberately.

They were trying to batter the outer door of the stables now, so she let them have it from behind. Shot pattered against walls and doors, but some of it must have found its mark because there were yelps of pain and they cursed before limping off into the darkness.

One stopped to yell, 'We'll be back.'

Would they really keep coming back? she wondered. Perhaps. Or perhaps something else would happen. Her cousin had made no secret of his annoyance that she owned this place and his determination to get hold of it. She'd better get that new will made out and signed quickly. After the scornful way Arthur had spoken to her and these recent events, she was determined that, whatever happened to her, he would not benefit in any way from her inheritance.

She'd inform the police about this second attack on her way to the lawyer's in Swindon, but had no faith in that young policeman. She must definitely find herself some protectors, perhaps men from the village. Arthur couldn't start an all-out battle, after all.

She sighed. She was finding it all extremely exhausting.

Stan made his way across to Bart during the lunch break. 'I spoke to my cousin last night. He's going to ask the other tram drivers if anyone took a fare from a woman with a heavy cold that morning. There wouldn't be many people out in such weather, would there?'

Bart shrugged and watched the entrance.

'Where's your food?'

'The boy's bringing me something.'

'If your daughters don't come back, you're going to need a wife.'

'Last thing I bloody need.'

'Don't you miss it, having someone in bed?'

'No. If I need it, I find someone. Don't need it as often these days, anyway.'

'The sort you find go with anyone for a drink or two.'

'I don't care what they do the rest of the time. Ah, there he is!' Bart heaved himself to his feet, sucked in his breath for a minute, then straightened up and waved to the boy.

Stan watched this, eyes narrowed. He'd seen Bart twitch with what could only be a sudden stab of pain a few times now, but hadn't said anything. He looked across and saw the foreman watching them too.

When Bart sat down again, he whispered, 'The foreman saw it.'

'Saw what?'

'You stop moving and wince.'

'I had a cramp in me foot.'

'Didn't look like your foot to me. You clutched your chest.'

'I'm all right, I tell you. Mind your own damned business.'

Stan shrugged.

During the next few days the invalid improved steadily, and was well enough for Jacob and the children to leave her alone and go to church on the Sunday.

After the service, the children were invited to

have Sunday dinner with some of their friends, which Jacob accepted. He refused the same invitation for himself, however, and went off home looking forward to a nice ham steak he'd bought from the village shop, which brought in meat orders twice a week.

When he went into the front room, he found Mattie sitting up in bed reading a book.

She looked up with a smile. 'Are you back already?'

He nodded. 'The curate doesn't preach long sermons. Folk round here wouldn't stand for it.' He smiled. 'And anyway, he's no good at preaching and cares more about the choir. He's a kind man, but he's a scholar and very impractical. No one understands half of what he says in his sermons, not even his bossy wife. Would you like a cup of tea?'

'Yes, please. If it's not too much trouble.'

'I'm having one myself.'

When he came back, he sat down and cradled his mug in his hands. 'You'll be needing some clothing if you're to get up properly tomorrow. I've got your clothes washed and dried, but I'm no hand at ironing, so they're all crumpled. I hope you don't mind. Oh, and there are some of Alice's things that might fit you, as well, near enough anyway if you can take the hems up. She was bigger built than you and taller.'

'Oh, I couldn't use those!' Mattie exclaimed involuntarily. 'That would be too painful for you, Mr Kemble.'

Jacob swallowed hard and shook his head. 'I know it's what Alice would have wanted. And anyway, it's time I did something with her stuff. It's been sitting there for over a year now. Can't waste good clothing, can we? And you've nothing but what you brought in that bundle. The things got stained with mud and water from when you fell. I can't get the stains out.'

Tears filled Mattie's eyes at his generosity, but she could only nod. 'Thank you, then.'

He sat on a bit longer but she could feel her eyelids getting heavy and couldn't stay awake. When she awoke from another healing sleep she was alone.

Strange how safe she felt with him now that she'd got to know him a little. Only a kind man would take in a stranger like this. And Miss Newington was kind, too, in her abrupt way.

Mattie had been very lucky that they'd found her and cared for her, she knew. And surely her stepfather wouldn't find her here? Jacob said there were only about thirty houses in the village and it was off the main road to Chippenham.

The following morning after the children had gone to school Mattie washed herself and got dressed.

That tired her so much, she made her way into the kitchen on shaky legs and had to sit down for a few minutes. As she looked around, she shook her head at the mess. Poor man, he worked so hard. But no one could do everything.

The table had been wiped clean, but through an open door she could see the morning's dishes piled on the wooden draining board in the scullery, and it looked as if a pan was soaking in the enamel washing-up bowl in the big square slopstone. There was no sign of Jacob, but when she looked out of the window, there he was, bent over his rows of plants. She smiled at the sight of him, such a kind man and as unlike her stepfather or Stan as any man could be.

She studied him, liking the way his fair hair blew about in the breeze, the graceful way he stepped between the rows of plants. He was tall and slim, not bulky like her stepfather and Stan. In fact, he was a very attractive man. She could feel her cheeks heat up at this thought. It was a long time since a man had affected her like this.

Beyond him was a small tree, its branches waving in the breeze, as if it was showing off its delicate white blossoms. It was going to be beautiful when it was fully in bloom. She stood and stared at it for a long time. And when she looked beyond it, there were others like it in the distance. Cherry trees, probably.

Although she wasn't strong enough to do much, she found some potatoes and peeled them for tea as she sat by the table, leaving them covered with water in a pan. She also tidied up a few things, working for a few minutes, then resting.

An hour later she felt so sleepy she decided to go back into the front room for another lie-down. It was so frustrating. She wanted to help them, not be a burden.

As she stood up the back door opened and Jacob came towards her. 'How are you?'

'Better, but I still tire easily. I was looking out of the window earlier. What are those trees, the ones with white blossoms? You have a small one and there are two bigger ones in the distance.'

'Cherry trees. That's why they call this Cherry Tree Lane.'

'They'll be beautiful when they're in full bloom. Even now, it's a pleasure to look out at them.'

He smiled. 'I love them, look forward to them blooming every year.' He looked at the table and said abruptly, 'You've been tidying up a bit, haven't you?'

She nodded.

'You shouldn't overtire yourself. You're looking very pale still.' He sounded disapproving.

'I only peeled the potatoes and put a few things away. And I was going to rest.' She swayed, feeling a little dizzy now.

'You shouldn't be doing anything yet. We don't want you relapsing.'

He picked her up without a word and she couldn't help crying out in shock and stiffening.

'I shan't hurt you.' He looked down at her, his face so close it made her breath catch in her throat for a moment or two.

'I was going to lie down,' she said as he continued into the front room and laid her on the sofa.

'Then I was just helping you do what you wanted.' His smile made her feel warm and cherished. 'You hardly weigh a thing.'

'I take after my mother. But I do need a rest now.' She sighed and snuggled down against the soft feather pillows.

He bent over to pull up the covers, pausing with his head just above hers. 'Have a good rest now. And thank you for your help.'

Her last thought was: *What a lovely man he is!*

When Mattie woke up she saw it was half past twelve by the clock on the mantelpiece. She yawned and stretched, and this time didn't feel dizzy. She made it out to the privy and back quite easily.

Of course, that attracted Jacob's attention and he came striding across to her looking anxious. 'Are you sure you should be outside?'

'It's quite warm today. I love the feel of sunshine on my face, don't you? I'm glad winter's over.' She turned her face up to the sun.

'Well, don't push yourself too hard. I'll come in now and make something for us to eat.'

'That'd be nice. I'm feeling quite hungry.'

Jacob thought how pretty she was when she smiled, but she was still so frail-looking he couldn't help worrying about her. He made sure she was comfortable in the rocking chair before he did anything else.

'I'm not normally ill at all. I'm sure I'll get better quickly now.' She looked down at herself ruefully, holding up one arm to stare at her wrist. 'I've lost a lot of weight, though.'

'You'll get better more quickly if you rest.'

'Nonsense. I'll just stay weak if I don't move around a little. I'd planned to sit by the window this afternoon, but I could do some sewing. Do you have any clothes which need mending?'

He smiled ruefully. 'I think most of ours do.'

'Good. I like to be useful.'

'But—'

She held up one hand. 'Please don't argue. That won't be at all taxing and I'd get bored with nothing to do. I'm a good needlewoman, I promise you. Do you have some sewing things?'

'You can only do it if you promise to have another lie-down when you're tired.'

'I shall. I'm not a fool, Mr Kemble.'

'I don't even know your second name. You just said Mattie before.'

'It's Willitt. But can't you call me Mattie? It seems more friendly.'

'Only if you'll call me Jacob.'

'Jacob, then.' She smiled at him.

He realised he was standing like an idiot, smiling back at her, so went to find Alice's sewing box. She'd always hated mending and sewing, poor lass, would rather have been outside working with him.

Mattie inspected the contents of the sewing box. 'Plenty of thread here and the needles haven't rusted. It'll feel good to pay you back a little.'

'I don't need paying back.'

'Well, I can't sit and read all the time, though you have some interesting books.' She gestured to the small bookcase, crammed with books of all sorts.

He loved books, sometimes picked them up cheaply at Swindon Market. 'You like reading?'

'I used to when I got the chance, which wasn't often. My stepfather didn't believe in it, said it was a waste of time, so I had to hide my library books and steal the odd half-hour with them during the day.'

'That's the man you're running away from? You'd better tell me his name so that I'll know him if I meet him.'

'He's called Bart Fuller.' She shuddered. 'And I pray he won't find me.'

'Is he the one who beat you so badly?'

Her colour deepened and a shamed look came onto her face. 'Yes.'

'Why?'

'Because I wanted to get married. He crippled the man I was to marry and he left town in a hurry.'

Jacob could see that he was distressing her, so didn't press the matter. But if that stepfather ever tried to touch her again, he'd take great pleasure in giving him some of his own medicine. Jacob never started fights, but he knew how to look after himself – and those he cared about. That thought made him blink, then he told himself it was natural to care about someone whose life you'd saved.

When he sat her at the table with some bread and cheese, and a wizened apple from last year's store, she said. 'Jacob . . . I couldn't help noticing that Sarah's clothes are too small for her. I'll try to let them out, but if you would purchase some material, I'd be happy to sew a new summer dress for her before I leave. It needn't cost more than a few shillings. Miss Newington might get some material for you. She's very kind, isn't she?'

He stopped eating, not liking the thought of never seeing Mattie again. 'You talk about leaving, but it'll be a while before you're fit enough to go. And where would you go, anyway? Do you have anyone who'll take you in until you can find work for yourself?'

Mattie shook her head, looking sad. 'No. But I'm a good worker. Maybe I'll find myself a job as a maid in a big house. Or in a hotel. You get bed and board that way.'

He felt relieved. 'Then there's no need for you to rush away. We could make you up a bed in the attic once you're well. We could do with a bit of help here, as you can see, a sort of housekeeper. There are two little bedrooms up there in the attic.'

'You're such a kind man.'

'It'd help us all to have you here.'

The back door opened and Miss Newington came in. He was sorry that stopped him and Mattie talking. His visitor was such pleasant company.

Emily looked across the room, pleased to see the invalid up and about. She saw the touch of colour in her cheeks, the way Jacob was smiling at his guest, and wondered what they'd been talking about. 'Are you feeling better, Mattie?'

'Yes, thank you, Miss Newington. I've just been thanking Jacob for saving my life.'

'He definitely did that.'

Jacob got up, looking embarrassed. 'Anyone

would have done the same. Now, I'd better get back to my garden. It's my busy season.'

'He's a fine man,' Emily said thoughtfully once the door had shut behind him.

'Yes, he is.'

'How do you get on with the children?'

'I haven't seen much of Luke, but Sarah seems to have adopted me and is treating me like a pet puppy.' Mattie chuckled. 'She's a delightful child, as kind as her father.'

'Good. Good.'

There was silence as Mattie closed her eyes and when Emily didn't speak, the younger woman's breathing deepened and she fell asleep again.

Emily studied her companion. She seemed a sensible sort and was pretty enough for any man, now she was looking better. She had lovely blue eyes and a nice, open expression on her face. You could tell a lot about people from their eyes, Emily always felt. She began to tidy up quietly, noting that someone had made a start on that. She began sorting out the washing, which was piled anyhow in a corner of the scullery. She'd send her scrubbing woman down one day to do it.

After an hour had ticked away, she woke Mattie. 'Do you need any help before I go back?'

'No, thank you. I'm a lot better today and I managed to get to the outhouse all right.'

'Very well.' Emily went to stand by the window

and watch Jacob work. She'd never seen him idle.

She made a cup of tea, chatted for a while, wanting to get to know the young woman better. As she walked slowly home, she admitted she felt rather tired today. She was getting old and it was frustrating not to be able to do all she wanted.

When she drew level with Jacob at the top corner of the field, she stopped and called, 'Can you come up to see me tonight for an hour? There's something I'd like to discuss with you.'

'Yes, of course. After tea be all right?'

'That'll be fine.'

She was very thoughtful as she walked home. She was sure she'd found the solution to Jacob's problems, but he was such a stubborn man. How was she to persuade him to do as she wished?

Chapter Six

After tea Jacob strolled up to the big house, enjoying the cooler air, glad the evenings were so much lighter now. He'd left Mattie helping Sarah read one of her story books, and Luke pretending not to be interested but listening all the same.

He went round to the kitchen door and found Lyddie clearing up while Cook toasted herself in front of the fire.

Lyddie greeted him as cheerfully as ever. 'Miss Newington is expecting you, Mr Kemble. Did you hear about our intruders? Isn't it exciting? Miss Newington's ever so brave. She keeps a shotgun in her bedroom an' she used it last night. Me an' Cook go to bed with our pokers right next to us an' our doors locked. Do you think they'll come back again tonight?'

'Stop gossiping and take Mr Kemble through

to the mistress,' Cook said. 'It's her he's come to see, not you.'

Jacob stopped beside her to ask, 'Are you all right?'

She nodded. 'But I don't know what it's coming to when a person has to use guns to keep their house safe in a Christian country. It's not as if we're ignorant heathens, is it? I mean, this is England!'

Smiling, he walked after Lyddie.

Miss Newington was sitting in the small drawing room at one side of the front of the house. It was shabby but still had a touch of elegance, and was decorated in colours which reminded Jacob of sweet peas just coming into bloom. Most folk used darker colours to be practical, but he supposed rich people didn't need to worry as much about such things. He'd never been in this part of the house before, though he'd supplied the former owner with fresh produce from time to time after old Mr Newington turned off most of the staff. Miss Newington usually received him in the morning room at the back, where they went through the accounts on the table where she ate her meals.

They didn't need as much of his fresh stuff these days at the big house, so Jacob took care to grow things that sold well at market in Swindon, including a few fancier items such as asparagus and artichokes for the better class of greengrocer. He picked his runner beans young and laid out his strawberries in little baskets, with leaves tucked in each side, or he had done when Alice was there to help him. He'd been improving his income gradually but since her death it had slipped back a bit.

When he was seated, Miss Newington stared at him disapprovingly. 'You most certainly do need a wife, Jacob Kemble. Just look at you!' She flicked one hand towards the big mirror over the mantelpiece.

He glanced at it quickly, shocked to see how scruffy his clothes looked, even though they were clean. 'Well, I don't want one. And even if I did, there's no one suitable in the village. I'd not touch a woman like that Essie Jupe, nor let her near my children.'

'I'd not ask you to. She's a shrew. But there is one woman who might be suitable.'

He frowned at her, racking his brain to think who she meant. But he couldn't come up with anyone, even on the outlying farms or among the people he dealt with in Swindon. 'Who do you mean?'

She clicked her tongue in exasperation. 'The woman you found in the lane, of course. Mattie Willitt.'

He couldn't frame a single word, so amazed

was he. This was the last thing he'd expected to hear.

'You must have a wife if you want that job – no, don't argue, I'm not employing a man who can't turn himself out smartly, not when he'll be dealing with moneyed folk. Just think about it for a minute or two. Poor Mattie is homeless. She's not a shrew, and she gets on well with your children. I'd guess she's a hard worker, because she's already trying to pay you back by doing your mending. And she's a fine-looking young woman. You're not telling me you're not attracted to her. I've seen the way you look at her. So what could be more suitable?'

He racked his brain for something to counter her arguments, could only come up with, 'But we don't know anything about her.' And even to himself it sounded feeble, both the argument and his tone of voice. 'She's not got the marks of a wedding ring, though,' he added before he could stop himself. He felt hot and flustered, didn't like the knowing smile on the old lady's face. 'I can't go marrying someone I've only just met.'

She folded her arms. 'Very well. If you're not going to even try, I'll find someone else to look after this house for me.'

He looked at her face and knew she meant it. She was a stubborn woman and used to getting her own way. He ought to have said no to getting wed, said it straight out, couldn't think why he hadn't. Well, if truth be told, his thoughts were in such a tangle he didn't know what to say or do. Because he did like Mattie Willitt. And he did need a wife.

Miss Newington stood up, saying calmly, 'Well, I've got things to do even if you haven't.'

He thought of all the benefits the job she was offering would bring, and in the end he said desperately, 'What if Mattie doesn't want to marry me?'

Miss Newington sat down again but her smile made him feel like an insect caught in a spider's web. 'You haven't spoken to her already?' he asked in horror, because if she had, he didn't know how he'd face Mattie when he returned.

'No. But I can do so tomorrow.'

'I can speak for myself – if I decide . . . anything.'

'In this case, Jacob Kemble, you'd do better with an intermediary.'

'I'll not have you threatening her or forcing her.'

'She's a determined sort of woman who ran away, ill as she was, rather than face a forced marriage with a man she disliked. I doubt that I or anyone else will be able to compel that woman to marry you if she doesn't want to. So I'll speak to her calmly and quietly about the possibility in the morning and you're not to say a word about this until I do. I want your promise on that.'

He nodded. He could only hope Mattie would say no or Miss Newington change her mind or that he'd think of some better argument for not rushing into marriage with a stranger. 'I'm still not sure.'

'You're a young man, Jacob. You need a wife. And Mattie needs a home.'

He found himself unable to summon up any further arguments. 'I'll be leaving, then.' He stood up, then turned to ask, 'What if the intruders come back tonight?'

'I've got my gun and Horace is also armed. We'll not be taken by surprise. No one is going to take my land from me. I'm going into Swindon tomorrow to make arrangements with my lawyer for a new will. When I inform my cousin what I've done, I think he'll stop these attacks.'

She didn't volunteer any more information, just escorted Jacob to the front door. He heard a key turn and bolts slide behind him. But you couldn't put bolts on window glass, could you? And windows were easy to break. It was a worry to think of an old lady like her alone at the house, with only the servants, two of them old and one very young.

He had his own family to look after, though. If there were intruders around, he didn't want them breaking into his home. Only he'd not heard of any other burglaries, just the attacks on the big house.

He walked back through the moonlit night, moving slowly because he had a lot to think about. He could sense spring doing its work around him, plants bursting forth, birds nesting, insects teeming. He stopped to lean on his own gate and stare across his field of carefully planted vegetables, fruit canes and bushes. It was wonderful the way things burst into life in the spring.

The thought couldn't be held back any longer. *What would he do if Mattie said yes to Miss Newington's suggestion?*

His body twitched at the thought and with a soft sigh he admitted to himself that he was definitely attracted to her. But was that enough? He'd gone to school with Alice and they'd walked out together for two years before he'd plucked up the courage to propose.

He simply couldn't imagine marrying a stranger and living so intimately together.

But he did like her . . . and he didn't want to lose this opportunity of a better job, either, for the children's sake . . . and Mattie had nowhere to go, no one to care for her. He couldn't turn her loose in the world.

What was a man to do?

When he went back into the house, all was

quiet. A lamp was turned low on the dresser and the fire was banked up. Luke would have seen to that. He was a good lad, but someone had swept up the ashes from the hearth, and Luke never noticed details like that. Had Mattie done that or had she suggested his son do it?

Jacob's eyes were still used to the dim light outside so he didn't bother taking the lamp as he peered into the front room to see if she was all right. There was enough moonlight spilling round the drooping curtain to show him how peacefully she was sleeping.

She looked so pretty he lingered there, studying her face. Then his eyes went back to the curtain and he realised why the moonlight was getting in. How long had it been hanging loose like that at the edge and why hadn't he noticed it before? Something was wrong with the end of the runner; he'd have to fix it when he had a minute. Only he never seemed to have a minute to spare.

He might have if he married, though.

He locked the back door, checked that Sarah had put the porridge pot on the edge of the hob to cook gently overnight and crept up to bed. But he didn't get to sleep for a long time because Miss Newington's suggestion had thrown both his mind and body into turmoil.

He was only thirty-one and his body had been making its needs plain for a while. The idea of marrying Mattie didn't seem as bad now he'd got over the shock. In fact, the thought of having a wife again was growing on him. No, not a wife, not any woman – her.

What would the children say? Should he do it? Would Mattie agree to marry him? And if she did, would she feel forced into it? That was the last thing he wanted for her.

Round and round his thoughts went and it was a long time before he got to sleep.

In the morning Jacob was tired and no closer to reaching a decision. He supervised the children's preparations for school, as usual. He was about to carry breakfast to his guest when the door to her room opened and she came out, pale still but again with a hint of colour in her cheeks. Definitely on the mend, thank goodness.

'Sit down and I'll get you something to eat. There's some porridge left or you could have bread and jam.'

'Porridge would be fine.'

'We have it every morning,' he said apologetically. 'Cooks itself overnight, so it's easy. We usually put a spoonful of golden syrup on it, or honey, and cream of course.'

'Porridge is very nourishing. Thank you. I'll . . . um . . . just nip outside first.'

When she got back, she washed her hands in

the scullery and sat down. He watched as she poured a little cream over the porridge. 'Take more. We've always got plenty of milk and cream because I trade fruit and vegetables for them with a neighbouring farmer. We never lack food, at least, even if I don't iron our clothes very often.'

She allowed herself some more cream and took a spoonful of golden syrup, dropping it neatly into the middle. 'This is a real treat. I'm feeling very hungry this morning.'

'That's good.' He poured them both a cup of tea and sat sipping his, wondering what she'd say when Miss Newington broached the idea, wondering if he should try to prepare her. No, he'd given his word not to mention it.

In the end, he set down his cup. 'I'll get out to work, then. I'll be back to make you something to eat at midday.'

'Thank you. But if you'll tell me what you want, I'll make yours. I'm sure I can manage that. If you have some vegetables, I could put some soup on to simmer.'

'That'd be a rare treat. We've a few shreds of ham on a bone. You could add that for flavour. Are you sure you're up to it?'

'I shan't overdo things.'

When he'd gone, Mattie continued to eat her porridge slowly and with relish. What had made him so stiff this morning? Did he wish to be rid of her? She didn't think she could walk far yet, let alone find herself a job. And she had very little money, one week's housekeeping only, not nearly enough to tide her over until she was well again.

No, he'd said they had bedrooms in the attic, that she could stay and be their housekeeper. Perhaps he'd changed his mind. Or perhaps he wasn't cheerful in the mornings. Some people weren't.

She pushed the bowl away, not able to finish the huge helping he'd given her. She hated to waste it, so covered the bowl with a plate, then cleared up the kitchen a little. But even that much exertion left her tired and then the coughing started again.

Still, she'd helped out a bit and if she had a rest, she'd be able to do more of the mending before she put some soup on for the midday meal.

She must show him she wouldn't be a burden.

Emily nodded to Jacob as she walked through the gate and along the neat gravel path to his front door. The plants looked to be flourishing. He certainly had a way with them.

She opened the kitchen door and found Mattie sitting by the window with a basket of crumpled clothes at her feet, darning a sock. Good sign, that. Emily couldn't abide idleness in young or old. 'Good morning, my dear. How are you feeling today?'

'A little better as long as I don't do too much. I started to clear up the kitchen, then had to lie down and rest. I fell asleep for a while.'

'You're doing well, though, looking a lot better. You can't hurry nature. Give yourself time to recover.' She sniffed. 'Something smells good.'

'Ham and vegetable soup.'

'Good, good.' Emily gestured towards the basket. 'There must be a lot of mending to do.'

'No one's done any for months, as far as I can see. I like sewing, even mending. It's such a peaceful activity. I've made all my own clothes since I was ten. My mother taught me and I taught my sisters. My stepfather wasn't generous with money, you see, except to himself.'

Emily sat down opposite her. 'What are you intending to do once you're better?'

Mattie let the darning drop into her lap and leant her head back. 'I don't know. Perhaps you could advise me?'

'You're safe here for a while. Jacob won't throw you out.'

'But he has to feed me, and he's not got a lot of money or he'd have hired a housekeeper, surely? I only have about a pound in my purse. I can't even pay for my own keep for more than a week or two.'

Emily hesitated. It was proving harder to make her suggestion tactfully than she'd expected. In the end she just said it. 'There is one thing you could do which would solve the problem of your future.'

'Oh? What?'

'Jacob needs a wife. You could marry him.'

Mattie stared at her open-mouthed. Emily waited patiently and when the younger woman didn't say anything, added, 'It'd be a good thing for both of you.'

'Did he suggest you ask me?'

'No. I told him it'd come better from me.' She saw disappointment in the younger woman's face and guessed the suggestion would have been more welcome if it had come from Jacob. That was a good sign, surely?

'I don't know what to say.'

'Say you'll think about it. I'm being rather selfish, I suppose, but he didn't need much persuading, and I can see from the way he looks at you that he finds you attractive.'

She watched Mattie stare down at the sock in her lap.

'Look, I think your marriage would solve all our problems. You need to make a new life for yourself. I need a man to act as my rent agent. Jacob would do that very capably, but he can't look after himself, his children and the house as well as caring for my interests. And also, he must dress respectably, which he doesn't at the moment.

He's always behind with the household tasks, as you can see, however hard he tries to look after his children and home. He manages to keep the family's clothes clean but they're nearly always crumpled and Sarah's grown a lot. She needs new ones. So . . . as I have to look after myself, I've only been able to offer him the job on condition he finds himself a wife.'

Another silence followed and she waited patiently. Nothing would be gained by rushing this.

Mattie looked down at her clenched hands, trying to hide her bitter disappointment. Jacob Kemble didn't want to marry her particularly, he only wanted 'a wife'. Any decent woman would do. 'And he . . . accepted your condition?'

'He didn't like it, but he wants the job so he's thinking about it. He's a shy man when it comes to women. He grew up here, married a girl he'd known all his life, and rumour has it that she asked him, even then. Now he has to take a more risky step – well, he does if he wants the job. So I gave him a nudge.'

Mattie looked at Miss Newington, trying not to show how upset she was. 'I can understand why you think he should marry, but why are you suggesting me? Surely there are other single women round here, people he'd feel more comfortable with? You know nothing about me.'

'There are no suitable women in the village. And there's one more thing.'

Mattie opened her mouth to protest, but Emily held up one hand, so she waited.

'Hear me out, my dear. There's one more thing, the most important reason of all. I should have said it first. I think you two will suit very well because I can see you're attracted to one another in the way a man and wife should be.'

Mattie couldn't look her in the face for a moment or two, because she was right. Jacob was a lovely man and she did like him.

Miss Newington's voice was low and persuasive. 'Why not take the chance?'

'I don't want anyone to be forced into marrying me!'

'If there were more time, if you lived nearby, I don't think I'd have had to give him a nudge. Jacob's not indifferent to you.'

'One of the reasons I ran away was that my stepfather was trying to force me into marriage with a friend of his. The friend had paid him money. He'd *sold* me!'

'I don't know what this other fellow was like—'

Mattie couldn't help shuddering at the thought of Stan Telfor. 'He was big, like my stepfather. No, not quite as bad, but I didn't like him to touch me. I think I'd have had a miserable life with him.'

'If you don't want Jacob to touch you, there's nothing more to be said. I'll help you find somewhere to live and we'll look elsewhere for a wife for him.'

Mattie blushed scarlet. 'I don't . . . It's not like that with Jacob. He's different, kind, caring.'

'Yes. You've only to watch him with his children to see what a gentle, loving man he is. Do you find him attractive in that way?'

For the life of her, Mattie couldn't deny that she did. 'I . . . yes, I do like Jacob, what I've seen of him.'

'He's a good man. You're a decent young woman—'

'Not so young now. I'll be thirty next month.'

'That seems quite young still to me. I'm seventy and thanks to my father, I never had the slightest chance of getting married and having children. I regret that bitterly now, very bitterly indeed.'

Mattie could hear the pain in the older woman's voice and that, more than anything, made her take the suggestion more seriously. She'd been feeling upset for years about not getting married, not having children of her own. It had hurt her to see women she'd been at school with pushing prams, walking along holding a child's hand, smiling fondly at a husband.

'Wouldn't a marriage which brings respect and liking from your husband – at the very least – be better than nothing at your age? You're not too old to have children. You get on well with Luke and Sarah . . .'

Mattie could only shake her head blindly. She was a fool, a romantic fool, worse than the heroines of her library books, but she wanted more than mere respect from a husband.

'Think about it, my dear,' Miss Newington said. 'Don't make a hasty decision. Take everything into account.'

'Very well. I will. But I'm not promising anything.'

That evening Stan came into the pub looking particularly pleased with himself. Bart, who was nursing a pint and wondering what to do about his washing, because he'd run out of clean shirts and the damned laundry charged a fortune for washing and ironing them, scowled at his friend.

'Want another pint?' Stan offered.

Bart nodded.

While they were waiting for the potboy to bring the beers, Stan leant forward. 'I found out which way she went.'

'Who?'

'Your Mattie.'

'She isn't my Mattie any more. I've washed my hands of her.'

'Have it your way. I shan't need to tell you

what I found out, then.' He took a long, slow pull of beer.

Bart tried not to ask, but in the end curiosity got the better of him. 'Where did she go, then?'

Stan wiped his mouth and murmured his appreciation of a good, well-kept beer.

'Where?' Bart repeated.

'Out of town. My cousin remembered a woman who could have been Mattie, remembers her very clearly. He said she got on his tram looking like death warmed up, white as a sheet and shivering, sneezing and blowing her nose. Her hair was soaking wet so it looked dark, except at the front, where it was sticky. He said she looked a right old mess.'

'Serve the bitch right.'

'She got off at the terminus and headed off along the road to Wootton Bassett. She wouldn't have got far walking in that condition, now would she? So I reckon she's quite close still. Why didn't she take the train with the others, that's what I want to know?'

Bart shrugged. 'She stole the housekeeping, but she wouldn't have had enough money to get far by train. I don't believe in women handling money, not more than they need anyway, or they waste it, so I kept my eye on every penny.'

'Some women are careful enough. My mother, for one.'

'Well, in my house, I'm in charge.'

'I'm going to have a look out Bassett way on Sunday. I've got a friend who's lending me his horse and trap. Do you want to come with me?'

'I suppose I might as well. Mattie'll know where her sisters are, that's all I care about.'

'I've got some news about them, too.'

Bart watched Stan raise his pint glass to his lips and take another leisurely swig to torment him.

'Your Nell's been seen meeting Cliff Greenhill, one of the upholsterers. His family lives up in Old Swindon. It'd have been a good match. Don't know why you didn't encourage it.'

'Because I want her to look after me, not another man!' Anger surged through Bart, beating at his temples, making his heart thump in his chest. 'How the hell did she meet him?'

'At church, I was told.'

'I'll kill the sod.'

'You'll have to find him first. He's disappeared too.'

'Ah! He'll be the one who's run off with her. But I reckon his family will know where he's gone.'

'Mebbe. Not my business.'

'No, but it's mine.'

'Don't do anything rash. They might not know anything.'

'If they don't know now, they're bound to

find out sooner or later where he is.' Bart quickly changed his mind about the way he was going to approach this. He intended to punch the hell out of Cliff when he found him, but Stan was right. The family might not know where the son was now, but if he threatened to hurt him, they'd never tell him. Bart must tread carefully and play the upset father, then they might be more inclined to share information with him once they did find out. 'And why's Renie gone with them? She isn't old enough to be interested in lads.'

'They could've took her with 'em. Might have been frightened you'd hurt her.'

'I'd have given her a leathering for not telling me, that's for sure.'

'There you are, then. She wasn't with Mattie, so she must be with them.' Stan drained the last of his beer and tapped his glass on the table as a hint.

Grudgingly, Bart bought him another pint.

'Don't you want another drink yourself?' Stan asked.

'This'll do me for a bit. Without the girls' wages, I have to be a bit more careful, damn them. I need to find someone to do my washing and that costs money. So from now on, we'd better each buy our own drinks. I don't know how you can afford to drink so much every night with only your wage to rely on.'

Stan tapped the side of his nose. 'Got ways of earning a bit extra.'

'I wish you'd show me, then.'

'Can't. Only enough for one in it.'

Which left Bart thinking hard as he trudged home to a dark house. What was Stan onto that he'd missed? If he'd ever needed extra money, it was now. As for Nell and Renie, they couldn't marry anyone without his permission.

It wasn't till he was in bed that he suddenly remembered that Nell had turned twenty-one not long ago. Mattie had wasted money on a fancy iced cake and sewed something for her. So Nell didn't need his permission to get wed. He smiled in the darkness. But she did need her birth certificate to prove her age and he'd got that hidden away.

Only he couldn't settle till he'd checked his box of papers. He got up, lit the gaslight and took the box of family documents down from the top of the wardrobe. It was still locked and hadn't been broken into. He nearly put it back once he was sure it hadn't been taken, but just to be sure, he took out his key chain and opened the box.

He cursed when he saw that none of the girls' birth certificates was there. How had they known where to find them? And how had they got hold of the key? Mattie always cleaned this room and she wasn't tall enough to see on top of the wardrobe. She always had to get the stepladders to clean up there when she did the spring cleaning and he hid the box inside the wardrobe then.

His fingers itched to take off his belt and give all three of them a proper lesson in obedience. As he'd once done to Mattie.

Stan was a fool to hanker after her. She was nothing but trouble, that one. But Bart was sorry he'd not now get the money Stan had been going to pay for marrying her, very sorry. She owed him for that as well as everything else. And he'd make her sorry for what she'd done.

Miss Newington left the house but didn't go across to speak to Jacob, who was working at the upper end of the field. She saw him staring at her and when she didn't make any sign of how she'd got on, he walked across to the wall, waiting for her to come up the lane.

'Well? Did you speak to Mattie?' he asked before she'd even come to a halt.

'Yes. She's thinking about it.'

'She is?'

'Yes, of course. Don't sound so surprised. You're a good-looking man.' She paused, amused to see a tide of red wash across his face. 'Of course, if you find her repulsive, we can still look for someone else. It's not too late.'

'I don't find her repulsive, but I keep telling you, I've not thought of remarrying, especially someone I don't know. Marriage is for life, not just something you slip into with anyone convenient.' But he'd known Alice and still been surprised at what it was like living with her, how limited her view of the world was.

'Well, think about it carefully, as she's doing. But remember . . . if she leaves here, you may never see her again, never even know if she's safe or not.'

Emily walked on without another word and he didn't call her back, but she'd seen from his expression that her parting shot had hit the mark. He'd looked shocked, definitely shocked.

Where the lane curved slightly to the right, she risked a quick glance back and saw that he was still standing there, hadn't moved an inch. She smiled. She felt pretty sure now that they'd get married.

She went and asked old Horace to harness the horse and trap, then drove into Wootton Bassett, leaving them at the livery stables as usual and taking the train from there into Swindon.

Frank Longley looked up as his clerk came to the door of his room.

'Miss Newington to see you, sir.'

He stood up and quickly checked that his tie was straight, because his wife said he had a habit of fiddling with it when he was thinking, then went out to greet her. For a man who had only opened his own rooms the previous year, every new client was important, but this one was quite a feather in his cap.

'My dear Miss Newington, please come through.' He waited till she'd sat down and then asked, 'How can I help you today?'

'I want to make a new will – and quickly. A very simple one, just a single legatee will do. I suppose there's no chance that you could do it for me this afternoon, is there?'

He blinked in shock at this. 'It usually takes longer than that to write a will. There are things to discuss and—'

'There's nothing to discuss this time. I wish to leave everything, unconditionally, to one person.'

'Well, I suppose I could draw up a simple will like that quite quickly. Is there some reason for the hurry?'

'Yes. My cousin Arthur is sending men to break into my house, trying to force me to sell it to him. Who knows what lengths he'll go to? I do want to leave the district now that you've told me I can rent out the house without breaking the conditions of my uncle's will, but I'm doing nothing until I've made sure Arthur can't get hold of the property if something happens to me.'

'Are you sure he's behind the break-ins?'

'Very sure.'

'But surely you don't think he'd . . . do something violent to you?'

'I intend to make sure he has no reason to.'

Frank didn't know what to say. She was an intelligent woman, sounded so certain. 'Tell me who your legatee is, then – another family member perhaps, or a close friend?'

She pulled a wry face. 'I've no relatives now except for Arthur and his family, and most of my friends have died in the last few years, so you can put this person down as legatee.' She took a piece of paper out of her handbag and gave it to him.

He stared at what she'd written in puzzlement, not recognising the name. 'Are you sure? Who is this?'

'Just someone I know and like. It's only temporary so that I can tell my cousin Arthur that if anything happens to me, he won't get the house. That should stop him, don't you think? And since at my age life is precarious, I want to make absolutely certain that he'll never get the house, whatever happens.' She held up one hand to stop him speaking. 'Don't worry. I'll make a proper, well-thought-out will later. This person doesn't know what I'm doing, so I'm not being coerced or flattered into it.'

'I see. Well, in that case, I'll do as you've asked. But I don't approve, I really don't.'

'You don't need to. Just do what I ask. I'll

leave a letter with you, explaining the reasons for my actions, if you like.'

'Yes. That might be useful.'

'And there's something else. I want to find a tenant for Newington House. You hinted that you might know of someone? Are these people still looking for a house to rent?'

'I can find out. What rent are you asking?'

They discussed this, then she looked at the clock which was ticking loudly on his mantelpiece. 'I'll go and buy myself afternoon tea and return in an hour to sign the will.'

She had left before he could stop her.

He sat lost in thought for a minute or two, trying to work out the implications of what she was doing. Surely Arthur Newington couldn't be behind the attacks on her house? He was a well-known figure in the county, not always liked but wealthy men didn't usually commit crimes to get their way. Only . . . there was a big estate at stake, and money had tempted people into crime before now.

Besides, you couldn't argue with clients who'd made their minds up, and though she didn't have a lot of money to spare, Miss Newington had enough to pay her bills, and always did so promptly. Which was more than some of his other clients did.

Arthur Newington's lawyer, James Parker,

had already made his displeasure about a young lawyer opening rooms in Swindon very clear. It was going to be . . . interesting working for Miss Newington.

Frank called for his clerk and they set to work on the will.

She would not find him lacking.

Chapter Seven

Embarrassed by what Miss Newington had done, Jacob avoided going into the house for a cup of tea and biscuit mid-morning. He slaked his thirst at the well and ignored his hunger. But though he continued working, he couldn't stop thinking about what Miss Newington had said. It did make sense for him to remarry, he admitted that, but to live intimately with someone who was little more than a stranger . . . to commit yourself to that person for the rest of your life . . . the thought of that worried him.

As the sun climbed higher in the sky, he couldn't postpone going into the house any longer. He was ravenous, needed his midday meal and had to make sure Mattie got hers too, or she'd not recover properly.

He took off his working boots at the door to

save tramping dirt into the house. As he stepped inside in his stockinged feet, he stopped to stare round in surprise. The room was tidier and the table already set. And Mattie was sitting in the rocking chair, waiting for him as if she was meant to be there. He thrust his feet into his slippers, which always stood ready, noticing for the first time how stained and worn they looked. He needed new ones.

As he turned, he tried to think of something to say, but couldn't.

Mattie glanced at him quickly, then looked away before their eyes could connect. She seemed as embarrassed as he was, which eased his nervousness a little. He didn't like bold women.

She cleared her throat. 'I saw you had some eggs in the pantry. I boiled some for sandwiches with our soup. Is that all right?'

'Yes. I hope you did plenty.'

'I did two for you, one for me.'

He remembered what Miss Newington had said. 'If you're trying to cost me as little money as possible, remember that I produce my own eggs and always have plenty. Since Alice died, I've not known what to do with them all, because I don't know how to bake cakes, even if I had time for it, which I don't.'

'Oh. Right, then.' She went across to put a pan on the hob, pouring water into it from the big blackened kettle that always stood to one side of the stove top to provide warm water when needed.

He let her work. She seemed very capable, her movements sure and graceful, a pleasure to watch.

Within ten minutes he was sitting down to a bowl of ham-flavoured soup and neatly cut sandwiches. He thanked her, then ate in silence, enjoying the simple meal but unable to think of anything to say except, 'This is good.'

As he pushed his plate away, Mattie said, 'Do you have any more of those wizened apples? I could make us stewed apple and custard for tea. And what do you want for the main course tonight?'

'Are you sure you're up to it?'

'I'm taking things slowly. I cleared up this morning, then had a little nap, then . . . um . . . talked to Miss Newington. I shall do the same this afternoon – have a rest, I mean.'

He liked the way she got flustered when she mentioned Miss Newington. She looked pretty today with her hair tied back and her face showing more colour. 'Better open a tin of corned beef. Could you make us a hash?'

'Yes.'

'I've not had time to get any fresh meat. I'll send to the village shop for something. They put orders in with a butcher in Wootton Bassett.'

'I make a good meat pie. If you get some stewing steak, I can do enough for two days.'

'That'd be good.'

Their eyes met and he could feel himself flushing, then got angry with himself for being such a coward and sat down again. He always told the children to face up to problems and should follow his own advice.

She looked at him warily. 'Is something wrong?'

He took a deep breath and said it quickly before he could lose his nerve. 'Miss Newington spoke to you, I believe? She made a . . . a suggestion.' He couldn't force out the words 'get married', just couldn't do it.

'Yes. It was . . . a surprise.'

'She shocked me too.'

'I'll perfectly understand if you don't want to . . .' Her voice trailed away and she flushed scarlet.

'I don't know what I want, and that's the truth.'

She let out her breath in a gasp that was almost a laugh. 'I don't, either.'

'You haven't refused, though?'

'No. You're still considering it, then, are you?'

'Yes. It . . . the idea does have some advantages, I must admit.'

Silence. She looked up just as he did and their eyes met. She seemed so anxious, he gave her a reassuring smile.

It was her answering smile that did it, shy and nervous. And how thin she was, how close she'd been to death. He felt responsible for her and he liked her. So did the children. He took a deep breath. 'All in all, I don't mind getting married, if you don't. But I don't want you feeling forced into it.'

She didn't look away, seemed a bit sad behind everything, but before he could ask her why, she spread her hands in a helpless gesture. 'All right.'

'You mean . . . you'll do it?'

She nodded. 'If you're sure.'

And suddenly he was sure, so he gave in to the temptation of taking her hand. 'I'll try to be a good husband to you, Mattie, provide for you as well as I can, treat you properly.'

Her hand turned to grasp his more firmly. 'I'll be a good wife to you, Jacob. I'll look after your children and work alongside you. I'm a hard worker.'

He gave her hand a little squeeze. 'And I wanted to say, in case you were worried: I won't ever hurt you. I don't believe in beating women or children. I never laid a finger on Alice.'

Jacob didn't know what to say next, so he let go of her hand and stood up. 'That's settled, then. I'll go and tell Miss Newington tonight.'

'I'll iron you a shirt. Do you have a better one than your working shirts?'

'Yes. I'll fetch my best one down.'

When he'd done that, he walked back out to the field wondering what had got into him. He'd more than half-decided not to remarry, even for the sake of the job. But Miss Newington was right. In many ways, it was a sensible solution to all his problems, and to Mattie's.

And she was pretty. He really liked her hair. And her smile.

If he hadn't offered to marry her, Mattie would have nowhere to go. He couldn't bear to think of her turned loose in the world with only just over a pound in her purse. Surely there was enough warmth between them, enough goodwill, for them to make a fair go of marriage?

He found himself smiling at the thought of her as he carried on working. Thinking how good it would be to come back to the house at dinner time and find her waiting, how good to see Sarah with a woman to guide her, how good to have Mattie in his bed.

Before she left the lawyer's rooms after signing her new will and writing a brief letter stating why she'd not left anything to her cousin, Emily borrowed a piece of paper and wrote a brief letter to that same cousin. She made a copy and gave that to Mr Longley, on the principle of not trusting her cousin an inch.

> Dear Arthur,
>
> It seems Mr Parker made an error when explaining our uncle's will to me, so in case you're under the same misapprehension, I'm writing to inform you of the real state of affairs.
>
> I am not obliged to live at Newington House but am free to rent it until the ten years are over, then I can sell it to whomsoever I choose.
>
> And as none of us are getting any younger, just in case anything should happen to me, I've made a will leaving everything I own to a person outside the family.
>
> Yours etc
> Emily

She signed the letter with a flourish, refused an offer to allow Mr Longley's clerk to post it for her and went to buy a penny stamp at the post office. She licked it, admired the King's head in shades of her favourite colour, green, then placed the stamp carefully in the corner of the envelope. She smiled as she slid the letter into the postbox, feeling as if a burden had been removed from her shoulders.

She was still smiling as she sat in the train. Arthur wasn't getting his hands on her land at some ridiculously low price. If he made her a better offer as a result of this, she'd consider it, but she wasn't giving the house away, to him or to anyone. She was still trying to decide what price would be fair as the train pulled into Wootton Bassett.

She let the horse go at its own pace, which was slow, as she drove out to the village. It'd been an eventful few days. Her cousin was a bully and always had been. She'd been glad when her mother persuaded her father to take up employment he'd been offered in Newcastle because Arthur had made the family gatherings of her childhood miserable. He'd pinched her when no one was looking, punching her in the stomach sometimes or pulling her hair hard enough to make her eyes water. He'd treated his male cousin the same way. Poor Jeremy was dead now. She still didn't approve of the Boer War. Why should Englishmen die so far away in South Africa? What good did such wars do?

Once her family moved away, she'd felt reasonably certain she would never see Arthur again. Only, after her uncle died, she'd had to come back and face him.

This train of thought led her to wonder once more why her uncle had left things so strangely. It could only be to create mischief. His son had been killed, something he'd never come to terms with, so out of resentment he'd made sure the niece and nephew who were still alive inherited problems, having either land or money, but not both.

Well, she intended to prove herself a match for Arthur this time.

Jacob was delighted to find tea cooked and ready to serve when he came in from his day's work. He sniffed appreciatively. 'Something smells good.'

Sarah rushed across to help him with his slippers, words pouring out of her. 'Mattie's made corned beef hash and she let me help with the apple crumble. There's custard to go with it and there are no lumps in it, none at all. Luke set the table, but he didn't want to, said it was girls' work.'

'Getting a meal ready is work for anyone who wants to eat.' Jacob gave his son a severe look. 'You never saw me grumbling about doing the cooking, did you?'

Luke shrugged and kicked the table leg, a habit he had when something annoyed him.

The food was simple but tasty and they ate up every mouthful.

'That was delicious.' Jacob smiled at Mattie, then turned to his daughter. 'And the crumble was good, too.' He waited for Luke to speak and when his son didn't, he asked quietly, 'Did you enjoy your meal, son?'

Luke nodded.

'Then why haven't you thanked our guest for cooking it?'

'Thank you for making tea,' Luke said, but he didn't sound grateful.

'You children can do the dishes, as usual,' Jacob said. 'Miss Willitt is very tired now. We all have to remember that she's not completely better yet.'

They didn't grumble, but he heard Luke snap at Sarah once or twice. 'I don't know what's got into our Luke,' Jacob said apologetically to Mattie. 'He usually has better manners than this.'

'It doesn't matter.'

'It does to me. I like my children to behave properly and show respect for their elders. Their mother would have wanted it, too.' He hesitated, then added in a low voice, 'You haven't changed your mind about what we discussed?'

'No. And you? I won't hold you to it if you have.'

'I haven't changed.' To his amusement she went pink again. He discovered that he liked to make her blush and had a sudden urge to touch her soft pink cheek.

At seven-thirty, Jacob went upstairs to change into his best shirt and Sunday suit for the call on

Miss Newington, finding them laid out neatly on his bed, the shirt beautifully ironed, with a stiff collar and collar studs beside it.

When he came down, Mattie was resting by the fire, looking tired, and he said, 'Luke, Sarah, don't let Miss Willitt do anything else this evening.'

'I'll look after her.' Sarah stationed herself beside Mattie's chair with a self-important air.

Luke mumbled something and Mattie shot him a quick, worried glance.

That boy needed a good talking-to, Jacob decided.

Lyddie tapped on the door and came into the small sitting room. 'Mr Kemble is here to see you, miss.'

'Show him in.'

Jacob came in and Emily noticed at once that he was looking much smarter than usual, no doubt due to Mattie's efforts. 'Please take a seat.'

He sat on the edge of the armchair opposite, looking ill at ease.

She frowned. 'Have you come to tell me you can't take the job?'

'No. I've come to tell you Mattie and I have agreed to get married and if it's still all right with you, I'd like to take the job.'

She beamed at him. 'That's wonderful news! What changed your mind?'

He fidgeted and ran one fingertip round the edge of his stiff collar. 'I felt sorry for her.'

That didn't please her. 'Feeling sorry for someone is no reason to get married.'

'And, well . . .' He flushed. 'I like her.'

'Ah, that's a much better reason. I like her too.' She beamed at him. 'I'm very pleased about this, very pleased indeed. We'll get a special licence tomorrow and we can have you married by the end of the week. April is a lovely month to get married in, don't you think?'

He blinked at her in shock and his voice sounded thin and scratchy. 'We don't need to . . . to rush things like that, surely?'

'We do. It isn't fitting for her to be staying with you if you're not married. And anyway, I wish to move back to Newcastle as soon as possible.' She didn't know why she felt to be in such a hurry but she did. She'd go into lodgings until she could buy a small house, somewhere in Jesmond Dene perhaps. Then she saw that Jacob was waiting patiently for her to continue and remembered that he was quite short of money. 'I'll pay for the extra expenses involved in the special licence. You'll be a married man by this time next week.'

She saw him mouth the words after her, his eyes widening in shock, and hid a smile. 'We'll go into Swindon tomorrow afternoon and make the necessary arrangements. I can see my lawyer while we're there and ask him if he's found anyone to rent this house yet. The job is yours, Jacob Kemble.'

His tense expression eased a little and he sat more upright as if he felt better for that news.

'Is that all?' she asked.

'I think so, unless you have anything else to discuss, miss?'

'No.' She stood up and he did too. His manners were always excellent. She held out her hand and he shook it without a word.

'I'll call for you in the trap tomorrow morning.' Then she had a thought and turned. 'Does your young lady have her birth certificate with her? I think we might need it.'

'I don't know. She had some papers, but they were sodden. I didn't look at them.'

'Better find out. If she hasn't got it, we'll see what my lawyer suggests.'

When he'd gone she allowed herself one glass of her uncle's fine brandy, sipping it slowly and smiling into the fire. Then she moved across to her writing bureau and began to make lists and plans for the move. She'd done her best to settle in here, her very best, but something was calling her home, and she felt she should go sooner rather than later.

That was her last thought before she fell asleep.

Home. She was going home. She'd soon be taking her daily walks along the seafront. That thought made her feel warmly happy.

Jacob walked back down the lane, feeling as if he'd been picked up and thoroughly shaken by a giant. It was all happening too quickly. What would Mattie say to such a hasty wedding? Would that make her change her mind?

He was surprised to find that he hoped not.

He found her sitting by the kitchen table, reading a book again. She looked tired, her face white and pinched, her eyes huge and, it seemed to him, her expression was rather apprehensive. She didn't even wait for him to sit down.

'Well? What did Miss Newington say?'

He went to sit beside her, turned towards her, leaning his left arm on the table and watching her intently. It seemed essential that he not miss anything about her expression. If she felt forced into this, afraid of marrying him, then he'd end it. 'She was pleased that we were getting wed. Offered me the job on the spot.'

Mattie let out her breath in a long sigh of relief. 'I'm so glad.'

'But she wants us to marry straight away, by special licence.' He wondered if he'd looked as surprised when Miss Newington said this to him as Mattie did now.

'Straight away!'

He nodded. 'If that doesn't suit you, I can go and ask her for a few more days, but she wants to get away from here quickly and go back to the north, which is home to her.'

'Oh. Well . . . I suppose it won't make much difference. Only . . .' Her eyes filled with tears.

He took her hand, didn't like to see her so upset. 'What is it?'

'I've nothing to wear. I'd hoped for time to make myself a pretty dress. And even then—' She broke off, covering her eyes with one hand.

He saw a tear trickle down her cheek and pulled her into his arms. 'There now, there now. Tell me what it is and we'll find a way to make it right.'

'I don't have enough money for the material. Oh, Jacob, I shall look so shabby!' She gestured to herself. 'I didn't leave home wearing my Sunday dress, and even that is . . . well, it's old-fashioned now. And my shoes have cracked after getting so wet. They were quite old too.'

'Did your stepfather keep you so short of money?'

She nodded against his chest, her voice muffled. 'I never had a penny of my own, even though I worked for two hours every day in a shop. He took all our wages and always wanted to know what I'd spent on housekeeping, right down to the nearest farthing.'

Jacob stroked her hair, marvelling at how soft it was and how well she fitted into his arms. 'I don't mind what you wear. It's you I'm marrying, not your clothes.'

'Any woman would want to look her best on her wedding day. I'm no different.'

He had a sudden idea. 'I've still got Alice's things. You can see if there's anything among them you could alter.'

'Wear your wife's clothes?'

'You're using her nightdress already.'

'It doesn't seem right to get married in her clothes, though. And anyway, that doesn't solve the problem of shoes.'

'She'd not mind you having the clothes. She was a kind woman, my Alice. You'd have liked her and I think she'd have liked you. And we can buy you some new shoes in Swindon. There are lots of shops in Regent Street. We're bound to find something there.'

Suddenly Mattie was sobbing even harder. He didn't know what to do to calm her, but rocked her to and fro, waiting for the storm to subside.

'What is it?' he asked when she lay quiet and spent against his chest. 'What have I done to upset you?'

'It's just . . . you're so kind. I've not been used to kindness from a man. It overset me.' She gave him a watery smile. 'I'm being silly. It's probably because I've not recovered yet.'

And because she was so upset, he found himself kissing her gently on the lips. 'You're not silly,' he said as he drew away. But because her lips were so soft and full, he had to kiss her again, properly this time. And she didn't protest or do anything but kiss him back.

When the kiss ended, he held her close. 'Funny old world, isn't it? Luke thought you were dead when he found you and now I'm going to marry you.'

'I was more worried about my stepfather catching me. I'm still worried about that.'

'Once we're married, there's nothing he can do.'

'He can attack you, hurt you badly. He prides himself on paying back anyone who's offended him. I think it's just an excuse for hurting people. He enjoys doing that, even in small ways.'

'He can try to hurt me, but I grew up defending myself against a lad who used to live in the village. Proper old bully he was when he was younger, and bigger than me. But it taught me to fight. He got into trouble for his rough ways and joined the army to escape. Went out to South Africa with Master Jeremy. Poor fellow, he died there as well.' When she didn't speak, he added, 'I do know how to defend myself, Mattie.'

'But you don't know my stepfather. He's a big man and he fights dirty.'

'I'll bear that in mind if he ever attacks me. But I promise you, as long as there's breath in my body, I'll look after what's mine, and that will include you from now on.'

She gave him such a luminous smile, it warmed his heart. He gave her hand a final squeeze. 'Well now, if that's settled, I'll make you a cup of cocoa while you get yourself to bed. I'll bring it in to you.'

When he carried it into the front room, he found she'd fallen asleep, her face peaceful as a child's, all traces of tears vanished now.

He smiled and was still smiling when he went back into the kitchen to drink the cocoa himself. This marriage was going to be all right, he was sure of it now. If Alice was up in heaven watching over them, he hoped she wouldn't mind. He didn't think she would.

And he knew his parents would have approved of Mattie.

How could you not approve of a woman like her?

Chapter Eight

The following morning Jacob again donned his best clothes, muttering under his breath as he tried to get the tie straight. So in turmoil was his mind that only at the last minute did he remember the birth certificate and ask Mattie about it.

'I did bring it. But it was in my bundle and it's in a terrible condition after getting soaked.'

'Can I take it with me?'

'Yes, of course.' She went into the front room and came back holding a crumpled piece of paper, its black ink water-smeared.

They peered at it together.

'I'd better write down the names,' she said. 'Some of them don't show up very clearly.' She did this while Jacob found an old envelope to put it in and stowed that in his inner jacket pocket.

'There. I'm ready.'

'Just a minute.' Mattie came across to straighten his tie, smiling up at him involuntarily. 'That's better.'

He too was smiling when he left, and kept thinking he felt the butterfly touch of her fingers on his neck.

In the middle of the morning, after she'd had a lie-down, Mattie went to try on Alice's shoes. They were far too big for her. She'd just have to polish up her own and hope no one noticed the cracked leather of the uppers till she could buy some new ones.

There were only a few clothes hanging in the wardrobe and from the way one of the dresses had been mended, she could tell that Alice hadn't been a good needlewoman. She muttered, 'Sorry to take your things!' as she went through them, because it seemed the right thing to do. After choosing a dress, she took it downstairs to unpick the seams. It was pale blue, a nondescript colour, not one she'd have chosen for herself, but it wasn't worn, so at least she'd be decent.

There was a Singer sewing machine in the front room, a very old-fashioned and heavy treadle type. When she pedalled the foot pad and tried it out on a piece of rag, it clanked and rattled and clearly hadn't been well cared for. She wondered if Alice had used it much and guessed not. It wasn't half as good as the one which had belonged to Mattie's mother, which she'd been using for years. She paused for a moment to wonder what her stepfather would do with her sewing machine and the few books her mother had left her. He'd probably hurl the books out into the yard or sell them to the rag-and-bone man.

She found it hard to concentrate as she unpicked some of the seams and pinned them to fit her properly. Her thoughts drifted and the dress lay unheeded on the table in front of her as often as not. She looked down at it with distaste, then got angry with herself. She should be grateful for these clothes . . . only she hated the thought of getting married in another woman's dress, absolutely hated it.

She looked round at another cause for irritation. Jacob had done his best, but she was aching to get the house clean. Physical activity still exhausted her, however, so she was saving her energy for cooking the meals and mending, which seemed the best way to help the family at the moment. They'd certainly been appreciative of her efforts last night. Well, Jacob and Sarah had been. Until prompted, Luke had offered only the unspoken appreciation of clearing his plate and accepting a second helping. He'd also scowled at her a few times. She couldn't understand why.

There was a knock on the front door and

almost immediately someone pushed it open and called, 'Mr Kemble? Are you there? It's only me.'

Mattie jumped to her feet, but it was too late to hide.

The woman who came in was dressed in dowdy, old-fashioned clothes but was clearly a lady, the sort who visited the poor but considered herself superior to them – though Jacob wasn't poor exactly and had no need of anyone's charity.

The newcomer stopped dead at the sight of Mattie, then drew herself up and said in tones of distaste, 'So they were right. I didn't believe it, but they were right!'

'I beg your pardon?'

'Who are you and what are you doing here?'

Mattie stiffened at the tone but for Jacob's sake tried to think of something conciliatory to say.

Before she could manage it, the woman took a step forward and said in an even louder voice, 'Well? Answer me this minute.'

Something inside Mattie rebelled. 'What business is that of yours?'

'Don't you dare take that tone with me, young woman.' She studied Mattie from head to toe and didn't seem to like what she saw.

'If you're looking for Jacob, he's out—'

'I deliberately chose a time when I knew he'd be working in the field, so that I could see for myself if rumour was correct.' Her expression became even more disdainful. 'And it is. He's keeping a trollop here.'

Mattie gasped at this insult and drew herself up. 'Please leave now.'

'I shall not leave until you've told me who you are and what you're doing here.'

'It's none of your business.'

'I'm Mrs Henty, the curate's wife, and it most certainly is my business if one of my husband's parishioners is living in sin. Just wait until Miss Newington hears about this. She'll be furious. If you have any concern for Jacob and what's right, young woman, you'll leave at once. Decent people don't want to live cheek by jowl with your sort.'

Mattie walked to the front door. 'I'll ask you one more time to leave.'

Instead Mrs Henty marched through to the kitchen door, opened it and bellowed across the field, 'Jacob Kemble! Jacob! A word if you please.' When there was no answer she called again, in a voice which would have woken the dead. No answer. After peering across the field, she turned back to scowl at Mattie. 'I'm not going anywhere till you tell me where Jacob is.'

'In that case, you'll excuse me if I get on with my work.' She had no intention of telling her that he was in Swindon, making arrangements for them to marry. It would sound apologetic, and she had nothing to apologise for.

Since the curate's wife was a stout woman, who must have weighed twice what she did, Mattie had no way of forcing her to leave. Ignoring the open door she sat down again and bent her head over her sewing, trying to hide the fact that her hands were shaking with suppressed anger.

'I've never met such impudence in my life!' The curate's wife moved to stand at the opposite side of the table.

'Nor have I.' Mattie raised her head to meet the other woman's gaze and held steady against it until Mrs Henty looked away. Then she bent over her work again.

It was a full five minutes before the curate's wife said loudly, 'You will regret this. I'm going up to see Miss Newington. Perhaps she can bring him to a sense of what's right.' She swept out of the room and slammed the front door behind her.

Mattie let her mending drop and buried her face in her hands. She hadn't thought to lock the door. People didn't usually barge into others' houses without being invited, not unless they were close friends or family, and she was surprised that Mrs Henty had done that. Perhaps they had different ways here in the country.

She hoped she hadn't done anything which would upset Jacob, but to be spoken to like that had made something snap inside her, and the temper that had been reined in by fear for so many years had taken over.

She had done nothing wrong – nothing! – and would not be treated like a loose woman.

Nor would she kowtow to anyone again, not if they beat her to death for it.

In Swindon, Miss Newington's presence at Jacob's side swept away all difficulties, because she could vouch for the bride, explaining to both the lawyer and the man at the registry office that she was a friend of the family and the bride was unfortunately recovering from the influenza and needed to rest.

'She's just lost the last of her family,' Emily said in a hushed voice, 'so she and Mr Kemble wish to get married earlier than they'd planned.'

Jacob signed papers when told, made the appropriate answers and found himself with a wedding booked for the following Tuesday morning.

Sitting in the train, Emily said suddenly, 'We need to find something for your bride to wear.'

'I've given her Alice's clothes and she's going to alter them.'

'What? You can't expect another woman to get married in your dead wife's clothes!'

'There isn't time to buy anything else.'

'Nonetheless . . .' She frowned for a moment

then beamed at him. 'I know! There are trunks full of clothing in the attics at Newington House. We'll take her up to the house in the trap and let her choose. There may not be time to have a dress made, but there's time to alter one. None of my things will suit her. I'm too tall, and anyway, my father didn't believe in ladies dressing flamboyantly.' She looked down at herself, sighed, then became brisk again.

'I'm not sure she'll accept charity,' Jacob said.

'She won't even hesitate. She'll wear anything rather than your wife's clothes. And besides, it'll be my wedding present to her.'

It felt like riding a runaway horse, he thought. Would Mattie want this? He didn't know.

They picked up the horse and trap in Wootton Bassett and Emily asked Jacob to drive it back. She enjoyed the pleasure of being able to study the scenery on the way back to the village instead of concentrating on driving, something she wasn't good at. When they got to the cottage, he would have handed the reins to her, but she started getting out of the trap before he could prevent her.

'You wait here. I want to have a quick word with Mattie.'

When she went into the house, she saw at once that the younger woman had been weeping.

'What's wrong? Do you not wish to marry Jacob?'

Mattie's lips trembled for a moment, then she said baldly, 'The curate's wife walked into the house this morning without so much as a by-your-leave. She accused me of . . . of being Jacob's trollop. She said the rumour had gone round the village. I shouldn't have let it upset me, because I know I've done nothing wrong, but it did. I seem to cry very easily at the moment.'

'Drat the woman! She will poke her nose into people's lives, whether they want it or not, and half the time she tells them it's at my behest, so they do as she wants, then blame me.' Emily hesitated, then went to give the younger woman a couple of quick pats on the upper arm. She wasn't one for mauling people around, but she had taken a liking to this young woman and didn't like to see her so upset.

Mattie blew her nose and squared her shoulders. 'I'm sorry.'

'Just ignore that woman. I'll have a word with her later. She's not going to blacken your name if I can help it. Now, get your coat and come with me. We need to find you a wedding dress.'

'I was altering one of Alice's.'

'Nonsense. You don't want to wear her things and if that garment is anything to go by, she had dreadful taste in clothes. She was a decent young woman, but more at home in the fields than in the house, and looked it.' Almost as an afterthought, she added, 'Oh, and everything's booked for Tuesday, so we haven't a minute to waste. We need to find you a dress quickly.'

'We're getting married on Tuesday!'

'Yes.'

Still Mattie hesitated. 'Are you still sure I should marry him, Miss Newington? People will think—'

'I'm very sure. It was the best thing that could have happened to Jacob, rescuing you. He'd let things get him down. I'll sort out what people think later. Now do come on.'

'But your dresses won't fit me, either.' And Miss Newington had even worse taste in clothes than Alice.

'I'm not offering you one of mine. There are trunks full of discarded clothing in my attics. I'm sure we can find you something suitable to wear, as long as you're prepared to alter it yourself. They're very old-fashioned, I'm afraid, and I can't help you with the sewing. I can embroider, but I'm no good whatsoever at dressmaking.'

'Oh. Well. All right. Um . . . there wouldn't be any shoes, would there?' She gestured down at her shoes.

'There may well be. Now, get your coat on. Hurry up.'

'Don't tell Jacob about Mrs Henty,' Mattie whispered as she was swept towards the door.

'Don't be foolish. Of course I shall tell him. He needs to know.'

Jacob listened in growing indignation as Miss Newington explained what had happened during their absence. He was furious on several counts. Fancy the woman daring to walk into his house without so much as a by-your-leave! He'd make it clear to her that she was not to do that again.

But what angered him most of all was that she'd upset Mattie. He hated to see her reddened eyes and think of her all alone, weeping. He heard her voice shake as she answered his questions and longed to take her in his arms and comfort her.

'What I don't understand,' he said at last, 'is how anyone knew you were there.'

Silence. The only other people besides themselves who knew about Mattie were his children. Had Luke broken his promise to keep quiet about their visitor? That thought upset Jacob. At eleven, Luke was old enough to know right from wrong. But Luke had been very sulky about Mattie's presence.

'It must be my son who let it out,' he said at last.

'You have a daughter too,' Miss Newington pointed out.

Jacob considered this, then shook his head. 'No. Sarah loves keeping secrets. And Luke's been in a bad mood lately. I reckon it's him.'

'They're only children,' Mattie said. 'You can't expect miracles of them. And it may not be Luke.'

'Nonetheless, I'm going to ask him,' Jacob said with quiet determination. 'Now, let's sort out this dress, then you must have a rest. You look exhausted even before we start.'

'I'm tired of resting.'

'It's the only way to get well,' Miss Newington said in her crisp, no-nonsense voice. 'Now, Jacob, would you carry your young lady up to the attics and help me with the trunks?'

'Of course.'

'I can walk,' Mattie protested.

'You're such a little thing, it's no trouble to carry you.' He picked her up and she put one arm round his neck. He liked the feel of her, the softness, the clean smell of soap and water. Her hair was shiny today. Had she washed it? It was tied back with a ribbon into a mass of waves. He had a sudden urge to kiss her again, but you couldn't do that sort of thing with an elderly spinster standing waiting for you at the top of the stairs.

He smiled at Mattie as he set her down on the attic landing. He was breathing heavily, but not

168

just from carrying her. He was surprised by his reaction. He hadn't desired a woman since Alice died.

Miss Newington's sharp voice brought them both to attention.

'It's this way. There's a big storage area at the rear behind the maids' bedrooms. I've started going through the stuff there, but it'll take me months to sort it all out at this rate. Hurry up!'

Mattie was amazed at how much stuff was lying around up here. Miss Newington seemed to know what she wanted, though. Jacob was told to fetch a rickety old chair for Mattie to sit on, then pull a big trunk closer. It proved to be full of discarded garments.

The two women pulled out clothes, none of which looked worn to Mattie. She couldn't help stroking the beautiful fabrics, which were like nothing she'd worn before. How much had these cost? 'They're too good for me.'

'I can't produce clothing of inferior quality just to suit you,' Miss Newington said sharply. 'This stuff is going to waste and costs me nothing. You must choose from what's available. This is no time to be picky.'

'I didn't mean . . . I'm not ungrateful . . . Oh!' Mattie reached for a dress in a soft green, holding it up reverently and trying it against herself.

'The colour suits you,' Miss Newington said, 'though the dress is far too big for you. Shall you be able to alter it?'

'Yes.' She'd do it if she had to stay up all night. It was such a beautiful colour.

'Then take it.'

Mattie could see Jacob smiling approvingly and couldn't resist accepting.

Miss Newington flapped one hand towards the trunk. 'Might as well pick two or three more while you're at it. No use leaving them here for the moths to feast on.'

Mattie opened and shut her mouth, then gave in to temptation and dipped into the trunk again.

The colours were like a garden of pretty flowers, the materials beautiful, some fine and silky, others of soft wool. They weren't practical clothes, but she wasn't in her dotage yet and had longed for prettier clothes for years.

'We'll have to find you a hat to go with that one for the wedding. And there were some ribbons in one of those drawers. Perhaps you could use them to trim a straw hat.' Miss Newington bustled about, fetching out some hatboxes, trying out their contents on Mattie, sometimes shaking her head, at other times nodding approval.

Finally, she looked down at the younger woman's feet. 'We need to find you some shoes.

These were worn out even before they got wet. Let's see . . .'

The shoes in the attic were more worn than the clothes, showing impressions of the wearers' feet. They were mostly too big, but just as Mattie was despairing of finding something suitable, they came across three pairs that were markedly smaller than the others.

'Try these!'

They fitted her perfectly and were as soft as gloves.

'I think they must have belonged to a young girl,' Miss Newington said thoughtfully. 'They're hardly worn. I wonder if she grew out of them quickly or . . .' She cut off what she'd been going to say. 'Anyway, you might as well have all those shoes. They're doing no good to anyone lying here.'

Mattie surprised herself by daring to give the older woman a quick hug. 'I can't thank you enough.' Her voice broke and she was near to tears.

Miss Newington flushed and for once seemed lost for words. Perhaps she wasn't used to being hugged. But she didn't seem annoyed, thank goodness.

Exhausted but filled with quiet joy that – for once in her life – she'd be well dressed, Mattie began to gather her new possessions together. As she did so, she thought of something she could do as a thank you. 'You should take that blue dress for yourself, Miss Newington. I could easily alter it for you. It was worn by someone as tall as you and that saxe colour would be very flattering on you.'

She thought for a moment or two that the older woman was going to take offence, then Miss Newington's expression softened and she picked up the dress, holding it against herself.

'Are you sure?'

'As long as you give me a few days, I can easily do it for you.'

'I meant, are you sure this will suit me?'

'Oh, yes. The tweeds you're wearing don't, because they're too muddy coloured, but that blue will. You have a pretty complexion.' She was surprised to see Miss Newington looking self-conscious, so turned quickly away, not wanting to embarrass her.

There was silence, then Jacob said, 'I'd better carry you downstairs again, Mattie, then I'll come back for the dresses. We need to get you home for a rest.'

'I'll bring the clothes,' Miss Newington said. 'But you can't leave for a few minutes. I want to write a note to Mr Henty. Horace can deliver it to him after he's taken you back in the trap.'

Mattie wondered what she'd say to the curate.

Was she going to complain about his wife? She hoped so. No one should judge someone without finding out the facts first. She let Jacob carry her down the stairs again, resting her head against his chest, feeling utterly boneless and weary now that the excitement was over.

She felt happy, though. She'd never had clothes like these. But as her benefactress said, they were just lying around in the attic, and wouldn't fit the older woman, so she didn't need to feel guilty about taking them.

Would Jacob think she looked good in that green dress on their wedding day? She did hope so.

When he saw the handwriting on the envelope, Ernest Henty showed it to his wife, not opening it, because letters from their local landowner often insisted on him doing things he found difficult. 'What can Miss Newington want with me, do you suppose?'

He opened the letter, but it contained only a summons to visit the landowner 'at his earliest convenience' and on his own.

'I was going to visit her myself.'

'You'd better not come this time. It doesn't do to go against her wishes.'

Her bosom swelled with indignation. 'I'll go and see her tomorrow. You were busy so I dealt with something today. That Jacob Kemble, who has always been impertinent, has a woman living with him, some trollop I've never seen before. Miss Newington will want you to do something about it.'

'How do you know she's a trollop?'

'Who else but a woman of low morals would live with a man to whom she's neither related nor married?'

'She may be a relative, for all we know.'

'She's nothing like him. She's not even as tall as I am, and he must be six foot, at least.'

'Have you seen her, then?'

'I called at the house earlier and there she was, as bold as brass. No respect for her betters, either. Miss Newington won't want a woman like that living in our village.'

He set off at once, worrying all the way up the hill. His wife was a very thorough sort of woman, who had taken control of every aspect of his life from the moment they first got married, but he sometimes wished she wouldn't interfere quite as much in his parishioners' lives. She shouldn't have gone into Kemble's house without being invited. He knew she meant well and she did wonders with the money he earned, but Jane wasn't the easiest of wives.

If they'd had children, it might have deflected her attention from him and the minutiae of parish life, but they hadn't been blessed. And she'd been a bit on edge lately. Well, they were both worried about what would happen to them if Miss Newington sold the estate. They couldn't afford a higher rent, not without the most stringent economies.

The person who'd bought the three cottages Miss Newington had already sold had immediately put up the rents, which had brought hardship to those families living in them and . . . He realised he'd reached the gate of the big house and stopped to mop his brow. The weather was very pleasant this evening, but his dark clerical garments were too hot because he couldn't afford both winter and summer weight clothing.

Emily stood by the window, looking out at the village below, as she often did. When she saw someone's head bobbing up the lane, she guessed it'd be the curate. She continued to watch until she could see him clearly. He looked hot and uncomfortable.

The poor man was completely under his wife's thumb and Emily would guess that it was probably Jane Henty who was preventing him from obtaining a parish of his own, because the woman had no tact, didn't even attempt to get on with the clergyman for whom her husband had been a curate for several years, let alone be pleasant to the bishop. Why did the dratted woman feel she had a right to stick her finger into every pie and tell the whole world what to do?

Well, this time she'd gone too far!

Emily went to take a seat by the fire and when the curate was shown in, she said nothing for a moment or two, staring at him in a way she knew made most people uncomfortable.

'You . . . um . . . asked me to come and see you, Miss Newington.'

'Yes. I suppose you'd better take a seat.' She waved one hand towards the chair opposite her and waited.

He cleared his throat. 'Um . . . how may I help you?'

'By controlling that wife of yours. She's angered me greatly today.'

He turned pale and swallowed visibly, his prominent Adam's apple bobbing in his scrawny throat. 'What has Jane done? I'm sure she didn't mean to upset you.'

'This morning she entered my rent agent's house without even knocking and then maligned a young friend of mine, who is residing there, with my knowledge and approval. Mattie and Jacob Kemble are getting married next week, but she's recently lost her home and has nearly died of pneumonia, so he and I have been looking after her.' She waited, seeing panic settle on her visitor's face.

'My wife has spoken to me about that. She was concerned about . . . um . . . immorality.'

'Does she think I am not? I can assure you nothing immoral has happened. That poor girl can hardly stand up still, let alone share a man's bed.'

'I'm sure you're right – honest mistake – we both have the utmost respect for you and . . .' His voice trailed away.

'I suppose it's too late to ask your wife to say nothing about my young protégée's presence?'

He flushed and stared at his feet.

'I see from your reaction that she's already spoken of this. Your wife, Mr Henty, is a meddling busybody with a tongue that never stops wagging. I should be grateful if you will tell her from me that there is no immorality whatsoever going on in that cottage. I would stake my life on it. Also, the people concerned have been engaged for a while and will be getting married on Tuesday in Swindon at the registry office. I shall be acting as witness for them.'

'Oh. I see.' After a moment's pause, he added, 'In the registry office? Would it not be better if they were married in the village church, in the sight of God?'

'No, it would not. They have friends in

Swindon who wish to attend.' She made a mental note to tell Jacob that. 'And anyway, if we held the ceremony here, your wife would intrude, as she always does. They want a quiet, pleasant ceremony with only their friends present, and that's what they'll get.' She rang the little bell that stood on the table beside her. 'I bid you good day, Mr Henty, and hope you will attend to this matter of your wife.'

'Oh, yes. You can rely on me. Now that I know . . .'

He was still trailing apologetic phrases as he was shown out.

Lyddie came back. 'Is there anything you want, miss?'

'A new curate.'

Lyddie was betrayed into a giggle.

Emily couldn't help smiling. 'I'd better tell you and Cook what this is all about.' She went to the kitchen and explained to them that Jacob was about to get married, again implying that she knew the young woman in question.

'I think it's so romantic,' Lyddie sighed, 'her coming to him for help like that.'

'Yes. And it's about time he found a mother for those two children,' Cook said.

'I agree. Perhaps we could have a festive tea for them here on Tuesday afternoon? Can you manage that, Cook?'

'It'll be my pleasure, miss. I do like to celebrate a wedding.'

Emily went back to her sitting room, where she did more work on her detailed calculations about what exactly needed to be done before she moved away from this house. She hoped the family her lawyer had mentioned were still looking for a house to rent.

As soon as that was arranged, she'd leave. She had such a hunger to see Whitley Bay again, to smell the sea air and watch the waves roll gently onto the beach.

Chapter Nine

On the Sunday morning Bart walked along the street, scowling at his friend Stan. 'I don't know why you insisted on coming with me. It's Mattie you're interested in, not the other two.'

'They might lead me to her, though.'

'Well, don't go spoiling things. Here. This is it.' He knocked on the door and tipped his hat to the woman who opened it. She looked a soft fool and her eyes were puffy and reddened, as if she'd been weeping. Serve her right for bearing a son like that. 'Mrs Greenhill?' he asked in his softest voice.

'Yes.'

'I'm Bart Fuller and this is my friend Stan.'

She took a step backwards, fear in every line of her body. As she tried to close the door on them, Bart put out one hand to stop her and she flattened herself against the wall, calling, 'Peter! Peter!'

A thin, weedy fellow came running to the door and stood protectively in front of her. As if that would stop Bart getting to her if he wanted to thump her! He'd have laughed his head off if this hadn't been so serious.

'What do you want, Fuller?'

'To speak to you about our children.'

The woman sobbed loudly and buried her face in her pinafore.

'You're too late,' the husband said. 'They've run away for fear of you, and I hope you're satisfied now.'

She uncovered her face to yell, 'Leave us alone! Haven't you done enough? We've lost our only son because of you.'

Bart felt his friend poke him in the arm to remind him to keep calm. He didn't need reminding. Thumping these idiots would do no good. 'Yes, well, I still think my Nell was too young to get wed, but I'm sorry now for frightenin' her like that. I miss my girls, and that's the truth. I was just wondering if you'd heard anythin'?'

The man shushed his wife. 'No, we've not heard a word nor do we expect to. Cliff said he wouldn't be in touch because he didn't want to risk you going after them.'

Bart studied the little twerp, reluctantly admiring his bravery.

Stan stepped forward, smiling at the couple. 'I think your son was mistook about my friend. He might have got angry with them, but he'd not have hurt them.'

'My Cliff wasn't mistook. You've a bad reputation in this town, Fuller. Everyone knows what you're like, how you got rid of your eldest's young man. And your Nell told us how badly you beat her sister as well. She's still got the scars, Nell said.'

Bart breathed deeply. 'Mattie was different. She's not my daughter, and she needed a firm hand keeping on her, that one did, or she'd have gone to the bad.'

'What was bad about getting wed?' Peter asked. 'I knew the fellow who was courting her, the one you injured. He was a decent sort and would have made her a good husband.'

'Well, I did what I thought best at the time, and I still think I was right. Besides, her sisters needed her. It was wrong to think of leaving her family, with them so young. Selfish, it was.'

Peter took a step back. 'Well, you've wasted your time coming here. We've nothing to tell you. We've not heard from Cliff and don't expect to.'

He tried to close the door, but Bart held it open. 'If you do hear, let me know, even if it's only to tell me Nell and Renie are all right.' But he could see from their faces that they wouldn't.

Stan pulled his friend's hand away and the door shut with a bang. There was the sound of a bolt sliding into place.

'Stupid sods!' Bart muttered.

The two men started walking back.

'You'll get nowhere, frightening folk like that,' Stan said.

'Frightenin' 'em! I was polite as you please, which is more than they deserved.'

'You talked polite but you frighten 'em by the way you look at 'em, an' the way you bunch your fists. If you're coming with me this afternoon, you'd better let me do the talking or we'll not find out anything.'

Bart shrugged. 'I'm coming, an' you can talk till the cows come home. I only want to find out from Mattie where the other two have gone. I'm not taking her back.'

'I keep tellin' you, you're not getting the chance. She's going to marry me.'

'If you can find her.'

'I've made a start, haven't I? I've found out which way she went when she left town.'

An hour later the two men set out in the borrowed trap. Stan was driving, but Bart could see he wasn't very skilled and would have laughed if he hadn't been in imminent danger of being tipped out. The elderly horse was stubborn about not going fast, but it had the habit of jerking to one side at the sight of any woman in a large hat decorated with flowers. He was surprised their husbands let 'em out of the house with those silly contraptions on their heads. It just showed how stupid women were.

The horse jerked again and Bart clung to the side panel. 'Can't you control that stupid creature?'

'You drive it, if you can do any better.'

He hadn't the faintest idea how to drive anything, horse or one of those newfangled motor cars. Didn't want to, either. Give him a nice, safe tram any day.

Once they passed the last tram stop and left the houses and churchgoers behind, the horse settled down a little. But after they'd clopped along the road for a while, Stan reined to a halt with a growl of annoyance.

'What's the matter? Why are you stopping?'

'Because there's no one around to damned well ask.'

'They'll all be at church at this time of day – or cooking their Sunday dinners. But if they saw her that night, they'll remember her. Mattie was in a terrible state.' After a moment's thought, he added with some relish, 'She might've died, then you'll not be able to marry her.'

'Not her. She's too stubborn to die young. But

you've give me an idea. Let's ask around for a doctor.'

'Ask who?'

'Anyone we meet.' Stan shook the reins and clicked his tongue. The horse ignored him, not moving till he yelled, 'Walk on, you stupid creature!' and shook the reins again.

Eventually they found an elderly woman dozing in the sun outside a small cottage. Beyond it, down a lane, other thatched roofs showed. Stan reined in the horse again and they got down, tying the reins to a horse rail at the edge of the road. The horse snorted and curled its lip at them. Bart moved hastily back.

'Could you tell us where the nearest doctor is, please, missus?' Stan asked.

She looked them both up and down. 'You two don't look sick to me.'

'We're not. We want to ask the doctor if he's seen a young woman what come out this way three Fridays ago and hasn't been seen since. She's run off from home, you see, and she wasn't at all well. We're afraid for her.'

She let out a cackle of laughter. 'I'd run off, too, if I was living with two sour faces like yours.'

Bart let out a growl of anger and took a step forward, fists clenched.

She stared at him unblinkingly. 'You don't frighten me.' She snapped her fingers at him. 'I could die like that, with my ticky heart, and I'd not care. I'm fed up of living like this, a burden to my family, so go ahead and hit me.' She jutted her wrinkled chin out at them.

Stan shoved Bart aside. 'Sorry about my friend, missus. He's worried about his daughter's safety. You didn't tell us where the nearest doctor is.'

'Swindon.' She closed her eyes as if that ended the conversation.

'There must be one closer.'

She didn't even bother to open her eyes again. 'Well, there ent.'

'Has anyone round here taken in a sick woman?'

She opened one eye. 'Folk in this village mind their own business. I don't know nuthen about no young woman.'

Stan dragged Bart back to the trap. 'It's no use. She's lost her wits, that one.'

'They should lock 'em away when they get like her.'

They drove for another mile or two, asking at every cottage, once turning along a short lane to a farm. But no one had heard of a young woman turning up in the district during the night of the thunderstorm.

In the end they drove home.

'You'll not find her,' Bart said. 'She's got away.'

'I'll find her.'

'Why the hell are you bothering?'

'Because I've set my mind on wedding her, and that's it.'

'You could find a dozen women easier to live with.'

'I don't want an easy woman, I want one with spirit and a bit of sense in her skull.'

When they'd returned the horse to its owner, they went round to the back door of the local pub and persuaded the landlord to sell them a jug of beer. He wasn't a stickler for the rules about opening hours, thank goodness, not with his regulars. They took the beer round to Bart's house, which was closest.

There he tried again to persuade his friend to see sense about Mattie, but to no avail.

'You've run mad,' he said when the beer was finished and Stan decided it was time to go home.

After that there was nothing to do for the rest of the day except wash a few dishes, which was women's work and the need for it added to Bart's sour mood. Only he didn't fancy eating his dinners off dirty plates, even if they were only pies or fish and chips, nor did he like mouldy crumbs on the tablecloth. A splash or two of tea was one thing, mouldy crumbs was another. Put you off your food, that did.

The hours passed and the emptiness of his house got on his nerves. Although he wouldn't have admitted it to anyone, he felt uneasy at the way his steps echoed on the stairs and his cough seemed to rattle the plates on the dresser. He couldn't remember when he'd last spent so much time on his own. It dragged your spirits down, being alone did, no one to talk to or watch. It wasn't natural.

'If I had that bitch here, I'd teach her a lesson, I would,' he muttered as he went to bed, thumping the pillow good and hard to get rid of some of his frustration.

What if something bad happened to Nell and Renie? If Cliff was anything like his stupid parents, he'd not be much use to them. They needed Bart to look after them properly. And he needed them for when he got old.

On the Tuesday Mattie woke feeling nervous. She got up and drew back the curtains of the front room, then dressed and folded up her bedding. She'd slept down here for the last time. Tonight she'd be upstairs in Jacob's bed. Her stomach churned at the thought of that, because she'd never lain with a man before and she'd heard it hurt the first time. And yet, the idea of not going through with this marriage made her feel even worse. She wanted to be his wife, couldn't believe she'd been so lucky as to meet a man like him.

She got dressed, not in her fine new dress,

which she'd finished altering by lamplight last night, but in her everyday things. She had trouble pinning up her hair tidily, it was so soft and fluffy. She'd had a bath and washed it again the night before, so that it would look nice.

In the kitchen she found Jacob sitting with a mug of tea in his hands.

'Brewed it a few minutes ago.' He pointed to the teapot covered by its bright, knitted cosy.

This was more of Alice's handwork, with a stitch dropped and running a ladder, Mattie noted. 'Lovely.'

When she returned from the outhouse, she found he'd poured hers and sweetened it just to her taste. She sipped her tea in silence, not sure what to say.

'I'll be glad when today's over,' he said suddenly.

'If you've changed your mind . . .'

He smiled and reached for her hand. 'I've not changed it and I won't. Stop worrying about that. I just don't like fuss and bother.'

'I wish we weren't getting married in Swindon. I'm afraid someone might see me and tell my stepfather.'

'Let them.'

She couldn't seem to make him understand that Bart Fuller was a vicious bully, a man people feared.

'You'll look pretty in that green dress,' he said suddenly. 'The colour suits you, with your hair.'

'Thank you.' She smiled as she poured them both another cup of tea. She was thrilled to pieces with the dress and had trimmed up a straw hat with matching ribbons and a flower she'd fashioned from scraps of material cut off the hem. She'd stiffened the flower with starch, and if she said so herself, it looked really pretty. The dress must have been made for someone very tall, because she'd had to cut a good six inches off the hem. She knew she'd never looked as good in anything, and that helped give her confidence.

'You've got more colour back in your face now.'

'I've still got a bit of a cough.'

'It's easing. Don't overdo things this morning, though, or after the wedding.' He waved one hand to take in the big farm kitchen. 'This place has been a mess for over a year. It doesn't need making perfect overnight.'

'I can't overdo things. I still get tired quickly.'

Silence sat comfortably between them for a while, then he said thoughtfully, 'It's strange how Miss Newington is taking such an interest in us, even coming to the registry office today.'

'Most women love weddings. And she's excited about going back home to the north, even though she tries not to show it.'

He shrugged, drained his tea and stood up. 'I'd better go and feed the hens.'

'Sarah said her mother used to look after them. I'll take over once I'm better, if you'll show me how. I've a lot to learn, I know. I've never lived in the country before. We went on a holiday trip once. I think it's lovely of the Railway Works to give all their employees a free day out on their trains every year. But we never went again because my stepfather didn't enjoy the outing. He said the concertinas and melodeons gave him a headache, and there were too many people crammed into each carriage. As if anyone cared about that when they were having a day's holiday. He wouldn't let us go again, not even when Mum cried and begged him to so that us girls could see a bit of the countryside.'

'He sounds a mean devil.'

'He is, in every way you can think of, spiteful, narrow-minded and unkind, not to mention stingy with his money.'

'I won't be stingy with my money, but we do a lot of bartering round here. We used to get all our cheese from swapping eggs. Good cheese country, this is. But I've only got a few layers at the moment. When you're well enough to take care of the hens, I'll get a few more in.'

When Jacob had gone outside, Mattie sat on for a few minutes longer, feeling content. They hadn't said anything important but it'd been nice to chat quietly before the day started. She would let the children sleep in a bit longer. They weren't going to school today because Jacob wanted them to come to the wedding.

Sarah was very excited about that and had had earnest discussions with Mattie about what to wear, so Mattie had put a bit of ribbon on the little girl's battered straw hat. Luke was more pleased about missing a day's school than about the wedding. His father had given him a good scolding for breaking his word and telling people about Mattie, and he'd said he only told his best friend, who had broken his promise not to tell anyone else.

Luke had been sulking ever since, seeming to blame Mattie for his troubles. He hadn't been rude to her, but he kept his distance and he gave her unfriendly looks when his father wasn't nearby. Surely when he had good food every day and clothes properly washed and ironed, he'd be won round? Most people liked to be comfortable.

She was sure she could be happy in this house. It was bigger than the one she'd left in Swindon, and she loved this kitchen, which was about twice the size of her old one. It jutted out at the back of the house looking over the field. Such a lovely, big room.

She smiled as she got the breakfast things out. Who'd have thought running away would lead her to this? It was like a dream come true. If fate was even half kind to them, she'd have a good life with Jacob.

Then her smile faded and she wondered how today would go. Her stepfather would be at work and if she kept her head down, perhaps no one would recognise her in the lovely dress and huge hat. She just wished they hadn't so far to walk from the station to the registry office.

But Jacob agreed with Miss Newington. He didn't want to be married in the village and have Mrs Henty poking her nose into their affairs, and anyway, that'd take weeks, what with having the banns called. So going into Swindon was a risk they'd just have to take.

Everything seemed different to Mattie today. She wasn't used to spending much time in the town centre, because she'd shopped and worked locally, and had always been in a rush.

When they left the station, Jacob offered an arm to each woman, but Miss Newington shook her head.

'Prefer to walk on my own, if you don't mind.'

So Mattie had Jacob to herself, with the older woman stalking along beside them and the children trailing behind. They needed reminding from time to time to keep up because they kept slowing to stare round, from which she assumed that they didn't often get into Swindon.

As they walked along Mattie was surprised when older gentlemen tipped their hats to her and other women eyed her clothes with envy on their faces. Even the few younger men they encountered smiled appreciatively at her.

Inside the registry office they sat waiting, not saying anything. The day seemed more than a little dreamlike by now.

Another wedding group was sitting at the other side of the room. They were very noisy, chatting away, laughing, teasing the bride and groom. She watched the young couple, glad to see them looking so happy.

At one point, the other bride nodded across the room to Mattie and she nodded back. They might be strangers but they were linked by the importance of the day and their roles in it.

Then the other party was invited into the room where marriages were performed.

Shortly afterwards the outer door opened and a gentleman entered the waiting area. Mattie was surprised when he came across to shake Miss Newington's hand.

'This is my lawyer, Mr Longley. I knew you needed a second witness.'

His presence and elegant clothes seemed to overawe the children.

When the lawyer shook the bride's hand, he stared at Mattie for so long she wondered if her hat was crooked and put up one hand to touch it surreptitiously. But it hadn't slipped. She knew that, really. So why was he still staring at her?

The other wedding party spilt out of the inner room suddenly, and the young bride stopped to say to Mattie, 'I hope you'll be very happy.'

'You, too.'

That brief encounter made her feel much better, as if some of the other bride's carefree joy had rubbed off on her.

When it came to their turn to go into the next room, Jacob took her hand rather than offering her his arm. His was big and warm, and her gloved hand looked very small against it. But it felt so good to be held like that.

She spoke the necessary words, added her signature to Jacob's, and then it was done. She was married, something she'd never expected to happen, something she could only marvel at. Married!

She smiled at her new husband and he squeezed her hand and gave her an approving nod.

'Kiss the bride, then,' Miss Newington said.

He swallowed hard, then bent his head to hers.

Mattie had expected a quick peck on the cheek, but he touched his lips to her, drew back an inch or two, then moved forward to kiss her soundly. She lost herself in that kiss, for it seemed to carry so many promises.

It was Miss Newington clearing her throat that made them both remember they were not alone. But Jacob's smile gave her the courage to face everyone, as did the lingering warmth of his lips on hers.

Mr Longley said, 'I wish you both happy!' Then he turned to his client. 'If I might have a quick word, Miss Newington?'

They stood aside in the waiting room to let a very small and subdued bridal party enter the inner room.

Jacob reached for Mattie's hand and she stood lost in quiet happiness, not in a hurry to move out into the crowded streets.

Emily went across to the Kembles, happy to see that Jacob was holding Mattie's hand. They looked so right together it made her breath catch in her throat. 'Perhaps you'd go ahead and wait for me at the railway station?'

She didn't wait for his agreement but let Frank escort her outside. 'What did you want to see me about?'

'The family I told you of, who were looking

for a house. They've found somewhere else to live. I'm sorry. I shall ask around and I'm sure we'll find someone to rent your house.'

'Oh. What a pity!'

'I'll walk with you to the railway station.'

'No need. I'd like a few moments on my own to think.' She consulted her little fob watch. 'The next train isn't due to leave for a while, so I'll just stroll there at my leisure. Thank you for coming to act as witness today.'

'My pleasure.' He raised his hat in farewell, set it firmly on his head and walked briskly off down the street.

She made her way towards the railway station, feeling very disappointed about his news. She'd been hoping to move back to the north quickly.

She stopped to stare in a shop window, wanting a few more minutes on her own before she faced Jacob and his new wife. The goods she saw reminded her that the two of them had received no wedding presents at all. That didn't seem right, so she'd buy them one.

Inside she chose a clock, a small but elegant timepiece. She left with it in a box, tied up with cord that formed a handle.

But her day was marred by the news from her lawyer, even though she tried not to let it show and spoil the newly-weds' day.

* * *

Fanny Breedon was walking past the station with a bag of shopping. She set it down for a minute and stared at a woman who was dressed so fine, envying her the beautiful green dress. She'd started to pick up the bag again when she suddenly realised who the woman was.

She turned away quickly, apologising to a man she'd bumped into, and pretended to look into a shop window as the woman and her family stopped in the entrance. She kept her back turned but could see their reflections clearly.

It was definitely Mattie Willitt! Everyone knew she and her sisters had run away and that Bart Fuller was furious about it. Well, when you lived on the same street you knew most things that happened. Everyone had decided Mattie must be far away by now. She'd be a fool to stay nearby because Bart would beat her within an inch of her life if he caught her. He'd done it before, hadn't he?

Even in the wavery reflection the green dress looked lovely. Where had Mattie got those fine clothes from? And who was the man she was with? Jealousy seared through Fanny as she looked down at her own much-mended garments, then suspicion crept into her mind. You didn't get lovely clothes by behaving yourself, that was sure. Had Mattie gone to be someone's mistress?

You'd never think it of her, but people surprised you sometimes.

Intrigued, Fanny kept her back turned till they went into the station, then hurried across the road, stopping just inside in the entrance. They were sitting on a bench now and if she went to stand behind that pile of boxes, she'd be able to see and hear better. She nipped quickly into place, delighted with this opportunity to find out what was going on. Just wait till she told people what she'd seen.

'Shall we call you Mum now you've married Dad?' the little girl asked.

She had a very penetrating voice and the words carried clearly. Fanny stiffened in shock and peered between the boxes, trying to see Mattie's left hand. But she was wearing gloves. And when she answered the little girl, she spoke quietly so that Fanny couldn't hear a word. But she noted how fondly Mattie smiled at the child and then the way she exchanged smiles with the man. The boy wasn't smiling, though, he looked sulky.

Mattie Willitt married! How was that possible?

And how come she'd never noticed before how pretty Mattie was? The younger woman had always seemed rather plain, a typical old maid, with her hair bundled back into a tight knot.

A tall, thin, elderly lady entered the station

and went across to join the small group, smiling at them. The man stood up, doffing his hat.

'I hope everything's all right, Miss Newington.'

She shook her head. 'It wasn't good news, I'm afraid. The people who wanted to rent a big house like mine have found somewhere else. So I'll have to wait a little longer to move back to the north.'

'I'm sorry to hear that.'

'Not your fault, Jacob.' She sat down next to Mattie.

A couple of minutes later a train puffed into the station and when the passengers had got off, Mattie and her companions went through onto the platform and boarded it.

Well! This was going to cause a scandal, an absolute scandal, but before the news broke Fanny was going to try to profit from being the first to find out what had happened to Mattie Willitt.

She waited till the train had left, then asked a porter where it was going.

'To Bristol eventually, and all stops in between.'

'Thanks.' That wasn't much use. She walked away, trying to work it all out. Was Mattie living in Bristol now? No, she couldn't be. If she was, she'd not be here in Swindon. Had she really got married today? It looked like it, what with everyone being dressed up fine. Mattie and her husband must be living somewhere along the line, then, somewhere much closer to Swindon than Bristol, or they'd not have come here to get married, it stood to reason.

Fanny walked back to her house, grimacing at the shabbiness inside and feeling envy of Mattie surge up again as she caught sight of her own reflection in the specked mirror over the mantelpiece, saw her sallow skin, the gaps where her teeth had fallen out, and the faded, shapeless clothes.

It might be better, she decided, to tell Stan Telfor about what she'd seen, not Bart. That one never parted with a halfpenny unless it was doing the work of a penny.

But Stan. Yes, he'd want to know. They'd read the banns out in church for him and Mattie, and he'd be furious at being made a fool of. He'd be much more likely to slip Fanny a shilling or two for bringing him the news. He wasn't a stingy old devil.

Decision taken, she waited impatiently for the rest of the afternoon to pass. When the hooter went at the Railway Works, echoing out across the town, she waited ten minutes, then put on her hat and coat, and went round to Stan's house, telling her husband she'd forgotten something at the shops.

Chapter Ten

As Jacob drove them back into the village, Miss Newington said to him, 'We're all going to my house now. Cook has prepared a special tea to mark this occasion.'

'That's very kind of you.' He turned to glance quickly at his wife, seeing how tired she was. 'Are you all right?' he asked softly.

'You'll have nothing to do but sit and be waited on,' Miss Newington said in a coaxing tone. 'And Cook will be so disappointed if there's no one to enjoy her cake.'

'I'm fine,' Mattie said. 'Just a little tired, that's all. It's very kind of you to do this for us, Miss Newington.'

Jacob would far rather have gone straight home but he pasted a smile on his face, added his thanks and drove up the lane, past his home.

When they stopped outside the big house, he helped the ladies down and let Horace take the horse and trap away. He grabbed Luke and Sarah's arms before they could start running round. 'Remember your manners, you two. Sit quietly, eat slowly and don't talk with your mouth full.'

Then he let them go inside with him, and saw with relief that the very size of the place had awed them into silence. It was, he realised, the first time he'd entered the big house by the front door as a guest. It felt different coming in this way, knowing he was going to be waited on.

Lyddie and Cook peered out of the servants' door at the rear of the hall, smiling at them.

'Come and greet our newly-weds,' Miss Newington called.

Jacob accepted the two women's congratulations, then allowed himself to be shepherded with the others into the small sitting room he'd been in before.

The food was brought in to them on a trolley and he saw they were expected to eat from plates balanced on their knees. He didn't dare let his children do this, was sure crumbs would go everywhere or they'd spill something on the beautiful carpet. 'I wonder if the children could eat at a small table,' he suggested. 'They're not used to balancing things.'

Miss Newington looked at him, head on one

side, like an alert bird. 'I should have realised that and had tea served in the morning room.'

'I can easily set the table there, miss,' Lyddie said. 'Won't take me more than a few minutes.'

'Good idea.'

Jacob tried not to show how relieved he was, but he saw by Mattie's fleeting smile that she understood his feelings. 'This is a lovely room,' he said, trying to make conversation. It was all done in pale colours with a mirror over the fireplace that had a fancy gold frame round it.

'It's my favourite room in the house. There is a bigger drawing room, as you've seen, but it isn't nearly as pleasant. Both rooms look down the drive towards the village, not across the countryside, so I can see some of the comings and goings, but this one hasn't got that walled garden in the way so I can see more from here. I often sit on the window seat and read.' She turned to the bride. 'Do you read much, Mattie? Jacob borrows books from me regularly and you're welcome to do so, too.'

'I've not had much time for reading, but I enjoy it when I can. My stepfather doesn't believe in wasting time with books.'

'He sounds to be a most unpleasant man.'

'He is.' Mattie didn't elaborate.

Jacob saw her shiver as she spoke. That part of her life was past now. Surely her stepfather wouldn't continue to pursue her now she was married, even if he did find out where she was? He'd have nothing to gain by it.

Lyddie appeared soon afterwards to say everything was ready and they all moved into a very pleasant room at the rear of the house, where a table was loaded with plates of sandwiches. In the middle stood a cake covered with white icing and the words JACOB and MATTIE in pink in the middle with two linked hearts piped underneath.

He could see that Mattie was pleased by this.

'Just a minute.' Miss Newington stood up and went out into the hall. She came back carrying the parcel she'd brought to the station. 'I bought you a wedding present.'

Jacob stared at her in surprise. 'Well, I didn't expect . . . It's very kind of you. Very kind.' He turned to his wife. 'You open it.'

She untied the cord and folded the box flaps back carefully to reveal a pretty clock with its cheerful face set in glossy wood. There was a brass ring round the clock face, which set it off nicely. It must have cost a fair penny, she thought, amazed.

'It's beautiful.' Mattie couldn't stop tears welling in her eyes. 'Thank you so much, Miss Newington. No one's ever given me such a lovely present.'

* * *

Her hostess went a bit pink but seemed pleased, and Jacob noticed that Mattie kept the clock in front of her on the table and stroked it a couple of times with her fingertips. He wished he'd thought of buying her a present, even something small. He'd used his mother's wedding ring for the ceremony, which fitted Mattie perfectly, thank goodness. But he should have bought her a present, too.

After they'd eaten, Cook and Lyddie came in for the cutting of the cake, which Jacob and Mattie were instructed to do together, both holding the knife.

By the time everyone had eaten a piece, Mattie looked chalk white with exhaustion and he was getting worried about her.

But Miss Newington missed nothing. 'I think we'd better send you home in the trap now, Mrs Kemble. Lyddie, could you go and ask Horace to get it ready?'

Mattie smiled. 'I want to thank you for making today special, Miss Newington. It means a lot to me.'

'I've enjoyed myself.'

Arthur Newington was driven up to the big house in the rear of a big Standard motor car just as Horace was about to drive the Kembles home in the dog cart. In spite of the fine weather, the hood of the motor car was up at the rear, where Arthur was sitting in solitary state.

The horse shied at the noisy machine and Jacob hastily put his arm round Mattie as they clopped past it, to hold her safe, remembering the accident that had taken his first wife's life. He was glad the children were walking home across the fields. Then he remembered that Miss Newington would be alone and asked Horace to stop.

'I'd better go back and make sure Miss Newington is all right. Her cousin is a bully and the man driving that car looks a rough sort to me. She's only got those two women to look after her. Will you be all right, Mattie?'

'Of course I will.'

Horace sighed. 'I'm glad you're a-going back, Mr Kemble. I can still fire a shotgun but I'm not much use in a fight any more. It's as much as I can do these days to look after the horse and do a bit of work outdoors. You wouldn't think it to look at me but I used to be a strong young fellow once. Make the most of life while you're young. It doesn't last.'

'I will, Horace.'

'Take care, Jacob,' Mattie called as he got out of the trap.

'I don't suppose there'll be any trouble, but she's been good to us, so just in case . . .' He waved Horace on and turned back towards the big house.

Luke and Sarah came running across the field to him. 'What's the matter, Dad?'

'Just keeping an eye on Miss Newington, son.'

'Can I come too?'

'No. I want you two to look after Mattie. She's still not well.'

Luke looked sulky.

Sarah said, 'I'll look after her, Dad,' and ran off towards the farm.

Luke looked pleadingly at his father, saw no sign of him weakening and followed his sister more slowly, feet dragging on the ground.

Jacob walked quietly up to the big house, staying out of sight behind the bushes. The two men had stopped the car, but had made no attempt to go inside the house. Instead Arthur was talking and pointing. The other man was frowning, even as he nodded.

Then the front door opened and Lyddie let Arthur in.

Jacob slipped quickly round the back and entered the kitchen, explaining why he'd returned. Cook heaved a sigh of relief.

Lyddie came in. 'I've to prepare a tea tray.' She looked at Jacob anxiously. 'He'll not dare do anything to her in daylight, surely?'

'I doubt it,' he said.

'He thinks he's God Almighty, that one does,' Cook muttered. 'Best to be on the safe side and keep an eye on her.'

There was a knock on the back door. From where she was standing Lyddie could see who it was. 'It's that fellow who drives the car,' she whispered.

'I'd better stay out of sight,' Jacob said in a low voice.

'You can go into the storeroom,' Cook said at once. 'There are boxes to sit on. It's that door round the corner.'

Jacob shook his head. 'I think I'd rather be within reach of your mistress.'

'Go into the room where you had your tea, then,' Lyddie said. 'She's got Mr Arthur in the small sitting room next to it.'

The man outside knocked again, more loudly, and she called, 'Coming!'

Jacob crept into the main part of the house, pausing to listen as Lyddie opened the door. He heard the driver ask if they had a cup of tea for a thirsty man and thought it rather cheeky. Someone would have gone out to offer him refreshments if he'd brought the car round to the back, only he hadn't done that. Why not? Why was it still standing at the front?

Moving on to the breakfast parlour, Jacob found he could hear Arthur Newington's booming voice quite clearly, because the door was open.

Everyone in the village had heard tales of when Mr Arthur was a boy and had played nasty tricks on his cousin Emily, and on any village child unlucky enough to be within reach.

Everyone in the village would band together if he tried to play any nasty tricks on her now, Jacob thought grimly. Gone were the days when the gentry could do what they wanted in their own districts. This was the twentieth century, not the dark ages.

And anyway, she was a nice lady, didn't deserve bullying.

Emily went back into the house after saying farewell to the Kembles, then heard a motor car chugging up to her front door. It couldn't be her lawyer because she'd seen him today. The only other person she knew with a car was her cousin Arthur. She went to peep out of the window and, sure enough, it was him. Her heart sank, but she didn't think he'd try to do anything to harm her in the daytime.

When Lyddie went to answer the doorbell, his voice boomed out, not asking if his cousin was free but stating that he was here to see her.

She glanced out of the window again and saw that he had his manservant Robins with him. Nasty fellow, that one, she always felt, though she had no proof of anything, apart from a brutal expression on the man's face, and hands that always looked more like a coal heaver's than those of a gentleman's personal servant. He'd stayed outside, however, so that was all right.

When Lyddie came in to ask if she was at home, Arthur followed her in without waiting to be invited.

'Of course she's at home! Where else would she be at this time of day?' he said.

'Do come in, Arthur,' Emily said, but her sarcasm was wasted on her cousin.

He went to stand by the fireplace, looking down on Emily, who had taken a seat again. 'Aren't you going to offer me a cup of tea?'

'If you wish. Lyddie, could you bring in a tea tray?'

'Yes, miss.'

When the maid had gone, Arthur pulled out a piece of paper and waggled it at her. 'What's the meaning of this?'

'As I can't see what "this" is, I can't tell you.'

'This letter you wrote to me, saying you're leaving the estate to someone who isn't family.'

'Oh, that. I should have thought its meaning was quite obvious. Given the latest attempts to break into my house, I wanted to make sure that I'd named someone to inherit in case anything happened to me.'

'Have you run mad? It's your duty as a Newington to keep the old place in the family. Even if you and I don't always agree, I have children to whom you might leave it.'

'I've made my choice and I'm sticking to it.'

'Who've you left it to?'

'None of your business.'

'I shall contest the will.'

'You're assuming you'll outlive me. I wonder why?' Her eyes flickered to his protruding stomach and his high-coloured complexion. 'You don't look like a healthy man to me.'

'I'm in my prime.'

She didn't bother to disagree. What did he think he'd gain by coming here today and hectoring her?

There was a knock on the door and Lyddie carried in the heavy tea tray. Any other gentleman would have gone to help her; Arthur made no such move.

Wondering how soon she could get rid of him, Emily poured him a cup of tea and offered him a biscuit.

He drank the cup dry in two gulps and held it out for a refill. 'I've decided to increase my offer for this place.' He made a broad sweeping gesture to encompass the house. 'It needs a lot of work, so it's not worth it, but I'll give you another two thousand pounds on top of my previous offer.'

'That's not nearly enough. I've had the place valued and it's worth another thirty per cent on top of that, even in its present condition.'

'It's only worth what a buyer will offer you. And I'm definitely not going up to your price.'

She set her cup down. 'You mean, you can't afford to. Well, I'd be a fool to sell for less, so you've wasted your journey today.'

'Easy enough to come here in a motor car. I see you're still driving around behind a horse.'

'If you have any more offers to make on the house, I'd be obliged if you'd go through my lawyer. And if that's all you came for, I'm rather tired and—'

'It ain't all. Mabel sent me over to invite you to dinner tonight. I can drive you over and then Robins can bring you back later.'

'No, thank you. As I said, I'm rather tired. If you've finished your cup of tea, Lyddie can show you out.'

'I'm not taking no for an answer.' He set down his cup and pulled her to her feet, keeping hold of her wrist.

Shock held her motionless for a moment or two, then she began to struggle. 'Let go of me at once!'

'Not till you agree to come back to dinner with us tonight.'

Suddenly she was frightened, because she

didn't want to go to his house, where she'd be in his power. She yelled at the top of her voice, 'Lyddie! Lyddie! Help!'

Arthur smiled. 'She won't be coming. My man's in the kitchen and he'll reassure them that you're in no need of help.' He tugged her forward.

'Do you think you'll get away with kidnapping me?'

'I'm only inviting you to dinner, then I'll send you back safely.' He smiled. 'I have a few papers at my place you might like to look at and sign before you return, though.'

'I shall sign nothing.'

'Oh, I think you will.' He began to drag her towards the door.

Jacob had heard enough. He went into the sitting room. 'Did I hear you call for help, Miss Newington?'

Arthur turned round sharply. 'Get out of here, fellow! How dare you intrude on your betters?'

'Do you want me to leave, Miss Newington?'

'Definitely not, Jacob.' Since Arthur had let go of her in his surprise, she moved quickly across to pick up the poker.

'Robins!' Arthur called.

There were pounding footsteps and the driver appeared in the doorway, his eyes scanning the room quickly.

'Get rid of this fellow for me. I'll deal with my cousin.'

'Lyddie!' Miss Newington called. 'Help!'

The young maid appeared in the room, clutching a rolling pin. Heavy footsteps followed her and Cook stood behind her, holding an iron frying pan.

For a moment, everything hung in the balance, then Arthur made a sideways cutting gesture with one hand and Robins stepped back. Arthur turned to his cousin. 'We've not finished this discussion, believe me.'

'We have as far as I'm concerned. And I'm going to report this assault to the police as well as the other incidents.'

He laughed. 'I'm good friends with those who command the police force in this county. Do you really think anything will come of a complaint against me? Or that they'll believe it, even? It'll be your word against mine.'

'I could hear everything you said today,' Jacob said quietly.

'Who'd believe the word of a labourer against mine?' Arthur let out a scornful sniff as he walked towards the door.

Robins backed out after him.

When the front door banged shut behind them, Miss Newington sat down suddenly, one hand pressed against her chest.

'See to your mistress,' Jacob said to Lyddie. He went to the window to watch the other two men leave, not stupid enough to follow them outside, where they'd be two to one. When Robins had swung the starting handle and got the motor going, he strolled round to the driver's seat, making a vulgar sign towards the house.

Only after the vehicle had set off down the lane did Jacob turn to see Lyddie fanning Miss Newington, who was as white as a sheet. He hurried across to her. 'Are you all right?'

'Just a bit upset by it.' She sat up and he watched her pull herself together by sheer willpower, but her cheeks remained ghost-pale.

'Is your cousin right about what would happen if you made a complaint against him?'

'Probably. But that won't stop me from making it, as well as sending a signed statement to my lawyer about the incidents in case anything happens to me.'

He was startled. 'Do you think they'll continue to hound you?'

'Probably. Arthur hates to be bested. But they'll not be able to do much once I've moved away.'

Cook came back with a cup of tea. 'I put brandy in it, miss. For the shock. Now don't argue, just drink it.'

Miss Newington grimaced but Jacob noticed that she did drink the tea, after which some colour gradually came back to her cheeks.

'You mentioned hiring a couple of young men from the village to keep guard here,' he said. 'Shall I do that for you? And please send someone into Swindon tomorrow to ask Mr Longley to come and see you here, so that you can ask his advice.'

'Are there men who'd come and keep an eye on things?' she asked, her voice a little stronger now.

'Yes. There are one or two who'd do it like a shot, young fellows who do all sorts of jobs to make a living rather than go into Swindon and get swallowed up by the Railway Works.'

'Then hire them for me, and I'm sorry to intrude further on your wedding day, but I think I should have them here straight away.'

'No trouble for me to nip into the village.'

'You'll . . . watch out for an ambush on the way?'

'I will.'

She nodded. 'Thank you.'

Lyddie appeared in the doorway. 'I've been round and locked all the doors and windows, miss, and as soon as Horace gets back I'll tell him what they did.'

'I told him he could go to the pub after he'd taken Mrs Kemble back and have a drink with his friends.'

'I'll tell him for you,' Jacob said. 'He'll come straight back when he hears, I'm sure.'

She nodded, then leant her head back and closed her eyes with a sigh. He was worried about how frail she looked.

As he went out into the hall, he heard her dismiss Lyddie and waited for the young maid.

'Has your mistress had any of these dizzy turns before?'

She looked over her shoulder and said in a low voice, 'Not that I've seen. But she'd not tell us if she did have one. Very independent, she is.'

'Keep your eyes open and those doors and windows locked at all times.'

He strode down to the farm, checked that his family were all right, explained quickly what had happened, then hurried on into the village. There he gathered a group of men together and told them what Mr Newington was doing. Some of them were older than him, some younger, but he'd known them all his life and trusted every one of them.

There was silence, then one said, 'We'd better all keep our eyes open, then. Good thing everyone has to go up that lane to get to the big house, so they either pass through the village or go past your place. He's a nasty sort is Mr Arthur, and always was.'

'Miss Newington wants one or two of you

young fellows staying up there, day and night. She'll pay you for your trouble.'

'Be nice to earn a bit extra,' Ben Summerhaye said at once. 'I'll do it.'

'Can you go up there tonight, Ben? I don't think anything will happen, not so soon, but just in case. Horace will tell you where to stay. Then we'll sort out a roster tomorrow.'

Only then did Jacob go home to his bride. It didn't feel like a wedding day now, though, in spite of the present and fancy cake.

Chapter Eleven

Arthur Newington sat fuming in the back of his motor car as they drove home.

When they arrived, Robins opened the door for him, saying, 'You should have let me have a go at him, sir. I could have dealt with him easy, and those two women as well.'

'Don't be a fool. There were too many witnesses. I should have dragged her out to the car as soon as that impudent maid left us. I'll not wait next time.'

'Will she let you into the house another time, though?'

'We'll send some men at night to get her. We'll give her a couple of days to think she's fooled us with that nonsense about her will, then pounce. This time we'll take enough men to deal with that stupid groom of hers and that Kemble fellow too if he pokes his nose in again. Once I have her under my roof, she'll have no choice but to sign those papers and a new will, then we'll think how to take care of her.'

Robins drew back a little. 'I'm not game for murder, sir. I draw the line there.'

'I am not contemplating murder. What the hell do you think I am? But if I could have her safely locked away for her own good, that'd do the trick just as well. She's obviously lost her wits, the way she's been behaving lately. Leave Newington House elsewhere, indeed! I'll make sure she doesn't do that, whatever it takes.'

Robins gave one of his slow smiles. 'You're a clever man, sir.'

'Yes, I am. If folk knew half of what I've got up to in the past few years, they'd be astonished. But it's filled my coffers and filled your pockets, too.'

'Always glad to be of help to you, sir. And I appreciate the money, I do indeed.'

'Then don't forget where your loyalties lie.' Arthur went up to his bedroom to wash his hands, staring round sourly, annoyed as always after a visit to Newington House. His place was much smaller and though it was modern, with every convenience, it somehow suffered in comparison. Why had his uncle left that big house to a dried-up stick of a spinster? And what had happened to the family money? His uncle had left him far less than people believed.

But he'd get hold of the big house one way or another. It wasn't stealing, taking what was owed to you. His uncle had clearly lost his mind in the last years of his life, saying one thing and doing another.

He knew why his uncle had done it. He'd wanted to cause trouble, had hated the whole world after his son's death, and had resented most of all the fact that his brothers had had children.

Dammit, Arthur had been promised that house! He was the only Newington who had children to carry on the family name. It was only right that they got it.

When Jacob went into the kitchen, he found the children sitting in front of the fire drinking cups of cocoa. 'Where's Mattie?'

Sarah put one finger to her lips and whispered, 'She went up to change out of her pretty dress and when she didn't come down, I peeped into your bedroom and guess what, Dad. She was fast asleep on top of the bedcovers. So Luke made us some cocoa and we're being quiet.'

'You're a good pair of kids and I was proud of you today.' He looked at Luke, who'd said nothing. 'Did you enjoy your special tea?'

The boy nodded. 'Was there trouble at the big house?'

'Nothing me and Miss Newington couldn't

sort out. Mr Arthur didn't stay long.'

'I'd love to ride in a motor car like that one.'

'You will when you're older, I'm sure. We had a good day, didn't we?'

'It was lovely!' Sarah said with her usual enthusiasm. 'But when I get married, I'm going to do it in church in a long white dress.'

Luke didn't comment and since Jacob knew his son still wasn't really reconciled to the marriage, he said quietly, 'I think we'll all find life much easier with Mattie to look after us. I'm glad you found her in the lane that day, son.'

Luke shrugged his shoulders slightly and Jacob added, 'I think your mother would be pleased, too.'

All he got for that was an indignant stare, then words burst out of Luke. 'Pleased at you marrying someone else? Pleased that another woman's taking her place? Why should she be? When Tom Peddle's dad married again, his mum's family were upset about it, said she'd be turning in her grave.'

'That's because he married someone who . . . um . . . wasn't a good housewife.'

'Then why did he marry her?'

'Because she was pretty.'

'Well, I don't see why Mam should be pleased about Mattie and I'm not calling her "Mam", not if you beat me senseless, I'm not.'

'Have I ever beaten you?'

Luke wriggled uncomfortably.

'Have I?'

'No.'

'Then why do you think I'm going to start now?' He let the matter drop with a sigh.

'Mattie looked lovely today, didn't she?' Sarah said. 'I want a green dress just like that one when I grow up.'

'She did indeed.' Jacob smiled at the memory of how proud he'd felt with his new wife on his arm.

'She let me try on her hat after we got back.'

'That was kind of her. And she's a good housewife, unlike the new Mrs Peddle.'

'How can you tell?' Luke persisted. 'She can't hardly stand up for more than an hour. What if she doesn't recover properly? Barry's aunt's an invalid. She spends her life lying on the couch an' they all have to fetch and carry for her.'

'Mattie'll recover. She's getting better every day. Good food and fresh air will finish the job. Now, it's time you two were in bed. It's been a long day and I'm sure we're all tired.'

Jacob banked the fire for the night, put the porridge on to cook slowly on the residual heat of the stove and locked the house. When he tiptoed into his own bedroom, he held the lamp so that it didn't dazzle her, but she looked so soundly asleep, he doubted it'd wake her even if he shone it directly into her eyes.

Setting the lamp down on the chest of drawers,

he moved her slightly so that he could pull the pretty green dress out from under her. She'd taken it off, put on her everyday dress, then fallen asleep. He hung the wedding dress carefully in the wardrobe, stroking the fabric gently. Beautiful, it was.

Then he moved Mattie so that her head was on the pillow and he could cover her up. She was still fully clothed, but he thought sleeping soundly was more important than wearing a nightdress, and anyway, it'd embarrass Mattie to think he'd undressed her, he was sure, even though he'd already done it while she was ill. They'd never mentioned that, but he'd not forgotten her slender body and soft skin.

When he slipped into bed beside her, he smiled wryly. Funny old wedding night, this was, but he'd already decided that he wouldn't make love to her if she was too tired, had half-expected it. They had the rest of their lives to love one another, after all.

He paused on that thought. Love one another. Surely love would grow between them? He was very fond of her already, she was such a courageous little thing.

He was stopped by a jolt of surprise as he realised this wasn't just a marriage of convenience, on his part at least. He'd truly wanted to marry Mattie.

But how did she feel? Did she care for him at all, or was she just glad to find a husband and home?

* * *

In the morning Mattie woke to find a heavy weight on her shoulder and felt something pressed across her body. When she opened her eyes she found Jacob snuggled up to her. She was in bed with him, but wasn't undressed. His head was on her shoulder and his arm flung across her possessively.

She was horrified when she worked out that she must have fallen asleep after she changed out of the pretty dress – on their wedding night, too! – and hadn't stirred until now. What must he think of her?

He looked very peaceful and she found it endearing that his chin was covered in tiny bristles, his eyelashes were longer than most women's and a lock of his soft, wavy hair was lying across his forehead. She smiled. Most women would die for those eyelashes and that fair hair, which had golden glints in it where a sunbeam had crept through a gap in the curtains and now slanted across the bed.

As if he could sense her staring at him, he made a sleepy sound in his throat, then opened his eyes. For a moment he stared at her as if he'd forgotten who she was, then his face softened into a smile. 'Are you awake now, sleepyhead?'

'Yes. I'm sorry I fell asleep on you and wasn't able to . . . to . . .'

'To what?' he teased.

'To do my duty as a wife.'

The smile vanished from his face. 'Is that how you think of it, doing your duty?'

'That's how the other women always talk about it. I don't know what else to call it.'

He frowned at her. 'I'd forgotten.'

'That it was me here, not Alice?'

'No, of course not. That you might be innocent still. You are a virgin, aren't you?'

She blushed furiously and didn't know where to look. 'Yes. I'm sorry. I'll do my best to . . . to do what's necessary in bed, if you'll show me how.'

'Mattie, we'll do our best to please one another, and I hope we'll succeed. It isn't a duty to make love to one another, or even a necessity. It's a pleasure and a joy.' He reached out to cradle her cheek in one hand. 'I promise I won't hurt or upset you.'

A weight seemed to lift from her chest. 'You're a kind man, Jacob Kemble. I really like that in you.'

'Good. Let's hope we grow to do more than like one another. There's love, too.'

Hope slipped tiny fingers into her heart. 'Do you really hope for that?'

'Of course I do. There's no reason why you and I shouldn't build a happy life together.'

'You make it sound so easy.'

'It isn't always. Life can be cruel at times. But two people have a better chance of surviving than

227

one on his own, don't you think? If they work together, anyway. Alice was a countrywoman, a tomboy when she was young, and she worked hard beside me in the fields. Shh! Let me finish. I don't expect that of you, or want it. But I'd like us to get on well, be companionable, talk, have fun, not just work.'

She nodded slowly. 'Oh, yes. My mother was happy with my real father. I can still remember that. But after she married Bart Fuller, she was very unhappy. I used to hear her crying sometimes. I was terrified of him, he's such a brute.'

'Why did she marry him?'

'He pretended to care for her at first, so he fooled her. She'd been left a little money and I expect that was what attracted him. As for her, she was lonely, missed being married. Strange how I'd forgotten about the good side of marriage . . . until now.' She smiled at him. 'I'll do my best, Jacob, my very best.'

'No one can do more.'

There was a sound from one of the other bedrooms.

'That'll be Sarah,' he said. 'She always wakes early and comes in to say good morning. I usually have to wake Luke, though.'

'I've heard you doing it. He's grumpy in the mornings, isn't he?'

There was the sound of bare feet pattering

across the landing. The door opened a little and Sarah peered round it. 'Are you both awake? Can I still come in, Dad?'

'Of course we're awake. Come and give me my morning kiss, then you can kiss Mattie too.'

Smiling, she marched round to Jacob's side of the bed, while Mattie marvelled that a man should show so much love to his family, and that a child should be so confident of being loved she'd come to give her father a kiss every morning.

Suddenly, Mattie wanted Jacob to love her like that. She wanted it so much it hurt.

Sarah came round to her side of the bed looking solemn. She hesitated, then kissed her quickly on the cheek.

Mattie put her arms round the child, pulled her close and gave her a proper hug. Sarah relaxed against her, gave her another kiss, then ran out to get dressed.

'She's such a loving child,' Jacob said fondly as he got out of bed.

Mattie averted her eyes as he got dressed and waited till he'd gone downstairs to get up and have a quick wash, then change into a dress that wasn't crumpled. She smiled as she did so. What a lovely start to the day! It had made her feel warm inside.

* * *

Fanny knocked on the door of Stan Telfor's house, a bit scared of what he might say and worried about whether he'd give her something as a reward. Just a few shillings would be such a help. She was always short of money to feed her hungry family.

He opened the door and looked at her with an unwelcoming expression. 'What do you want, Fanny? If your Jimmy's kicked his ball over into my yard again, I'll go and throw it over the back wall.'

'It's not that, Stan.' She looked over her shoulder, then back at him. 'It's something I thought you ought to know, but you won't want anyone else hearing it.'

'Look, Fanny, I know you enjoy gossip, but—'

'It's about Mattie Willitt. She—' Fanny let out a little cry of shock as he dragged her into the house and slammed the door shut.

'What about her?'

'I saw her today.'

'What? Where did you see her?'

She hesitated. 'You'll give me something for my trouble, won't you, Stan? I've not told anyone else.'

'Just get on with it!' he said in a tight, low voice. 'Then we'll see.'

'I saw Mattie at the station with a man and two children. I sneaked across and got close enough to hear them talking. And Stan . . . she's gone and married him.' She flinched at the ugly expression on his face.

'She can't have got married,' he said at last.

'She has. I reckon she'd just done it today. She was all dressed up in a fancy dress and she looked . . . well, she looked pretty. I didn't think she had it in her. I never saw her looking so fine before.'

He stared at her so angrily she began to edge towards the front door.

'Come through into the kitchen!'

She didn't dare refuse.

He made her go over it all again, questioning her about every single detail, and then she suddenly remembered the older lady who'd joined the family group, so mentioned her as well.

'Who was she?'

Fanny frowned, trying to remember the lady's name.

'Well?'

'Don't rush me. I'll forget everything if I get agitated.'

He moved away, jingling the coins in his pocket, then spun round and came back to her, holding a handful out. 'Look. These are all yours if you can remember the lady's name.'

Fanny stared at the coins longingly and racked her brain desperately. 'New-something,' she managed at last.

'Newman, Newstead?'

She shook her head.

It was his turn to rack his brain for more names. 'Newton?'

She brightened. 'That's more like it, but it's longer. Please don't get mad at me, Stan, I can't remember any more.'

He controlled his anger and nodded. 'You've done very well to come to me.' He tipped the coins into her hand.

As he did so, she said, 'Oh. I've remembered something else, not about the lady. The husband's name was Jacob.'

'Well done. Now, are you sure that's all you can think of?'

A pause, then, 'Ye-es. I think so.'

'If you remember anything else, anything at all, you'll come and tell me, won't you?' He looked meaningfully at the coins.

'Oh, yes, Stan. I'll come straight round.'

'And don't mention this to anyone else, or I'll come for my money back.'

'I'd never do that, Stan.'

After she'd gone, he began to pace up and down the room, anger burning hotly through him. How could Mattie have met and courted this Jacob fellow without anyone knowing? In these streets folk knew if you coughed twice.

How was it possible?

And who were these people she was with?

He'd find out. No one played tricks like that on him. She'd promised to marry him, damn her, and he wanted to know why she'd broken that promise.

He sighed. He'd never wanted a woman so much as he wanted Mattie, couldn't understand why. He had to know why she'd run out on him.

Mattie felt shy as she went downstairs. But the kitchen hadn't changed overnight and by the time she'd served the porridge as usual she was feeling more at ease.

'I've already fed the hens.' Jacob ate quickly, with an eye on the clock, then stood up. 'Will you be all right? There are a few things that need doing, what with me missing yesterday. I need to water some of the younger plants because it's not rained for a day or two.'

'Of course I'll be all right.'

He went out of the back door, leaving it open to the beautiful spring morning. She could see him lacing up his boots and as he got up, he turned to call, 'Don't overdo it today, Mattie! Luke, hurry up! You've still got your chores to do before school.'

Sarah finished her porridge, then cleared the table without being asked and got out the bread. 'We need to make sandwiches for dinner. It's too far to come home, so some of us stay at school.'

Mattie smiled. 'I know. But I'll make them for you from now on. What do you like best?'

'Cheese. But Luke likes ham best. And we take an apple or a carrot, pea pods sometimes, whatever Dad has plenty of. When Mum was alive, she used to make cakes. Do you know how to make cakes?'

'I do indeed. Give me a few days to finish getting better and I'll make plenty of cakes and scones for you.'

They stared at one another across the table.

'I'm glad Luke found you,' Sarah said suddenly. 'Dad's a lot happier since you came. He keeps smiling. He didn't smile much after Mum died.'

Tears filled her eyes as she said that and Mattie went quickly across to give her a hug. 'My mother died when I was fourteen and I still remember how unhappy I was.'

Sarah snuggled against her for a minute, then pulled away and got herself ready for school, soon smiling again.

When Luke came in from doing his chores, Mattie had to remind him to wash his hands properly before he set off for school. He scowled at her but did as he was told.

Once the house was empty she allowed herself a few minutes to sit and take stock of her situation, which felt to have changed. This was her home now, she had a husband, stepchildren ... A thought suddenly occurred to her, such a wonderful thought that she could hardly breathe for a moment. She might even have children of her own as well, if she was lucky. She was only thirty, not too late. She so longed to have children.

There was only one sadness left, and one worry. She worried about what her stepfather would do when he heard about her marriage, as he was bound to do one day, and she felt desperately sad about her sisters. She thought about them several times a day, wondering how they were, what they were doing, where they were living and if Cliff had found a job.

In two years, they'd agreed, he'd write to his family and then she could find out from them where he and the girls were. That seemed a long time to wait for news about people you loved, people you'd seen every day, shared a bed with, laughed and cried with.

Whatever the risks to herself of her stepfather seeing her, she'd visit the Greenhills at the end of those two years to ask about her sisters. If they had an address and it was safe, she'd write to her sisters. If not, at least she'd know they were all right.

She didn't know how she'd bear it if there was no news.

Chapter Twelve

Emily got up feeling exhausted. This had happened to her a few times lately and she'd dismissed it as old age. Mostly she managed not to think about being seventy, but when she looked at the age spots on her hands and arms, or stared into the mirror at her grey hair and wrinkled face, it was hard to avoid the knowledge that her days were numbered.

. She wondered how the newly-weds had got on last night, wondered what it was like to sleep with a man, have him put his arms round you. That made her sigh for the girlish dreams that had faded to nothing so many years ago . . . no, not nothing, because you still dreamt of a better life, however old you were. She'd longed to marry, longed for children too, but men simply hadn't been attracted to her. She was too tall and thin, with a rather beaky nose, and she didn't have any money to sweeten that pill. And anyway, her parents hadn't encouraged men to call on her, had made it plain they expected her to stay at home and look after them.

She'd had no choice about it, unlike these modern young women who learnt to use typewriters and went out to work, even those from good families. She'd been totally dependent on her parents, and it was only after her father's death that she'd had some choice about what she did with her life – the choice of which employer to work for because most of his income had died with him.

She'd been astounded when her uncle left Newington House to her, wasn't sure even now that it had been worth the trouble of leaving the few friends she did have and coming down to Wiltshire to keep this old place going. She'd been very lonely here.

But that didn't mean she was prepared to hand the place over to her cousin Arthur for so much less than it was worth. He was a horrible man, just as he'd been a nasty little boy, and he didn't deserve such a gift. The trouble was, she still hadn't come up with an alternative so that she could make a final will instead of the temporary one. She smiled at the thought of her temporary legatee inheriting. That would throw the cat among the pigeons.

She stabbed the last hairpin into her bun and stood up from the dressing table, clutching it hastily as the room spun round her, then sitting down again with a bump.

When she could move without feeling dizzy, she went downstairs for her breakfast. It wasn't her custom to complain about her personal health so she said nothing to the servants. In her opinion, you just got on with things and kept your aches and pains to yourself.

Her young maid was as cheerful as ever, bringing in the crisp toast with butter and jam, which was all Emily ever wanted in the mornings.

'Lovely day, ent it, miss?'

She murmured an answer, let Lyddie run on and scraped butter across a piece of toast, then some of cook's delicious strawberry conserve. When the maid had gone, she forced herself to eat the whole slice, because you had to keep up your strength, but she didn't feel at all hungry today.

When she got up from the table she had another dizzy turn and the next thing she knew, she was lying on the floor and someone was screeching, 'Cook! Cook! Come quick.'

She wanted to tell them to be quiet, but couldn't form the words or open her eyes because her lids felt so heavy.

'Ooh, miss, are you all right? Miss! Speak to me. Cook! Where are you?'

Emily tried hard to speak, but couldn't manage it. As someone carried her to the sofa in her sitting room, she made a huge effort and managed to open her eyes briefly, seeing it was Lyddie and Cook. One of her legs felt numb. She must have been lying on it awkwardly when she fell.

Lyddie rushed off, shouting, 'I'll fetch some pillows and a blanket.'

She was back almost immediately and with a sigh of relief Emily laid her head on the softness and closed her eyes.

There were still voices nearby, but she couldn't summon up the strength to work out what they were saying. She'd just have a little rest first.

As Jacob straightened up from his weeding, he saw the maid from the big house come running down the lane, skirts flying, cap missing. Before he could walk across to her, she clambered nimbly over the wall and ran to where he was standing.

'Mr Kemble! Oh, I'm so glad I found you!' She gulped in air, clutching his arm.

'What's the matter?'

'Miss Newington's fainted and she won't wake up. She's just a-lying there and we don't know what to do.'

He stabbed his hoe into the soft earth and struck his hands together to get the worst of the dirt off, then tipped the watering can over them and dried them on the back of his trousers. 'Fetch Mattie. I'll go straight up to the big house.'

'Please hurry, sir. Me an' Cook are that worried.'

He followed her example, not going round by the gate but clambering over the wall and hurrying up the lane.

Inside the house he found Cook sitting with Miss Newington, who was lying with her eyes closed.

'She's not come to properly yet, Mr Kemble.'

He knelt beside the couch. 'Miss Newington. Can you hear me?'

Her eyelids flickered and she opened her eyes but didn't seem able to see him properly. She was squinting – no, not squinting. He'd seen it before, that drooping in one eye.

'Send Horace for the doctor. I think your mistress has had a seizure.'

When Cook had gone, he bent over Miss Newington again. It didn't seem right to pick her up without a word, so he said gently, 'I'm going to carry you up to your bed. You'll be much more comfortable there.'

'Mmm.'

Was she trying to respond? He hoped so, because that would be a good sign. He scooped her into his arms, surprised at how light she was, and carried her up the stairs. At the top he paused, not sure which room was hers, so fumbled with the nearest door handle.

The room seemed musty and unused, so did all the ones on this floor, so he went up another flight of stairs. The big room at the front of the house there had a hairbrush and comb on the dressing table, so he laid her in the bed, unbuttoning her blouse at the neck because the upright collar seemed so tight.

Then he waited, unable to think of anything else to do except hold her hand, reasoning that the gentry needed comforting just like anyone else.

But he was relieved when he heard footsteps and women's voices.

Mattie went into the room, looked at the still figure on the bed, then at Jacob.

'I think it's a seizure,' he whispered.

She studied Miss Newington again, seeing the slight droop to one lip as well as to one eye. 'Yes. But I don't think it's a bad one.' There was a slight frown on the older woman's face and she wondered if the poor lady was aware of what was going on, so tried to offer comfort. 'One of our neighbours had a mild seizure and she looked like this. It took her a few weeks, but she got better again.'

Jacob put down the hand he'd been holding, stood up and gestured to the bed. 'I reckon you should sit with her till the doctor comes, Mattie.' He looked down at himself. 'I'm all dirty.'

She glanced across at the young maid who was still looking terrified, and said, 'Why don't you go down now, Lyddie?' Then she took the chair, picking up the hand Jacob had laid down and patting it. 'It's Mattie here, Miss Newington. I'm going to sit beside you till the doctor arrives. You're going to be all right, I'm sure. Just lie still.'

The fingers squeezed hers slightly. She was sure she wasn't imagining it. That was a good sign . . . wasn't it?

It seemed terrible that the poor lady had no family to be with her at a time like this.

When Jacob went outside he found Horace trying to harness the horse to the trap. The old man looked very upset and was all fingers and thumbs as he tried to buckle a strap. 'Here, let me do that.'

'Young Ben has gone home or he could do this. We should keep two of them here day and night, Jacob lad. Mr Arthur won't give up, you know. He's a terrible stubborn fellow, always was, even as a young 'un.'

When the horse was ready, the old man looked at Jacob pleadingly. 'Can you go for the doctor? I'm all of a dither. If she dies, we're all out of a home and job, you see. No one else will take me on, not at my age, and I've no close family. It'll be the workhouse for me.'

Jacob knew how hard life could be for people who were getting too old to work, in spite of the old-age pension of five shillings a week, so patted Horace's shoulder reassuringly. 'Tell me who to fetch.'

'That new doctor in Wootton Bassett, Crawford he's called. She don't like the old one. He wouldn't come out to see Cook when she had a bad turn, thought it was beneath him to visit a servant. The younger doctor came, though. Nice young fellow he is.'

Jacob sent Horace to tell Mattie what he was doing, then drove the trap into Wootton Bassett.

The 'young doctor' must have been at least fifty years old, which made Jacob smile wryly. He explained what had happened and Dr Crawford agreed to come out straight away.

As Jacob drove back, he couldn't help worrying about his own future if Miss Newington died and her cousin Arthur inherited the estate. He had a wife as well as children now, very little money saved after the winter and although he could make a decent living for them, he couldn't see Arthur letting him do that in peace. Indeed, he was pretty sure the man would try to drive him away.

When Jacob got back to the big house, he went

in via the kitchen. Cook and Lyddie both looked upset. 'Is she still . . . all right?' he asked, afraid she might have died while he'd been away. People often died during the few hours after a seizure.

Lyddie, who'd clearly been crying, used her apron to wipe away more tears. 'The mistress hasn't got any worse. Your wife's sitting with her, said we were to get ourselves a cup of tea. She seems to know what to do.'

'I'm making some barley broth because it's strengthening,' Cook said. 'Chicken broth would be better, but we've not got any hens now.'

He saw how her hand was trembling and agreed that this was a good idea. Whether Miss Newington was able to eat the soup or not, it'd be better to keep the old servant occupied.

By that time the doctor had arrived and Jacob went to the kitchen door to let him in.

Dr Crawford left his horse and gig in Horace's hands, not seeming at all upset at being invited to enter by the servants' door.

'Up here.' Jacob led the way.

Mattie looked up in relief as the doctor entered. 'She's a little better, I think.'

'This is Dr Crawford,' Jacob said. 'My wife.'

'Morning, Mrs Kemble. Perhaps you'd stay with me and your husband can wait outside.'

The doctor took her place by the bed and

examined Miss Newington, who opened her eyes and seemed aware of what he was doing.

'I agree with Mr Kemble,' Dr Crawford said, sitting back. 'You've had a minor seizure, Miss Newington. You'll feel dizzy and disoriented, but you stand a good chance of making a full recovery.'

The patient managed a slight smile, one side of her mouth rising more than the other.

'Do you want me to send for your family?'

Miss Newington immediately grew agitated. 'No. No. Not . . . tell them.'

Mattie leant forward to wipe the saliva that ran from the affected side of her mouth. 'She doesn't get on well with her family, Doctor, and if she was known to be helpless, they'd push their way in here and take over. Am I right, Miss Newington?'

The invalid nodded. 'Don't . . . want . . . them. Want . . . lawyer.'

'We know who he is,' Mattie said soothingly. 'So I can easily send for him.'

Miss Newington grasped her hand and nodded, keeping hold of the hand.

The doctor looked down at the joined hands. 'She seems to trust you, Mrs Kemble.' As the sick woman's eyes closed, he gestured towards the door.

Mattie bent to say, 'I'll be back in a minute,

Miss Newington.' She went with him to the door.

He spoke quietly, still keeping an eye on his patient. 'Don't do anything which makes her agitated. She needs to be kept peaceful. Unfortunately, there's nothing I can give her to help her recover. In this situation, the body does its own work.'

She shared her biggest worry. 'I've known people have a second seizure soon after the first one.'

'Yes. We can't predict who will do this, though, so just look after her as best you can and pray for her recovery. Do you know how old she is?'

'Seventy, I think.'

He shook his head as if this wasn't a good sign.

She went downstairs with him and found the other three in the kitchen. She listened as he explained the situation again, in case she'd missed something, but she hadn't.

'She wants her lawyer.' Mattie glanced at the clock.

'If I write a quick note now,' Jacob said, 'could we trouble you to put it in the post, Doctor?'

He too looked at the clock. 'Yes, of course. It should just catch the second post.'

'I'll show you where the mistress keeps her writing things,' Lyddie said.

Cook poured the men a cup of tea, muttering

to herself at intervals, obviously very upset still.

'The servants all seem fond of her,' the doctor said to Jacob as he went outside with the letter safely in his pocket.

'They are. But they're afraid of her cousin, Arthur Newington. She definitely won't want him coming here and taking advantage of her weakness.'

'She'll need someone with a bit of sense in their head to stay with her, though. Those two servants mean well, but an old woman and a young girl aren't going to stand up to anyone, are they? I don't suppose you and your wife could move in temporarily? I don't have anyone free to nurse Miss Newington at the moment, I'm afraid. Everyone's having babies at the moment in Bassett.'

'Yes, of course. We'll help in any way we can.' He didn't allow himself to sigh about this. Fate didn't seem on his side where consummating his marriage was concerned, but you couldn't let people down when they needed you.

Upstairs he found Miss Newington dozing. Mattie, who was again sitting beside her, raised one finger to her lips in warning. However, the noise of his footsteps must have woken the older woman, because her eyes fluttered open and she looked round with fear on her face. She relaxed as soon as she saw him. He could guess what she'd been afraid of.

He waited till her eyes closed again, then beckoned to his wife, wanting to speak to her alone. But as she stood up, Miss Newington reached out for her.

'Don't . . . go.'

'I just need to talk to Jacob. I'll only be a minute.'

'Jacob . . . stay.' Her voice was slurred but she persevered, managing to say a few words with great difficulty. 'Can you . . . all . . . stay here, help me?'

Mattie didn't even wait for Jacob, but said at once, 'Of course we can. As long as you don't mind us bringing the children, that is.'

'Bring them.'

'And we've written to Mr Longley. The doctor's taken the letter to post. Your lawyer will be here tomorrow morning, I'm sure. If anything needs doing, he'll see to it. You'll be in a better state to talk to him then.'

'Good.'

Again her eyes closed and Jacob exchanged pitying glances with Mattie. To see a brisk old woman brought to this helpless state was very sad.

When he went down, Jacob heard Lyddie talking to the postman, telling him what had happened. He cursed under his breath that he hadn't thought to tell her to keep quiet about it. There would be no stopping Kenneth now. He was the main carrier of news and gossip in the village and beyond.

He went to join them. 'Can you do me a favour, Kenneth?'

'Certainly.'

'Miss Newington has asked me and my wife to stay and—'

'So it is true!' Kenneth said triumphantly. 'You hev got married again.'

'Er . . . yes.'

'Who is she?'

'No one you know. She's from Swindon. You'll meet her in the next day or two, I'm sure. Now, what I wanted to ask was if you'd tell young Ben Summerhaye to come and stay here for the next few days, and young Peter too.'

'I can do that. Are you still afeared Mr Arthur will come back?'

'Yes. You won't forget, will you?'

'Not me. And we'll all keep our eyes open. Don't want them rough types causing trouble in our village, do we?'

Kenneth cycled off, whistling tunelessly, seeming impervious to the bumpy surface of the lane.

Jacob turned to the maids. 'I think you'd better lock the doors and windows again, Lyddie.'

'In the daytime?'

'Better safe than sorry. We don't want Mr Arthur walking in unannounced, do we? And tell Horace to move into the main house tonight. He can leave the lads to keep watch outside.'

'You think them rascals will be comin' back, don't you, Mr Kemble?' Lyddie said, her voice shaking a little.

He did but he didn't want to make her panic. 'I think it's best to be prepared, just in case. But Mattie and I'll be staying, the children too, so after you've locked up, perhaps you can find us some bedrooms.'

Her anxious expression lightened. 'Oh, that's good! I'll feel a lot safer with you here, in charge, like. So will Cook, I know. But just in case, I'll go to bed with that poker beside me again. Miss Newington druv 'em off with a poker that first time. Brave, she was.' She dabbed her eyes. 'Good mistress, she is, too.'

He patted her shoulder. 'Yes. I know.'

The letter Jacob had written just caught the lunchtime collection and arrived at Frank Longley's rooms in Swindon by the second post instead of the next day. It was taken straight through to him, since it was the only one delivered. He exclaimed in shock when he saw what Jacob had written, then sat thinking hard, not liking the sounds of this. What if Miss Newington died?

She'd made a will, but only as a temporary measure. If she died now, the estate would go to a most unsuitable person.

He looked at the clock and decided to go out to see his client straight away. There was no time to be lost. If she was at all lucid, she must make a new will.

Then he scribbled a note to let his wife know why he'd be late and told his clerk to see it was delivered. As he set off for the railway station, he prayed Miss Newington would still be alive. Matters couldn't be left like this.

Ben strolled up to the big house, whistling and feeling pleased to be earning money merely for staying up there at night. Nothing had happened so far, but if it did, he'd be ready.

His dad said he was a fool and shouldn't mess with the gentry, especially nasty types like Mr Arthur, but Ben reckoned the gentry had had their day and ordinary folk were what counted now. Decent folk, who didn't get rich and leave others to want. His dad hated him expressing such views but Ben wasn't going to tug his forelock to anyone.

Which was why he wasn't working in Swindon. If you went into the Railway Works, they thought they owned you body and soul. He'd always found a way to earn enough to manage on, and he'd kept his freedom so far. And that meant freedom from girls, too. They'd come a-chasing him, but he wasn't getting married till he was a lot older and had made something of himself.

When Ben got to the big house, Jacob explained what had happened to poor Miss Newington and asked him if he could make up a roster for the young fellows who'd be staying at the house turn and turn about.

'Yes, I can do that, Jacob. I'm good at organising things and I know who I like to have on my side in a fight.'

'Right. I'll leave it to you. But keep my son out of it, eh? We're all staying here for the time being and Luke will be bursting to join in.'

'He's too young, but he's got a good heart. I'll keep my eye on him.'

'School should be out soon. When the bell goes, can you find him and Sarah and tell them where we are?'

'I'll do better than that. I'll walk up with them.' Strange thing to do if you expected trouble, take your children into the heart of it, Ben thought, but then Jacob had no one else to leave them with.

He set off again, happy enough to walk round in the afternoon sunshine and earn money for doing it. And happy to organise things, too. He enjoyed that sort of thing.

* * *

When Mrs Henty saw the postman, she stopped to give him a letter to post for her, which would save her a walk.

Kenneth leant closer. 'Hev you heard the news, Mrs Henty? Miss Newington's been took bad . . .'

After her shock had died down, Jane began to feel annoyed that the Kembles should be the ones to be helping out at the big house, when obviously it was her duty as the curate's wife to perform this service and make sure those two servants didn't take advantage of the confusion to slack off.

She went home to share the news with her husband and he was as shocked as she was about poor Miss Newington. She sent him on his way to his monthly meeting with the clergyman whose curate he was, and after fidgeting around the house for a while, decided to go up to the big house to see for herself what was happening.

She puffed her way up the hill and hesitated, wondering whether to go round to the kitchen, then shook her head. She might be a mere curate's wife but she was a lady born and bred, and had a right to enter by the front door. When no one answered, she knocked again, harder this time, annoyed at being kept waiting.

As she was raising her hand to the knocker for

the third time she heard footsteps and the door was opened by Jacob Kemble.

'Miss Newington's not well, I'm afraid, Mrs Henty. She can't have visitors.'

'I know she's not well. The postman told me about it. I've come to help.'

'She's got enough help, but I'll tell her you called.'

When he tried to close the door in her face, she stuck her foot in it, because whether it was a ladylike thing to do or not, it was a tactic sometimes necessary when visiting the poor, who were an ungrateful bunch on the whole.

As he was still barring her way, she snapped, 'Let me in this minute!'

'Look, it's very kind of you, but—'

She took him by surprise, shoving him out of the way, and since she knew he'd not dare lay hands on her, made her way towards the stairs.

'Come back!' he roared, forgetting to keep his voice down. He ran after her and pushed in front of her.

'Get out of my way this minute, Kemble! How dare you try to stop me seeing Miss Newington!'

Since Mrs Henty was famous for being able to make herself overheard above a whole church hall full of people talking, her voice easily penetrated into the sick room. Mattie recognised it at once and frowned, remembering the woman's visit to the cottage and how rude she'd been. Unfortunately, the noise had woken her companion.

She bent over the bed. 'It's Mrs Henty. Do you want to see her?'

Miss Newington shook her head, mouthing the word 'No'.

'I'll get rid of her, then.'

Mattie managed to get the bedroom door closed before the unwelcome visitor reached it. When she looked at the curate's wife, she was reminded for a moment of Bart Fuller – the woman had the same angry red hue to her face as he got when annoyed, the same staring eyes, and even the plumpness of face reminded Mattie a little of her stepfather's double chins.

Suddenly the years of bullying boiled up inside her. She was free now of the need to put up with this sort of treatment. Drawing herself up to her full five foot two inches, she folded her arms and waited.

'Open that door!' the foghorn voice ordered.

'I told Miss Newington you were here and she said she didn't want to see you.'

'Of course she wants to see me. I'm here to help nurse her.'

Mattie shuddered at the thought of being nursed by this loud-voiced bully. She looked at Jacob. 'Why did you let her come up?'

'She pushed past me before I knew it. I could hardly manhandle her.'

'Well, she'll not push past me.' Mattie stared at the older woman. 'And I'm quite prepared to manhandle her if I have to, to protect Miss Newington.'

'Let me through at once!'

Mrs Henty reached out to push her aside, but it was Jacob who grabbed her hand and pulled her away. 'You'll not touch my wife.'

'How dare you lay a hand on me!'

'I'm obeying the mistress of this house and keeping you out of her bedroom. I think you'd better leave now. You're causing a disturbance and she needs peace and quiet.'

The curate's wife made no effort to leave, continuing to berate them at the top of her voice. But Mattie neither flinched nor did as she was told, and Jacob stood beside her as solid as a rock, his eyes watchful.

When the other woman ran out of steam, Mattie looked at her husband. 'Will you please show Mrs Henty out, Jacob? And if she won't go, then she'll need helping on her way.'

He took a step towards Mrs Henty, who hesitated.

When he took another step and raised his hand to take hold of her arm, she took a hasty step backwards. 'You'll be sorry for this! I'm quite sure Miss Newington didn't mean you to keep me out!'

'I said your name to her, so she did mean it. And I'm never sorry for doing what's right,' Mattie declared. 'Jacob?'

'I'll be back with someone in authority,' Mrs Henty threatened.

'Doesn't matter. Miss Newington is still in charge here, and what she says goes.'

Only when the front door had slammed behind the curate's wife did Mattie sag against the bedroom door as reaction set in. Then she remembered the sick woman inside and hurried back to the bedside, suddenly afraid she'd gone too far. What if that loud encounter had so upset Miss Newington that she'd had another seizure?

But as Mattie approached the bed, she saw that the other woman was smiling at her, crooked mouth and all.

'Well done!' the invalid said and let out the faint husk of a chuckle.

Chapter Thirteen

Frank Longley was worried about this visit to his client, because Arthur Newington had a lot of power in the district. Why, he might claim that the young lawyer was too inexperienced and had misinterpreted Miss Newington's wishes. Frank had been told to his face that he was too inexperienced when he set up his rooms – several people had said that – and been advised to continue working for an older lawyer till he learnt his business.

He'd already worked for a few years in London and saved hard, so he knew he was ready. He'd come back to the town where he'd been born to set up his own practice, determined to work in a more modern way, helping ordinary people, trying to see that justice was done, not merely supporting the rich. Times were changing and he believed the way the law was applied should change with them.

But he still needed to protect himself and his client from those who wielded power, so he walked down the street to the nearby public telephone box to call his friend, who lived in Wootton Bassett. Sam Painton worked in his family law practice there. They had a private telephone in the rooms and Sam owned a motor car. It was only a small Riley, but it was his pride and joy, with three-speed transmission and wire-spoked wheels. Sam had been known to clean these lovingly with his carefully ironed pocket handkerchief, to his mother's intense annoyance.

If Sam would drive him out to Shallerton Bassett, Frank knew his friend would make an impeccable witness, and by using the car he could get there and back tonight.

He slipped a coin into the slot in the door of the telephone box to gain access to the phone itself, picked up the handpiece, bent down to be near the fixed mouthpiece on the wooden wall panel, which wasn't designed for tall people like himself, and asked to be connected to Mr Painton's rooms.

When he was better established, he intended to have a telephone installed in his rooms, too, but couldn't yet afford the expense.

To his relief, Sam was there and agreed to

come with him. The little Riley got them to the turn-off for Shallerton Bassett very quickly, then putt-putted its way up the bumpy lane, going more and more slowly. At one stage it seemed as if the engine was going to fail, then the car seemed to summon up just enough momentum to crest the rise and find its way to the front door.

Jacob Kemble opened it before they could knock. 'How did you know to come here?'

'Your letter reached me by second post today.'

'Thank goodness for that!'

Frank watched in amazement as he locked the door behind them. 'Is Miss Newington so nervous she must have her doors locked all the time?'

'She is since her cousin tried to force her to leave with him,' Jacob said bluntly.

'Force her?'

'Yes.'

'Why would he do that?'

'He wanted her to sign some papers, apparently.'

'You're sure of this?'

'I was there and helped prevent it. There's nothing wrong with my eyesight, or my hearing either. I heard what he said.'

Sam let out a low whistle of surprise, which reminded Frank of his manners. 'Ah, this is my colleague, Mr Painton, who has kindly brought me here in his motor car. This is Jacob Kemble,

Sam, who collects Miss Newington's rents for her.'

The two men shook hands, then Jacob gestured to the stairs. 'Would you like to go up? It's on the second floor. I'm sure Miss Newington will be delighted to see you.'

'How is she?'

'She's regained consciousness and seems in full possession of her senses. The doctor says if she doesn't have a second seizure, she'll probably make a good recovery. But she's very anxious not to let her cousin Arthur take over while she's ill, which I think is why she wants to see you.'

'Ah. Who's looking after her?'

'My wife and I, with the maid's help. Although the servants are very loyal, they aren't capable of standing up against Mr Arthur, so the doctor suggested my wife and I move in temporarily.'

'The doctor suggested it?'

'Yes. And we're glad to help, since the poor lady has no one else.'

'She's not paying you to do this?'

Jacob looked affronted. 'I don't need paying to help a neighbour.'

'Very commendable. Could you take us up to her, please?'

'She gets tired easily. Perhaps your friend could wait down here?'

'Considering the power of Arthur Newington,

it'd be better if Mr Painton stays with me and witnesses what she says.'

'Ah. I see.' Jacob hesitated, then added, 'I've been obliged to hire young men from the village to stay here too, just in case there's any more violence.'

'The police haven't found the people who broke in?'

'No, sir. I don't think they've tried very hard, but we all have a fair idea of who's behind it.'

'Hmm. Well, it won't hurt to have the men here, I'm sure.'

As they followed Kemble up the stairs, Sam whispered to him, 'I can't believe such precautions are necessary in this day and age. Are you sure this man isn't exaggerating?'

'Once you're out in the countryside, you don't have the police to hand, or even neighbours in a place like this,' Frank said. 'And besides . . . I don't know whether you've ever met Arthur Newington?'

'Yes. He's an acquaintance of my parents. I don't know him well, but he's a gentleman and surely he'd not descend to that sort of thuggish behaviour?'

'Who else could be behind it? He was very angry about not inheriting the house.'

'Yes. I've heard him talk about that to my parents.'

'As long as these young men from the village give my client peace of mind, it costs her very little. And if there is something in the story, well, once again we'll have witnesses to hand.'

'Can't beat that.'

The bedroom was large, with a window slightly open to let in the fresh air. Miss Newington looked frail, her face almost as pale as the pillows against which she was propped up. It took only a quick glance round the tidy room for Frank to see that she was being well cared for.

Mattie bent over the bed and said quietly, 'Mr Longley's here to see you, Miss Newington.'

The old lady opened her eyes and to Frank's relief, the same intelligence shone in them, even though one side of her face was drooping a little. When she spoke, her speech was slurred, but he had no problem understanding her.

'Good. Leave us . . . Mattie.'

Mrs Kemble nodded to Frank. 'I'll be in the kitchen. You've only to ring that bell if you want me, sir.'

When she left, Sam escorted her to the door, keeping it slightly open for a moment or two, then shutting it and mouthing, 'She's gone.'

Frank agreed with this caution. You couldn't be too careful when dealing with elderly clients who could be taken advantage of. He sat down next to the bed. 'How can I help you, my dear lady?'

'The will.'

'You want to change it. I can write a temporary one quite quickly and—'

'No. Want it . . . to stand . . . as it is.'

'Are you sure?'

'Yes.'

'Does anyone else know how you've left things?'

'No. Only you.'

He didn't like this, but had to respect her wishes. 'What did you want to see me about, then?'

'Want Jacob Kemble . . . to have power . . . to look after me . . . if . . .' Her voice tailed away and she closed her eyes for a moment.

'If you're incapacitated,' Frank finished for her.

'Yes.'

'You trust him that much?'

'Yes. Good man. But make it him . . . and you together.'

'Good idea. Though we'll hope it isn't necessary and that you make a full recovery. I can easily sort out the paperwork for that. Sam, will you go down and make out a deposition? I'm sure Kemble will show you where to find paper and a pen.'

Emily's fingers plucked at Frank's hand. He turned to her and called, 'Wait!'

Sam stopped by the door.

'Say . . . not my cousin,' she said. 'Not Arthur.'

Just to be certain, Frank repeated, 'You want the deposition to say your cousin Arthur is not to look after you if you're incapacitated, and Kemble and I are?'

'Yes.'

'Very well.'

When Sam had left, Frank waited quietly until his client opened her eyes again. She seemed very tired, as if every word was an effort. 'Are they looking after you properly, Miss Newington?'

She nodded. 'Very well. Very kind.'

It was a while before Sam returned. She dozed, leaving Frank to his thoughts. It was a strange business, and he could see big trouble ahead if she died, especially when the beneficiary was revealed. But . . . it was what she wanted and she was definitely in her right mind, which was the only ground on which the will could be contested.

Sam returned, bringing Cook with him. 'Witness,' he said at Frank's questioning look. He held out a piece of paper.

Frank scanned it quickly and nodded approval, then turned to Miss Newington. 'I shall read this to you before you sign it.' He did so, then at her nod, took the fountain pen his friend was holding out and placed the paper against a book, so that she could sign it. What a good thing it was her left side that was affected by the seizure! Even so, the handwriting was shaky.

He beckoned to Cook. 'You must sign here to say your mistress understood what this paper contains and that she signed it of her own free will.'

'Yes, sir.' She traced out a round, childish signature and stepped back.

'Now my colleague must also sign it in your presence.'

'I understand, sir. I've witnessed other people's wills, and it's the same sort of thing, isn't it?'

'Yes.'

When she'd gone, he turned to Miss Newington. 'It's all finished and been done properly.'

'Thank . . . goodness.'

'Did Arthur Newington really try to force you to go with him?'

'Yes. Him and Robins. Kemble stopped them.'

They looked at one another and shook their heads in amazement, then Frank rang the bell.

When Mattie came, they left Miss Newington to rest, with the young woman keeping watch.

'I'd not have believed this if I hadn't seen and heard it with my own ears,' Sam muttered as they walked down the stairs. 'Good thing there are two of us, eh? There'll be all hell to pay when it comes out that her cousin's to be kept away.' He stopped. 'I take it she hasn't left her property to her family?'

'No.'

Sam let out a long, low whistle.

Downstairs, Lyddie came forward to say, 'We've put some tea and scones in the small sitting room, Mr Longley. Cook thought you might be hungry.'

'Thank you.' Frank pulled out his pocket watch. 'Might as well have a quick bite before we leave. I must admit I'm getting peckish and I'll not be home till well past dinner time.' He turned to the maid. 'Could you ask Mr and Mrs Kemble to join us, please? We need to have a word with them. Perhaps you could sit with Miss Newington in the meantime?'

Half an hour later the two lawyers were on their way.

Jacob spoke to Ben and the other young men from the village, sending them out with old Horace, who was to show them round the outbuildings and rear gardens – not that they hadn't seen it all before, because most lads from the village had scrumped apples from the big house, or gone up there for a dare. But you couldn't admit that.

Luke hovered nearby and Jacob left his son with Ben, with strict instructions not to get in the way. The lad was bored already here, not used to being on his best behaviour for so long, and full of energy after a day shut up in school. Ben winked at Jacob and told Luke to stay with him.

Sarah was in her element, helping Cook and then helping Lyddie to set the kitchen table for a high tea.

As he was going back into the house, Jacob heard another motor car coming up the hill. He went to peer out of the front window, sighing when he saw that it was Arthur Newington. How had the man heard the news so quickly? He wished the two lawyers were still there and hoped he could deal with this.

He heard footsteps behind him and turned to see Ben in the doorway.

'Thought you might need some help, Jacob lad.'

'I might. I'll try to send him away. Where's Luke?'

'Safe in the kitchen. Back door's locked.'

There was a hammering on the front door. As Jacob went to answer it, Mattie called his name and ran lightly down the stairs.

'Miss Newington says if it's her cousin, you can show him up to see her, but anyone else is to stay outside. And you and I are to stay with her while he's there.'

'All right. You go back up.' He waited until she'd reached the landing before opening the door.

Arthur Newington stood there, with his driver

behind him. 'I've come to see my cousin. I hear she's had a seizure.'

Jacob didn't move. 'Yes, sir.'

'Well, let us in, damn you!'

'You can come in, sir, but no one else. Miss Newington's orders.'

'How can she give orders if she's had a seizure?'

'It's only a mild one. She's in full possession of her senses and can still speak.'

As his master entered the house, Robins tried to follow him, so Jacob beckoned Ben forward. For a moment it seemed as if the fellow would still push forward, but his master made a gesture to stay back.

'Wait there for me, Robins.'

Ben went to stand to one side of the hall, arms folded, expression grim.

Jacob locked the front door behind them and turned to see that the visitor had already started up the stairs.

Catching up with him on the landing, Jacob moved swiftly past him, leading the way up the stairs to the next floor.

'Why did you put her up here?'

'It's the bedroom she's always used. She didn't like the master bedroom, apparently.'

He knocked on the door, barring the way until Mattie opened it.

She looked past her husband. 'Miss Newington

269

will see you now, Mr Newington, but only for a few minutes. She's very tired.'

Arthur pushed past her without a word, which made Jacob breathe deeply. Mattie went to stand beside Miss Newington.

Jacob listened in disgust as Arthur put on a plummy, sympathetic voice, which sounded as false as it probably was.

'Good evening, Emily dear. I'm sorry to see you in this condition.'

She gave a slight nod.

Arthur turned to the Kembles. 'You two can leave now. I wish to speak to my cousin in private.'

It was Mattie who answered. 'I'm sorry, sir. Miss Newington has asked us to stay with her while you're here.'

'There's no need whatsoever for that. What do you think I'm going to do, hurt her?' He turned back to his cousin. 'Tell them to leave.'

'No. They stay.'

His face went red and the look he threw sideways at them was thunderous.

Jacob smiled slightly, folded his arms and leant against the door. Mattie stayed where she was, beside the bed.

Left on his own, Robins went round to the rear of the house, but to his annoyance, two more strapping young men were standing just outside the kitchen, chatting to the young maid through an open window.

'Did you want something?' one of them asked.

'Just stretching my legs.' He carried on round the side of the house but the taller one followed him. He turned. 'If you're wise, you'll not anger my master. When he inherits this place, you could be thrown out of your home.'

The young man grinned. 'Our cottage don't belong to the big house no more, so that's a bit hard for him to do, ent it?'

'You've been warned.'

'Shaking in my shoes, I be!' He laughed.

Robins continued without a word till he got back to the car, where he leant against the bonnet. He'd make personally sure that young fellow regretted his impudence.

Upstairs, Arthur drew in a deep breath and forced a smile to his face. 'Emily, my dear, my wife and I would like you to come to us, so that you can be properly cared for.'

'Staying here.'

'But you've no one to make sure you're all right.'

'Mattie and Jacob.'

'Who?'

'She means us, sir,' Mattie said.

'They're strangers, Emily. You need family at times like this.'

He glared at the maid, but she didn't seem to care that he was angry, any more than her husband had. Young people today had no respect. In his father's time, folk like these wouldn't have dared defy their betters. He turned back to his cousin. 'Do be sensible.'

'Seen . . . my lawyer. He's keeping an eye . . . on things.' She paused, closed her eyes for a minute as if gathering her strength to continue. 'Don't want you . . . here again.'

The words came out slowly and it was clear that it took a huge effort for her to speak. Arthur wished with all his heart that the damned fool of a woman would drop dead and be done with it. He didn't believe she'd really left the house to anyone outside the family, and if she had, he'd contest the will and claim undue influence. No, she'd have left it to his children or grandchildren, and they knew better than to cross him, so they'd let him take charge. 'I think you're wrong, Emily.'

'My choice.'

For a moment or two she stared at him in that knowing way that had always made him feel as if she could tell what he was thinking. There was nothing else he could do tonight, but if she thought he was giving up, she was wrong. 'I shall leave you, then, but I'll be back tomorrow to make sure you're all right. I'll bring my wife.'

'No. Stay away.'

'You don't know what you're saying. Of course we'll be back. We're your only family.'

'No.'

'My dear Emily—'

She seemed so frail and tired, Mattie looked at Jacob and he stepped forward.

'I'm afraid I must ask you to leave now, sir. Miss Newington has said what she wants to and must rest.'

As they were going down the stairs, Arthur asked, 'What did Dr Blair say about her condition?'

'It was Dr Crawford who came, sir.'

'What? That fellow deals with the poorer folk. Why on earth did you send for him?'

'Cook says he's been Miss Newington's doctor for a while now, so naturally we sent for him. And he said she should make a full recovery if she rested and was careful.'

'He said that?'

'Yes, sir. It's quite a mild seizure, apparently.'

'Then let's hope he's right.'

But once they'd driven away, Arthur stopped hiding his anger. 'Those damned Kembles have wormed their way in with my cousin. Did you try to get in the back way?'

'They've got two other men stationed there, sir.'

'Then force won't do it. We'll have to try something else, won't we? Good thing I have friends in useful positions.'

Chapter Fourteen

Towards the end of the morning Sam went for a stroll along the street, giving himself a rest from dusty documents and boredom, wishing his father didn't believe young lawyers couldn't be trusted with anything except the simplest of everyday transactions. When he saw Arthur Newington striding along the street and then entering the rooms of Thaddeus Ransome, the local magistrate, he stayed where he was, half-hidden by a horse and cart.

What was Newington doing there? Was it just a coincidence or did it have something to do with Miss Newington?

Sam hesitated, then strolled along and turned into the back alley that led to the rear of these buildings for tradesmen's deliveries. On such a beautiful day, most windows were open to let in the pleasant spring air. He knew which was the room Ransome used and with a wry smile at himself for doing this, he crept along until he could stand between an outhouse and the house itself.

Praying that no one would come out and discover him, he wondered if he was close enough to hear anything. But since both men were a little hard of hearing, he had no difficulty listening to the conversation.

What he heard had him hurrying off to the post office to send a telegram.

When he got back to his father's rooms, he found that Ransome was now closeted with his father and the clerk was waiting for him.

'Mr Painton is annoyed that you left your office, Mr Samuel, and asked me to remind you that those papers are wanted today.'

'Yes, all right. I'll get them finished. Just needed to clear my head.'

The clerk's expression said he didn't approve of young men having the freedom to do this. Like master, like man, Sam thought as he sat down at his desk with a sigh.

He wondered what Ransome wanted with his father and got up on that thought, slipping into the stockroom and opening the window there, from whence he could hear most of what they were saying.

Second time I've eavesdropped today, he thought with a grin. The smile soon faded as he heard what they were discussing.

Frank Longley had spent a restless night worrying about the situation. He wasn't certain what to do next, but couldn't neglect his other work in order to keep going out to Shallerton Bassett, so went into his rooms as usual.

Just before one o'clock the telegraph boy turned up. Frank ripped open the envelope with a sense of foreboding. The little strips of white paper glued to the beige-coloured form rarely brought good news and this one was no different.

AN HAS VISITED MAGISTRATE. PLOTTING TROUBLE. BETTER COME QUICKLY. SAM.

Frank cursed under his breath, then slung things he might need into his briefcase and rushed out to catch the next train. In Wootton Bassett he ran all the way to Sam's father's rooms.

As soon as the clerk heard his name, his attitude changed and he refused point-blank to disturb Mr Samuel.

After arguing for a few minutes in vain, Frank went outside, wondering what to do next. As he paced up and down, he saw the alley which led to the rear of the building. He and Sam had played there as lads. With a smile, he slipped into it, climbing over the locked gate to knock on the window of his friend's office, which looked out onto the backyard.

When he explained that he'd been denied entry, Sam looked grim.

'What's going on?'

'I'll tell you what I know and what I suspect once we're on our way. I'll just get my hat and join you in a minute. Can you get back over the gate?'

Frank grinned. 'I haven't lost my old skills.'

As he waited at the front of the building, he heard his friend arguing with his father from the big bow-windowed office at the front. They were both shouting but the words weren't clear.

When Sam came out to join him, he was flushed with anger. 'We're going to have a hard time getting justice done. They're ganging up on her – and you.'

'I feel guilty about involving you.'

'I'd rather know now what my father's like when push comes to shove. I didn't become a lawyer to support rich folk who break the law. And if that makes me an idealistic young fool, I don't care. And it'll not upset me too much to work elsewhere. He hasn't trusted me with anything beyond what a clerk could deal with since I started.'

'That's why I set up my own rooms.' Frank clapped his friend on the shoulder. 'Thanks, Sam.'

'You're welcome. Now, let's get my car started. It's just down the street.'

As they drove out of town, they didn't speak for the first mile or so, then Sam said, 'I wonder if you'd like to take on a partner in your practice? I have a small legacy. I can put some of that in as my contribution. I'm not sure whether I've just resigned or whether he's sacked me, but either way, I'm not going back to work there.'

'Oh, hell, I didn't mean you to lose your job.'

'I didn't believe Pa would go this far to support his friends. I thought he had more integrity.' He sighed. 'Well, do you want a partner?'

'Of course I do. But you won't be earning much for a while.'

'Doesn't matter. My godmother left me enough to manage on. I'll have to move out of home, though.'

'We could fix up the top floor of the building, turn it into a flat. There are several rooms up there.'

'Done.'

But Frank still felt guilty about his friend. And worried about whether they'd be too late.

Two cars drove up to the house in the early afternoon and the watchers upstairs and down saw Arthur Newington get out of one, smiling and surveying the house with a distinct air of triumph. An elderly gentleman got out of the other vehicle.

Jacob groaned. Thaddeus Ransome, the local magistrate, a man the poorer people in the district detested. Jacob had never been involved with the law, but knew the man treated offenders harshly. He didn't know how he'd manage to hold out against him.

The driver strode up the steps, grinning broadly, and knocked on the door.

Jacob waited until Robins had knocked again before going to answer it. He told Ben to stay close by as he opened it. The man outside looked at his master, as if asking for permission to push inside, but was waved aside.

Arthur Newington mounted the steps in a leisurely manner and waited for his elderly companion to join him at the top before speaking to Jacob. 'We're here to see my cousin.'

Jacob had received his orders and intended to stick to them. 'Miss Newington has instructed me not to let you in, Mr Newington, but—'

Arthur turned to the other man and said, 'See! This fellow keeps people away from her. It's a plot. They're taking advantage of her.'

His companion poked a finger in Jacob's chest. 'I'm the magistrate and—'

'I'm well aware of who you are, Mr Ransome. If you'll let me finish speaking, please? I can take your name up to Miss Newington and ask if she'll receive you.'

'I'm here on official business and whether she wants to see me or not, I'm coming in.' He suddenly thrust the flat of his hand against Jacob's chest, taking him by surprise and shoving him backwards. 'Do not try to stop me or I'll have you arrested for interfering with an officer of the law going about his duties.'

Jacob hesitated, then gestured to Ben to let the two of them past. However, when Robins made to follow them, he shoved the man back far enough to close and lock the door.

'What are you doing?' a voice roared from the foot of the stairs.

'Following Miss Newington's orders, sir,' Jacob said. 'Keeping the doors locked at all times.'

'Stay down there.'

But he followed them up the stairs.

'Did you hear me, fellow?'

'I've been appointed officially to—'

'Stay where you are!'

Jacob hesitated, but it'd do no good for him to be charged with contempt, or whatever imaginary offence those two chose to drum up. He turned to Ben and murmured, 'Get one of the lads to send a telegram to Mr Longley. Ask Cook to give you the money.'

Ben nodded and slipped out towards the back.

Jacob ran lightly up the stairs, disgusted by Arthur's behaviour and fearful of how this visit would affect a sick woman.

Mattie didn't wait for the men at the door of the bedroom because she was afraid they'd shut her outside before they started bullying Miss Newington. She'd watched what was going on over the banisters and only a deaf person could have failed to hear what was being said.

The two men didn't even offer Miss Newington the courtesy of knocking on her door, but pushed it open and walked in.

'Get out, you!' Arthur snapped, pointing to Mattie.

Miss Newington clasped Mattie's hand. 'She . . . stays.'

For a moment there was silence, then she added, 'Mr Ransome . . . send my cousin . . . away.'

'It's at his behest that I'm here.'

'Send him away. You stay.'

Mattie could see how white the old lady had gone and ventured to say, 'Excuse me, sir, but the doctor said Miss Newington was to be kept quiet and peaceful.'

The magistrate glared at her, looked down at the hand clasped around her wrist, and said sharply, 'If you wish to stay in this room, then you're to keep quiet. Is that clear?'

'Yes, sir.'

He turned back to the invalid. 'Your cousin, Mr Arthur Newington, has asked me to give him the authority to look after you properly. And I can see why he's concerned, when servants try to order their betters around. These people have taken advantage of you and are no doubt feeding you lies.'

'Mattie is . . . following my orders. My lawyer has . . . signed deposition . . . about my wishes. And my new will.'

'Wills can be made under undue influence, dear lady. And you are not yourself at the moment.'

'I am . . . in full possession . . . of my senses. My body is . . . improving. I do not need . . . my cousin . . . whom I detest.'

Mattie watched Mr Arthur out of the corner of her eye, saw him go bright red and start to speak, then snap his mouth shut.

'I think in these circumstances, I must be the best judge of what's needed,' the magistrate said.

'No!'

But he ignored Miss Newington and said loudly, 'My finding is—'

* * *

At that moment there was the sound of another car driving up to the house. Arthur nipped across to the window. 'That damned young lawyer has disobeyed his father and brought the other one with him – what's he called? Longley, I think. And there's someone else sitting in the back of the car. Can't quite see who.'

Mattie didn't wait. She slipped out of the room and bumped into Jacob.

'Go and let Mr Longley in! Quick!'

As he ran down she went back into the bedroom, standing near the door, trying not to draw attention to herself. While both men continued to stare out of the window, she had a sudden thought. Taking the key out of the lock, she resumed her position by the bedside and slipped the key under the pile of pillows.

Miss Newington beckoned to Mattie and fumbled for her hand again.

The men turned from the window and walked across to the bed.

'My lawyer will be able to tell you . . . what's been arranged.'

'He can't stop me from making a judgement,' Ransome said.

'I'll . . . sue you.'

Arthur leant over the bed. 'You'll be in no state to sue anyone. Hurry up, Thaddeus.'

Mattie saw the magistrate hesitate.

'Put that maid outside and lock the door. There are things I need to say, to make it legal.'

'My pleasure.' Arthur came round the bed and dragged Mattie to her feet. But when he got to the door, he stared at the lock and snapped, 'What happened to the key? It was here a few minutes ago.' He shook Mattie hard. 'You must have taken it. Give it to me this minute.'

She struggled against him as he fumbled for her pocket, outraged at the way his hands were making free with her body. Hearing the front door open, she shouted at the top of her voice, 'Let go of me, you brute!'

There was an exclamation from downstairs and someone raced up the stairs. Mattie sagged in relief as Jacob burst into the room.

He pushed Newington away from his wife and stood between them. 'How dare you manhandle my wife!'

Outside other footsteps pounded up the stairs.

Frank came into the bedroom, throwing an angry look at the magistrate as he went across to the bed. 'I came as quickly as I could, Miss Newington. This must be very distressing for you, so I've brought Dr Crawford with me.'

'Thank you.'

The relief on her face made Frank want to

punch her cousin. He even found his hands clenching into fists.

He watched the doctor move to the bedside, feel her pulse and study her face. 'Clear the room of everyone except Mrs Kemble,' he ordered. 'Miss Newington needs to rest. I can't believe you've come here and upset your cousin, Newington. Are you trying to kill her?'

There was dead silence in the room.

'I'm trying to look after her,' Arthur said.

'She's perfectly capable of managing her own life. How many times do I have to tell you that she's utterly lucid. Now leave me to speak to my patient.'

The men filed out, but Mattie stayed.

On the landing Ransome turned to Jacob. 'Find us a room, fellow. I need to make careful enquiries from these two about what's going on.' A scornful gesture indicated he was speaking about the two young lawyers. 'I'm not at all satisfied with the situation here. I've never heard of anyone preventing their only close relative from looking after them and I greatly fear that the poor woman has been misled, and that you two have mishandled things.'

'Does he have the right to do this?' Jacob asked Mr Longley in a low voice.

'We don't want him to claim he was prevented

from making a proper inquiry. And it won't hurt to set him straight about what the real situation is. Though I'm not sure he'll care about the facts. He's a close friend of Newington.'

Jacob raised his voice. 'We can use the dining room, I suppose, sir.' He led the way downstairs and opened the door, following the others inside.

'There's no need for you to stay, fellow,' Ransome said.

His tone set Jacob's teeth on edge. He hated it when rich folk spoke in such a patronising way, as if being rich made them superior, which it damned well didn't. He turned to the young lawyer. 'In the circumstances, I think I ought to stay, don't you?'

'You most certainly ought.' Frank turned to the magistrate. 'Mr Kemble is involved in this and needs to be present. Shall we be seated?'

The two young lawyers sat on one side of the table, the older men on the other. Jacob took the end chair without being told, folding his arms, refusing to be cowed. He wasn't letting Mr Arthur get hold of Miss Newington, not if he had to outface the King himself to do it!

Frank pulled some papers out of his briefcase. 'These are copies of papers signed by my client yesterday. Before I let her sign them, I checked with the doctor that she was in full possession of her faculties. And I had Mr Painton with me at every stage, so he can bear witness to the truth of what I'm saying.'

Looking sour, Ransome held out his hand, read the pieces of paper carefully, letting out a snort of disapproval, then passed them to Arthur, who wasn't hiding his anger. He slapped them back down on the table after reading them.

'As you can see, Miss Newington has made Mr Kemble and myself jointly responsible for her welfare in case of any incapacity. There is no mental incapacity at the moment, so she's able to make her own decisions, but she's very weak physically. Therefore Mr Kemble and his wife are staying here to make sure she's carefully nursed until she recovers. Dr Crawford tells me it was a fairly mild seizure and—'

'I shall question him myself about that,' Ransome put in.

'Certainly, sir. I'll let him know once he's finished attending to his patient.'

'Whatever he says, that fellow' – he jabbed a forefinger in Jacob's direction – 'had no right to try to stop her cousin seeing her.'

'May I remind you that Miss Newington specifies in her deposition that she doesn't want her cousin to enter her house, or to deal with her in any way. She made that clear to him as well yesterday, so I'm surprised he's come here today, knowing her wishes. Mr Kemble has merely been trying to follow her orders.'

Arthur leant forward. 'I came because Emily was misled, influenced by the Kembles, who're no doubt out for their own gain. And as for you two, I think you should consider carefully what you're doing today. You're young and less able to judge your fellow men than those of us with greater experience of the world. If this matter goes any further, with you supporting common persons against gentlefolk, you could be doing your reputations a great deal of harm.'

'My first duty is to my client, sir!' Frank said frostily. 'Who is also of gentle birth. And I don't believe there is anything wrong with my judgement, legally or morally. Can you say the same?'

Arthur glared at him, then turned his attention to Sam. 'I'm surprised your father has let you get involved in this mess.'

'No one could stop me from defending the truth.'

Jacob was pleased to see the two younger men standing up to the old bullies. They didn't look down their noses at you, those two didn't.

Mr Arthur turned to him next, as he'd expected.

'You should also think very carefully about what you're doing, Kemble. If anything happens to my cousin . . .' He didn't make an actual threat, but it was implied.

'I shall continue to do what's right,' Jacob said. 'I'd never let a neighbour down who needs my help. Nor would my wife.'

Arthur turned to the magistrate. 'Surely those stupid papers can't stop me from looking after my cousin?'

Ransome stared down at them, drumming his fingers on the table. 'I need to speak to the doctor first. I'm sure I can get him to . . . be sensible . . . and let her family look after her.'

Arthur scowled at him. 'Then I suppose we'll have to wait until he comes down. You!' He looked at Jacob again.

'Yes?' He didn't say 'sir' because he didn't think the man deserved any respect.

'Tell one of the maids to ask the doctor to speak to us when he's finished.'

Jacob folded his arms. 'No need. We'll hear him coming downstairs.' He was pleased to see Mr Arthur's face go even redder and watched as the magistrate laid a hand on his friend's arm and shook his head warningly.

After that they waited in silence. The clock had a very loud tick and Jacob found himself counting the sounds it made, tapping his forefinger in time to them. When he stopped himself doing that, his foot jerked to the rhythm.

Eventually they heard footsteps on the stairs and Jacob got up to intercept Dr Crawford in the hall, speaking loudly enough for those in the room to hear every word he said. 'Mr Ransome would like to speak to you before you leave, Doctor.'

Crawford followed him into the room. 'And I'd like to speak to Mr Ransome. How dare you come and badger a woman recovering from a seizure! Are you trying to kill her? Let me tell you, if anything happens to her, it'll be because of you, and I'll complain to a higher authority than you about your abuse of power today.'

'Is she all right?' Jacob asked anxiously.

'I don't know. I'm worried about her, I must admit. Her pulse is very irregular and I'm concerned about the stress this day's events have placed upon her.'

Frank caught his eye. 'Could we ask you about her state of mind? Is she still in full possession of her senses?'

'Of course she is. I told you that yesterday and I said it again today. How many times do I have to repeat myself? She may only be able to speak slowly, but what she says shows a good deal of sense, which is more than I can say about some people.' He glared at the two older men.

Speaking in a more conciliatory tone, Arthur said, 'I wanted to be sure she was safe. It can't be right for a woman in her position to be cared for by two servants.'

'That's what I thought, so I asked Mr and Mrs Kemble to stay here.'

Jacob saw the two young lawyers exchange smiles.

'*You* asked them to stay?' Ransome said in tones of disbelief. 'You're sure they didn't hint about this?'

'Of course I'm sure. Her two women servants are very willing but I didn't think them capable of dealing with what might happen, so I asked the Kembles to stay – he's her rent agent, after all, so she must trust him, and his wife's a very sensible woman. It seems as if I've been proved right about the need for their presence here.' He nodded to Jacob.

Ransome stood up, giving a quick shake of his head in response to Arthur's questioning look. 'Well . . . er . . . I'm glad to have seen for myself that things are being dealt with properly here. I'm sure Mr Newington can be forgiven for his overzealousness. After all, his cousin is seventy now and—'

'A year younger than he is, I gather,' the doctor said. 'And if your high colour is anything to go by, Mr Newington, you too are heading for a seizure! Now, I think you should leave the occupants of this house in peace.'

The two older men walked outside, both stiff with anger.

Sam let out his breath in a long whoosh of relief. 'We arrived just in time, eh?'

Crawford was still looking grim. 'I hope so, but I fear damage has been done. It's not safe for a woman in her condition to be upset and harassed like this. It's a good thing you stopped me in the street and brought me out here. Now, if someone can take me back into Bassett, I'll come out here under my own steam this evening to check that she's still all right.'

When Sam had driven off with him, Frank looked at Jacob. 'It's a bad business.'

'Yes.'

'You did well standing up to those bullies. It can't have been easy.'

'I try to do what's right. My wife had to face up to them as well. She's a brave lass.'

'You've made a bad enemy there. Newington may be getting old but he's still got a lot of influence in the district and is determined to bulldoze his way through life as he did in his youth. He forgets we're in the twentieth century now.'

'I'm not the only one to have made an enemy, I reckon. That magistrate wasn't looking too happy with you and Mr Painton.'

'We do what we have to for our clients.'

There was silence for a few moments, then

Jacob remembered his manners. 'Perhaps you'd like some refreshment. I'm in need of a cup of tea, even if you aren't. I'll just go and tell Cook.'

'And I'll go up and check that my client is all right, make sure she understands what we've done.'

In Swindon that same evening, Stan waited for Bart after work. As the long lines of tired men filed past on their way home from the Railway Works, he fell into place beside his friend. 'We need to talk. We'll go to your place.'

At Bart's house he looked round in disgust. 'Can't you get some woman to come in every day and sort this place out for you?'

'That'd cost too much. I've one coming in to do my washing and give the place a bit of a clear-up once a week, but I'm not wasting good coin on dusting. When I get my girls back, they'll clear the place up again.'

Stan looked at him in surprise. 'How do you know you'll get them back? We've not found a sign of them yet. It's only Mattie we can trace.'

Bart looked at him quickly. 'You've found her?'

'I've found out there's a family called Newington with property out beyond Wootton Bassett. Landowners. Rich. I set a friend on to make enquiries at the registry office and he found out about the wedding. Your Mattie got married to a fellow called Kemble – a widower, he was. He lives out that way, too. I'm going to find 'em next weekend. You can come too if you want.'

'I might as well. She'll know where the others have gone. They're thick as thieves, them three girls are.' He frowned. 'But I don't see why you want to bother with her now. She's wed to someone else, and you're well shut of her if you want my opinion.'

'I want to see her.'

'She's not worth the trouble.'

Stan shrugged. 'I know, but I still want to see her.'

'You've gone daft.'

He knew that, but he had to find out why she'd rejected him when he'd promised to treat her right, which was more than Bart did.

Chapter Fifteen

Once they'd routed her cousin, Miss Newington said she was tired. She lay so quiet and still that Mattie began to worry about her. Even after her seizure Miss Newington had tried to speak, struggled to move her sluggish limbs, made plans. Now, she was just staring into the distance. She didn't want to eat or drink, didn't try to speak, thanked her helpers only with a faint smile when they tried to make her more comfortable.

'She's going to die, I know she is,' Lyddie said when she came to take away a tray of food that hadn't been touched.

'Shh!' Mattie glanced over her shoulder, went out onto the landing and closed the bedroom door. 'Why do you say that?'

'My gran were just the same. She give up tryin'.'

'Well, I don't want you saying anything like that where Miss Newington can hear you, and if I can make her want to live, I shall.'

Lyddie looked at her with a sad smile. 'She's lucky she's got you and Mr Kemble.'

'She's lucky she's got you and Cook, too.'

'We're not the same. We're just servants.'

As she went back into the bedroom, Mattie wondered what she and Jacob were. If not servants, then what? Everyone else round here seemed quite sure of each others' place in the scheme of things. She wasn't sure of anything about her new life, except that it was better than the old one and . . . that she both liked and admired Jacob. She wished she could be with him now, be married properly, building a home and family together.

But they were needed here in this big, near empty, echoing house. You couldn't leave a sick old woman on her own, you just couldn't. So Mattie and her new husband, and his children, would stay here for the time being and move back to their own home later.

When Dr Crawford came back at six o'clock that evening, he asked Mattie to stay and spent some time with Miss Newington, trying to get her to talk while observing her carefully. After he'd finished, he said a cheerful goodbye.

'I'll just give your attendants instructions about how to use the calming medicine I'm going to leave here for you. I'll be back in the morning.'

He shook the sick woman's hand and she held on to it for a minute, the first sign of her old self.

'Thank you, Doctor.'

He stared down at her. 'I do my best.'

'My will . . .'

He waited, then prompted, 'Yes. Your will?'

'Is as I want it to be. Everything's going to a good person. Remember that.'

Her eyes closed and he waited a minute, but they didn't open again. He gestured to Mattie to leave the room. 'Do you know anything about her will? Is there some problem?'

'You'll have to ask Mr Longley about that, Doctor. I don't know anything about it.'

'Let's find that husband of yours. I need to talk to you both.'

'Is something wrong?'

His voice was brusque. 'I don't want to keep repeating myself.'

She knew then that something was indeed wrong. Well, she'd sensed it already, hadn't she? It was as if the magistrate's visit had drained Miss Newington of energy – and Lyddie was right. The old lady had lost the will to live, looked so frail you felt a strong wind would blow her away.

Mattie wasn't usually fanciful but like Lyddie she'd seen the same thing before. Her mother. One week struggling to live, the next waiting calmly to leave this life.

They gathered in the small sitting room.

Dr Crawford declined an offer of refreshments, took a deep breath and said, 'I'm afraid we're going to lose her.'

Cook let out a cry, then muffled her tears with her apron. Lyddie patted her shoulder.

Jacob broke the silence. 'They've killed her, then!' His voice was angry and his hand tightened on Mattie's.

'They've probably hastened her death, yes. But her heart has become very fluttery and weak and I don't like her lethargy. I'm deeply sorry her last days have been marred by such unpleasantness.'

Mattie watched the maid take out her handkerchief and wipe away her tears, but others followed and the girl didn't seem able to stop weeping.

'Stop that!' the doctor said sharply. 'Save your weeping till she's gone. Do you want to surround her with gloom and tears? She'll see it if you have red eyes, you know.'

Lyddie gulped and blew her nose, struggling to get her emotions under control. It was Cook's turn to comfort her.

Mattie held on tightly to Jacob's hand.

'I think you should take it in turns to sit with her tonight,' the doctor went on. 'Just in case.'

They nodded. No one wanted the poor lady to die alone.

'And don't hesitate to send for me if you need me – at any hour. One final thing: should she die, don't touch her, don't change anything. No laying out till after I've seen her.'

Mattie looked at him in puzzlement.

'We don't want to give her cousin any excuse for saying things have been tampered with, that you hastened her death.'

Lyddie and Cook looked scandalised and Jacob let out a little growl of anger.

'Her lawyer is coming out to see her again tomorrow, and every day thereafter. He and I agree that it's best we keep an eye on her until . . . things are resolved. And now I'd better get back to my family.'

Jacob saw the doctor to the door, then rejoined the others, who were still sitting there in numb silence. 'The doctor's right. We must try to be calm and cheerful when we're with her. She won't want to be surrounded by miserable faces.'

They nodded.

'She knows, though,' Lyddie said suddenly. 'She knows she's going to die.'

No one contradicted her.

* * *

Mattie took over from Jacob at three o'clock in the morning, as agreed. 'How is she?'

'She's hardly stirred.' He pulled his wife to him for a moment, holding her close, then stepped back with a yawn. 'I'd better get some sleep. Are you going to be all right? You're not long recovered yourself.'

'Of course I'll be all right. I slept soundly till you woke me and I'm feeling better every day.'

She sat down by the side of the bed, lost in thought, thinking through all that had happened to her in the past few weeks. Who would have thought she'd end up married?

Just as it was starting to get light, Miss Newington stirred, then opened her eyes and stared towards the door, as if someone had entered the room.

Mattie turned round, but there was no one there except herself. She looked back to see Miss Newington smiling and hold out one hand, as if greeting someone. Then the old lady's head fell sideways and she didn't move again.

Mattie had seen death enough times to recognise it at once. She closed the staring eyes and said a quick prayer, adding, 'Goodbye, Miss Newington. I'm sorry I didn't know you better.' Then she went to fetch Jacob.

They stood by the bedside together, hand in hand, looking down. Mattie loved the feel of his hand in hers, the feeling it gave her that she was no longer alone. He'd never offer her fancy words, she knew, but if he continued to offer her his hand, she'd do very well.

'How did she go?' he asked.

'It was very peaceful. You couldn't ask for a gentler death.'

'I'm glad about that, at least.'

'We'd better send for the doctor.'

'I suppose so. I'll drive into Bassett for him. Make me a cup of tea first, will you? And could you find me something to eat? It sounds heartless, but I'm always ravenous in the mornings.'

As they sat together at the kitchen table while Jacob quickly ate a slice of bread and jam, Mattie asked the question that was uppermost in her mind: 'What's going to happen to us now? Miss Newington said her cousin wouldn't inherit, but who will?'

'I don't know. Can't even guess. Don't fret. Even if I lose the rent agent's job, I reckon I can always earn enough to put bread on the table.'

'I'll be an extra burden on you.'

Jacob looked at her in surprise. 'You're my wife, not a burden.' As if that settled the matter, he ate the last corner of bread, sucked a blob of jam off his thumb and stood up.

Mattie tried to smile at him, but she couldn't manage it.

He pulled her to him and gave her a quick hug. 'I meant that.'

She looked at him in wonderment and raised her hand to his cheek for a brief caress, then allowed herself to lean against him for the sheer comfort of it.

His breath was warm in her ear. 'Far from you being a burden, Mattie Kemble, you've been a godsend. I don't know what I'd have done without you these past few days, and that's a fact. And you were lovely with Miss Newington. I'm sure you made things easier for her.'

'I'm glad, too. And I'm very glad I married you, Jacob Kemble. I'm looking forward to our life together.'

'So am I.' He glanced at the clock and moved her gently aside. 'I'd better get going. We want that doctor here before anyone else hears the news.'

When he'd gone, the warmth of his words lingered inside her, but outside, the early morning stillness seemed heavy and threatening today, as if a storm was about to break upon this house. She shivered. Not like her to be so fanciful. She tried to banish such thoughts, but the feeling persisted.

Then Lyddie came into the kitchen, yawning, and Mattie was at last able to forgot her strange fancies, because there was a great deal to do.

* * *

Mattie sent the children to school. She'd not told them of Miss Newington's death and had asked the others not to mention it, either. But as Cook kept wiping her eyes and the normally cheerful Lyddie was sad and quiet, it was obvious something was wrong.

Ben and one of the others had slept in the barn and came up to the house for breakfast. She asked Ben to stay behind afterwards and told him what had happened. For some reason she trusted him implicitly, young as he was.

'What's going to happen now?' he asked.

'I don't know.'

'I'll stay near the house this morning, shall I?'

'I'd feel better to have you around,' she admitted. 'I hope Jacob doesn't take too long to find the doctor.'

He grinned at all the women. 'You're a fearsome lot and I'm sure you'd hold your own without us men. I'd not like to meet you three when you've got pokers in your hands, that's for sure.'

He didn't just sit there as the clock slowly ticked away the minutes, Mattie noticed. He brought in wood for the fire, carried things to and fro for Cook, and generally made himself useful. A good man, Ben Summerhaye.

It was two hours before Jacob returned, by which time Mattie was starting to feel anxious.

'Dr Crawford's out at a birthing, but he'll come straight here afterwards.' Jacob looked at the three women and Ben. 'You didn't tell the children what had happened?'

They shook their heads.

'I don't like to think of the poor mistress lying there untended,' Cook said. ''Tisn't right.'

'We must do as the doctor ordered,' Jacob said.

Cook wiped away her tears with the back of her forearm, then turned to her cooking. 'Best be ready for visitors. Won't look good if we've nothing to offer them. We don't want anyone thinking we took advantage of the mistress to slack off, do we?' She went into the pantry and came out again. 'You don't have any spare eggs, do you, Mr Kemble? I've only got two left.'

'I can get you some. I'll have to go and feed the hens, anyway.'

'Take care,' Mattie said involuntarily.

'I doubt anything can happen to me just going down the lane.'

But as he walked out of the house, she turned to Ben. 'Could you send one of the other lads to stand at the gate? We don't want anyone taking Jacob by surprise.'

'I'll go and do that myself and send Percy to stay in the house with you.' He turned to Cook. 'He'd appreciate a snack if you have anything.

Not got a lot to eat in his house, and he's always hungry.'

She nodded. 'I can find him something. I don't like to see lads as need their strength lacking food.'

The lad in question was twenty, nearly six foot tall but bony and with a hungry look to him which Mattie had seen before among poorer people.

She went to help Lyddie with the housework, rather than fret around the kitchen, ignoring the maid's protests that this wasn't right.

As Jacob carried the bowl of eggs back to his house to wash his hands, a man slipped round the corner of the building. He tensed till he saw it was one of his nearest neighbours.

'Did you know someone's been watching the big house and wandering round your place?' Walter asked.

'What? Who is he?'

'Says he's a cousin of yours, but I ent heard you talk about no cousins.'

'That's because I've not got any living near here.'

'Thought as much. I sent him off with a flea in his ear. He has a bicycle hidden down the lane, near the main road. Why would he hide it there if he was coming to see you? And why hasn't he come out of hiding now you're here?'

'Because he isn't my cousin. Thanks for keeping your eyes open.'

'If neighbours can't help one another, who can we rely on?' He hesitated. 'Everything all right at the big house?'

Jacob hesitated, then decided to trust a man he'd known all his life. 'Miss Newington died in the night. We're waiting for the doctor now. I'd appreciate it if you'd keep the news to yourself for the moment.'

'Never been one to flap my tongue at the world.'

'I know.'

There was the sound of a horse in the lane and he spun round, stiffening, ready to rush back to the house. But it was the doctor's vehicle which came into view. 'I know you're busy, but can you find someone to keep an eye on things here? I'll give them a florin just to stay around the place.'

'I c'n find someone easy enough. You expectin' trouble?'

'Could be. Arthur Newington's already tried to take over at the big house. Miss Newington didn't want him there, though. Sent him off with a flea in his ear, ill as she was.'

'He's her only relative, ent he?'

'Yes.'

'Then he'll be inheriting.'

'I've heard she's leaving it to someone else, but I don't know who. Keep that to yourself as well.'

Walter let out a low whistle of surprise. 'Let's hope it's someone decent. Now, you'd better get back to the big house, Jacob. I'll see an eye's kept on your place.'

'Thanks.'

He was grim-faced as he walked up the lane with the bowl of eggs. If Arthur Newington got hold of the big house, his peace would be over. And probably his livelihood too. Easy enough to damage a field of fruit and vegetables.

Mattie accompanied Dr Crawford up to Miss Newington's room.

'You've not touched the body?' he asked.

'I closed her eyes, that's all.'

'You can leave me to my work now. I'll come down when I've finished.'

'Shall I put a jug of water in the next room for you to wash your hands in afterwards?'

'Thank you.'

She found Jacob in the kitchen and Cook exclaiming in pleasure over the big bowl of eggs he'd brought.

He turned to Mattie. 'I see the doctor's here.'

'Yes. I'm just going to take him up a jug of water to wash in afterwards.'

'I can do that, Mrs Kemble,' Lyddie said.

'Thank you. Leave it in the room next door with a towel.'

It was half an hour before the doctor came down, by which time Jacob was pacing up and down the hall and Mattie was sitting watching her husband through the open door of the small sitting room. She liked this room best of any to sit in. How lucky people like Miss Newington were to have such space and comfort. Until she ran away from home, Mattie had never even had her own bedroom.

When she heard footsteps, she went to the doorway.

Dr Crawford came quickly down the stairs like a man half his age. 'I'd appreciate a cup of tea, if it's not too much trouble.'

Mattie nodded and for the first time ever rang the bell for Lyddie, because she didn't want to miss what the doctor said.

He waited till she'd sat down before taking a chair himself. 'It was as I'd expected. She died of natural causes, and I'd guess from the peaceful look on her face that she felt no pain.'

'She didn't,' Mattie said quietly, and explained what she'd seen.

'I've written out the death certificate and shall send it to her lawyer. He's going to arrange the funeral.'

'He's coming here today,' Jacob said. 'Do you want me to give the certificate to him?'

'No. Better for me to do that. If I meet him on the way back, I'll stop him and hand it over.'

'Can I lay her out now?' Mattie asked.

'You could leave that to the funeral company. No doubt her lawyer will let them know they're needed.'

'I don't want to wait and leave her in a mess. I've laid people out before and I know what to do. We always helped one another in our street.'

'Then I'll leave you to it.'

The house seemed quiet since the doctor left, with nothing for them to do except wait. But it was an uneasy silence, as if a storm was threatening. Jacob went down to work on his plants, nodding to a youth he found sitting outside his back door, with a thin, alert-looking dog by his side.

'No trouble?'

'No,' the lad said. 'Easiest money I ever earned, this. Any trouble and I'll send Rover home. Dad'll know to come running.'

'Can't be too careful,' Jacob said. 'So stay alert.'

There it was again, he thought as he put in an hour's work. Friends looking after one another.

He took care of what was urgent but didn't stay any longer because the lawyer would be coming soon and he didn't want to be caught all dirty from the garden.

Mr Longley arrived at the big house just before midday, driven again by his friend Sam.

When Jacob heard the motor car in the lane, he abandoned what he was doing, which was pulling up weeds from the garden at the big house. He wasn't a man to sit still and watch the grass growing where it shouldn't. Washing his hands hastily under the garden tap and stamping his feet to shake loose any soil, he went back to the house.

He found the two lawyers sitting in the morning room, enjoying a piece of cake and some freshly made scones with Mattie.

They all looked up when he went in.

'I've set a place for you,' Mattie said. 'I knew you'd come in once you saw the car.'

'We're waiting for the funeral company to bring the coffin and finish laying her out,' Frank said. 'She left detailed instructions for her funeral. She wanted her body to lie at rest here, then the will to be read in the drawing room after the funeral. I'm afraid we can't avoid inviting her family this time, but she wanted you two present at the reading of the will as well.'

'What concern is that of ours?' Jacob asked in surprise.

Mr Longley gave a slight shrug and an apologetic smile. 'I'm just obeying her instructions. Oh, and could you stay on here until the funeral and keep an eye on things? Would you mind?'

'I can continue working from here easily enough.' Jacob hesitated. 'Me and Mattie are worried about what'll happen to us if Arthur Newington or one of his family takes over the big house. They'd not make easy neighbours.'

All he got in response was another enigmatic smile, which, as he said to Mattie afterwards, was not much help to a man with a business to run and a family to feed.

Chapter Sixteen

At three o'clock on Saturday afternoon, the hearse, a modern motor vehicle instead of the old-fashioned carriage drawn by black horses, drove up to the big house. Mattie and the servants went to peer out of the window of the small sitting room.

''Tisn't right to take her to church in a smelly, noisy machine like that,' Cook grumbled.

Ben laughed softly. 'It's the way of the future, so you'd better get used to it. And anyway, the coffin will be in the back, in the glass part. She'll do just fine there.'

'I still don't like them motor cars,' Cook said defiantly.

'You'll learn to put up with 'em, though. Everyone got used to trains in my great-grandma's time, didn't they, even though people said they'd frighten the cows and burn the crops? Which they didn't. Well, they'll get used to motor cars just the same. And it'll be a better world for having them, they're so much quicker than horses and they don't foul the streets.'

'We've got trains when we need to go anywhere quickly,' Cook said sourly. 'And you'd be cheerful if the sky fell in, young Ben.' She went to glance in the mirror over the fireplace to make sure her best hat was on straight. 'Just you make sure no one breaks into this house while we're at church.' The worries about her appearance settled, she went back to her post by the window.

The hearse was followed by four other motor cars and several village urchins ran up the lane after them, not daring to come right up to the house, but peeping at them from beyond the gates.

'Look at them kids. They'd love to ride in a car,' Lyddie said. 'So would I, come to that. Have you ever rid in one, Cook?'

'No, and I don't intend to, neither. We'd better get back to the kitchen now, don't you think, Mrs Kemble? The guests will be coming inside soon.'

Mattie nodded and as she went through the servants' door at the back of the hall, glanced back to see that Mr Longley was the first to enter the house. He'd brought his wife with him and beckoned to Mattie.

'Is there anything I can do to help?' Mrs Longley asked, after the two women had been introduced.

She had such a friendly smile, Mattie didn't feel offended. 'Not really. Cook is very capable. We've plenty of food for the mourners when they get back from church. It's set out in the morning room. Come and look at it, tell me if it's all right.'

Mrs Longley studied the table. 'There's more than enough and you've set it out beautifully.'

'It's Cook who did that. My husband found some port wine in the cellar.' She pointed to the decanter on the sideboard. Not that she'd be drinking it. She'd never had a glass of wine in her life and although she'd tasted beer once or twice, she didn't really like it. Give her a freshly brewed cup of tea any day.

'The Newingtons are coming into the house,' Mr Longley called. 'We'd better go and greet them, my dear.'

'I'll wait in the kitchen with the others.' Mattie hurried off.

Lyddie stationed herself at the partly open door to the kitchen area and kept up a running commentary for the others.

'Mr Arthur looks in a bad mood again. He's got

his wife with him, ooh, and his son and daughter-in-law, but his daughter isn't there. They're all wearing black.'

So were the servants. Mattie had had to do some quick alterations on another of the dresses from the attic to make sure she was decently clad. It was tacked together loosely in parts and she was praying the stitches would hold.

She wished today was over, wished they knew who would inherit this house, knew Jacob was worrying about that too, however much he pretended to be cheerful. He was outside now, talking to the young men who were still helping keep an eye on the house. She kept looking out of the window at him, thinking how attractive he was, how lucky she was to have met him.

She saw Lyddie watching her and felt herself flushing. The young maid gave her a knowing, but friendly smile, as if she'd guessed what she was thinking.

Did her feelings for Jacob show so clearly, then? Mattie wondered. She'd grown fond of him so quickly.

In the hall, Frank took on the role of host, which immediately set Arthur's back up.

'I'd have thought it'd be for me, as Emily's closest relative, to receive the guests today,' he said in his overloud voice.

Frank kept a smile pinned to his face. 'My client left very clear instructions for the funeral. I can show you them if you wish. Perhaps you'd like to go into the drawing room?'

Arthur's wife tugged his arm and he moved on, still grumbling. His son followed, saying nothing and ignoring the lawyer's outstretched hand. His daughter-in-law didn't trouble to hide her boredom and disinterest.

Their wealth and comfortable lifestyle clearly didn't make these people happy, Frank thought.

Although he'd not been invited, the magistrate walked into the house, his eyes challenging the lawyer to try to deny him entrance.

'Mr Ransome. What a pleasant surprise to see you here.'

'Newington invited me.'

Well, both of you are in for a few shocks today, Frank thought, but said only, 'Through there, please.'

In the drawing room, the Newingtons sat with Ransome, looking down their noses at the Longleys and Sam Painton.

The ones who really cared about Miss Newington are in the kitchen, Frank thought. These people care only about her will.

'Is there to be a viewing of the body?' Mrs Newington asked unexpectedly.

'No. My client didn't wish for that.'

She let out a huff of displeasure and said no more.

When the coffin, which had been lying on the big dining-room table, had been carried outside, everyone got back into their vehicles to be driven in state the half mile to the village church.

The Kembles followed the gentry in the dog cart, driven by Horace and accompanied by Cook and Lyddie. It was a bit of a squash, but Sarah sat on her father's knee and Luke squeezed into the last six inches of the bench seat, sitting sideways.

Both children were very quiet today, Mattie thought. They're probably overawed by the company and the circumstances.

And so am I. But she held her chin up and tried not to let her nervousness show.

At the church Jacob took his place near the hearse with the other pall-bearers, all of them men from the village except for Mr Longley. This left Mattie to take the children in, so she slipped into the church with the servants and they found seats at the rear. The place was crowded with villagers paying their respects.

But just as she was settling down, Mr Painton came to the rear of the church and stopped at the end of their pew. 'Places have been saved for you and your husband next to us, Mrs Kemble.'

Mattie looked at him in shock. 'There's no need

for that, sir. We'll be quite comfortable here.'

'It was Miss Newington's wish and Mr Kemble is a pall-bearer so will be sitting there. Please join us there.' He looked at the children. 'Perhaps you two can stay with Cook and Lyddie?'

They nodded in obvious relief.

Since he was still standing there, drawing everyone's attention, Mattie didn't like to argue and moved forward. But she stopped in panic when he gestured to her to enter the front pew of all, which was usually reserved for the leading figures in any community. She'd never sat in a front pew in her whole life.

The Newingtons and Mr Ransome were in the other front pew, looking across at her with outrage on their faces.

In the pew behind them, Mrs Henty was also glaring across at her.

She didn't look that way again but took a seat next to Mrs Longley and bent her head in a quick prayer.

Then the organist played a long minor chord and started a slow tune that Mattie didn't recognise. Everyone fell silent.

She glanced quickly over her shoulder to see the coffin being slowly carried in by the six pall-bearers, with her Jacob and Mr Longley at the front. It seemed to take a long time till they set their burden down on the velvet-draped stand and took their places in the pews, leaving Mr Henty at the front with the coffin.

A quick glance sideways at Jacob as he sat down next to her showed him to have a wooden expression on his face and Mattie guessed that he too was finding it uncomfortable to be at the centre of attention. His hand sought hers. He gave it a quick squeeze and kept hold of it underneath the folds of her skirt. That made her feel a lot better.

Mr Henty stumbled his way through the service, seeming unnerved by the presence of the Newingtons and the magistrate, because he kept glancing their way and stammering.

It was hard to pay attention and Mattie heard bits and pieces only:

'I am the resurrection and the life, saith the Lord: he that believeth in me, though he were dead, yet shall he live . . .

'We brought nothing into this world, and it is certain we can carry nothing out. The Lord gave, and the Lord hath taken away . . .'

That set her thinking. She'd brought nothing to Shallerton Bassett with her, and yet fate had given her a husband and a home. She prayed to be worthy of that wonderful gift and gave heartfelt thanks to her Maker for it.

When Mr Henty had finished, Arthur Newington stood up, clearly intending to deliver the eulogy, but Mr Longley moved quickly to the front.

Although he spoke quietly, Mattie was close enough to hear him say to the irate gentleman, 'Sorry. I've got instructions about this part of the service as well.'

'I don't believe she'd exclude her relatives.'

Frank produced a piece of paper and Arthur snatched it out of his hands. He scanned it, said, 'Shameful!' in a very loud voice, thrusting it back at the young lawyer, not caring that it missed the outstretched hand and fluttered to the floor.

Frank picked it up, then went to stand behind the lectern. He waved the piece of paper. 'My client left instructions for her funeral with me a while back, which I'll try to follow. She wanted me to tell everyone how much she'd appreciated the welcome she got from the people of Shallerton Bassett when she inherited the house unexpectedly and came to live here. And she particularly wanted me to thank the three servants at the house for their loyal and willing help, also Jacob Kemble and his wife.'

At the rear of the church, Cook let out an audible sob and buried her face in her handkerchief.

Jacob blinked his eyes and sniffed a couple of times.

'And she wanted me to tell everyone that she'd

made her will in the full knowledge of what she was doing. She hopes you'll treat the new owner of Newington House as kindly as you've treated her.'

Another glance showed Mattie that the villagers were nodding their heads to one another, clearly pleased with these acknowledgements.

'Didden mention her cousin, did 'er?' an old man near the back said suddenly, his voice echoing clearly round the church. He was hastily shushed by his relatives.

'Well, 'er didden,' he said defiantly.

Mr Longley moved to the coffin again and gestured to the other pall-bearers to join him in carrying it outside to its final resting place.

Mrs Longley smiled at Mattie. 'We'll let that lot go first,' she whispered, gesturing to those in the pew across the aisle.

As if she'd have tried to push ahead of them, Mattie thought.

The sun was shining so brightly as she stepped out of the porch that she was dazzled and stopped moving, then realised she was holding up the rest of the congregation and moved on hastily. She would be glad when Jacob's duties let him come to stand by her side again.

Everyone gathered round the open grave, the villagers at a respectful distance from the funeral party, the Newingtons and Ransome on their own at one side. A quick glance showed Mattie that Luke and Sarah were standing next to Lyddie.

At a nod from Mr Henty, Arthur Newington picked up a handful of dirt and cast it down on the coffin. As his wife and son did the same, Mr Henty began the final part of the service and the other mourners followed suit.

'Forasmuch as it hath pleased Almighty God of his great mercy to take out of this world the soul of our sister here departed, we therefore commit her body to the ground . . .'

When the coffin was in its grave and enough earth had been ceremonially scattered over it, Arthur Newington made no pretence of bowing his head to say a final prayer, but led his family at a rapid pace back to their vehicle.

'Did you leave your guards on duty?' Frank asked Jacob.

'I did. No one will get into the house till we're back.'

'Then we needn't hurry,' Frank smiled. 'See you up there.' He strolled back to Sam's car with his wife.

Jacob beckoned to his children and they all got into the dog cart again. This time it was the first vehicle to leave, because the driver was having trouble starting the Newingtons' car. People from the village were standing around it, smiling broadly, and someone from the back of the crowd asked if it'd been fed today.

The driver's face was dark red with anger, just like his master's.

When they got back, Horace reined in the horse at the front door while Sam stopped his car nearby.

'Not here, Horace. Take us round to the back,' Jacob said.

'No. I ent doin' that. Miss Newington wanted you two in the funeral party, so you should go in the front way, like the others.'

'He's right,' Cook said. 'But we'll carry on looking after the children for you. I daresay you two would like something to eat, wouldn't you? And you'll be comfier in my kitchen.'

Luke nodded enthusiastically.

'Mind your manners, then,' Jacob said and led his wife into the house. They waited in the hall for the young lawyers to follow them inside.

'Surely I'm not needed now?' Mattie said to Mr Longley, when he gestured to her to lead the way into the drawing room. 'There's a lot to do in the kitchen. I should be helping Cook.'

'You're needed at the reading of the will, Mrs Kemble. I'm sure Cook can manage perfectly well.'

'Why am I needed?'

'All shall be revealed in due course.'

With a sigh she took Jacob's arm again, but pulled back when the lawyer tried to seat her and Jacob at the front of the room, at a right angle to the others. 'Not here!'

'Please trust me on this. I need you to be here.'

So they sat down, and judging by his stiffness, Jacob felt as uncomfortable as she did. He ran one finger under his shirt collar, wriggling uncomfortably, and she gave him a quick nudge in the ribs and whispered, 'Sit still!' She didn't want to give that horrible man any reason to insult them again. Not that he needed much excuse.

When the Newingtons came in, Arthur stopped to glare at the Kembles, turned to his son and said loudly, 'Damned upstarts! In my day servants knew their place and didn't try to keep company with their betters, let alone take places at the front of the room.'

'*I* asked Mr and Mrs Kemble to sit there,' Mr Longley said coldly. 'And for a good reason.'

Angry at Mr Newington's rudeness, Mattie raised her chin defiantly, but it was difficult to keep a calm expression on her face with all four of them looking at her as if she was a lowly worm.

Mr Longley cleared his throat and rustled his papers. 'If everyone is ready, I'll begin.'

Suddenly, they were all attention.

Into the silence, he said, 'The will is very

simple indeed. Miss Newington left everything she owned to her young friend Matilda Willitt, who is now Mrs Kemble, with minor legacies to her three servants.'

There was dead silence, then Arthur roared at the top of his voice, 'Then my cousin had definitely lost her wits and I shall be contesting the will.'

Mattie heard Mr Longley's words but it was a minute or two before their meaning sank in fully, then she gasped and put both hands up to her mouth in shock. It couldn't be true! It just couldn't.

Jacob took hold of her hands and pulled her round to face him. 'Are you all right?'

She looked at him in bewilderment. 'There must be some mistake. She can't have left all this to me.' She gestured round them.

He kept hold of her hands. 'I suppose it must be true, if her lawyer says it.'

'But she hardly knew me. Why would she leave everything to me?'

'I don't rightly know what to think. We'll ask Mr Longley later. He must know. It's . . . puzzling, I must admit.'

As they turned back towards the lawyer, the magistrate stood up and walked forward as if he was God come down to earth on the day of retribution.

He looked so threatening, Mattie reached out for Jacob's hand and clutched it tightly, not caring how that looked.

'I'd like to see that will, Longley,' Mr Ransome said.

Frank gave him a piece of paper from the table. 'I took the liberty of having a copy made for Mr Newington. I'm sure he won't mind you looking at it. The original is locked away safely in the bank, but I'm happy to let you see it if you have any doubts that this is a true copy. You can make an appointment to do that through my clerk.'

He passed the paper to the magistrate, who scanned it quickly, scowled even more deeply, then handed it to Arthur, who had joined him at the front.

He read it, then repeated, 'I'm definitely going to contest this ridiculous will.'

'On what grounds?' Frank asked.

'Emily not being in her rightful mind.'

'You haven't a chance with that one. Dr Crawford has given me a signed statement that Miss Newington was in full possession of her senses until the very end, as I could see for myself.'

'It seemed otherwise to me when I saw her,' Ransome snapped.

'To me also,' Arthur chimed in. 'And she's my cousin so—'

'A cousin whom you rarely saw because you didn't get on with one another, which is, she put in writing, the reason she didn't leave anything to you. That antipathy should be fairly easy to prove as well. It's commonly known.'

Sam stepped forward to join his friend. 'So it'll be your word against two lawyers, a doctor, her servants and the people caring for her, Newington.'

'Then we'll cite undue influence as the reason.'

'Mrs Kemble didn't even know she was the legatee, so how could she have been exerting any influence?'

'Don't let her fool you. She's a good actress, that sort always is.'

Frank reined in his anger. 'Should you continue to insult Mrs Kemble, I shall advise her to bring a charge of slander against you. We have, as you can see, a room full of witnesses.' He wouldn't do any such thing, but that made the arrogant sod snap his mouth shut.

Ransome took over. 'I shall be happy to support Mr Newington in his claims.'

Frank looked sideways at his friend, who nodded and moved forward.

'A word with you, if you please.' Sam took Ransome aside to the bay window, lowering his voice so that no one else could hear them. 'If you continue making these false claims and trying to help your friend bully his way into someone else's inheritance, you can be sure that I shall complain to the Law Society about your unprofessional behaviour.'

'What the hell do you mean by that?'

'It's strange the way you threatened my father to make him try to coerce me into falling in with your wishes about this matter.'

'Did he say that?'

'No. He didn't need to. I overheard you speaking to him myself. You have a rather loud voice, which carries easily through open windows.'

'It'll be your word against mine, then. Your father will bear me out that I did no such thing.'

'You may frighten him into doing as you wish, but there was another witness present with me, one who has an immaculate reputation and who won't lie under oath.'

'Who?'

'I shan't tell you, but I shall produce the person in court, if necessary, and it won't look good for a man in your position to have such a case proved against you.'

The magistrate drew back, his mouth open in shock for a moment, then he bent his head forward and said in an equally low voice, 'You might find yourself out of a job, if you don't take care.'

'I've resigned from the family practice and have already joined another. I'm no longer on good terms with my father and am not likely to want my old job back, so I'm afraid that threat carries no weight with me. It wouldn't have done, even if I were still working with my father. I believe in the law, Mr Ransome – and in justice, which isn't always the same thing.'

For all their lowered voices, the air around them was fairly crackling with anger.

Arthur called across the room, 'Is everything all right?'

Sam looked at the magistrate and raised one eyebrow questioningly.

'Damn you!' Ransome pushed past him. 'I think we should leave now, Arthur.'

His friend nodded, but turned to toss a final word at Frank. 'You'll be hearing from my lawyer.'

The whole family left the house.

The two young men stayed in the bay window for a few moments longer, talking earnestly.

Since no one was paying attention to them, Jacob took Mattie's hand. 'Are you all right?'

'No.'

'What's wrong?'

'I can't take it in. I can't believe it's true.'

They were both silent for a moment or two, then Frank came across to join them and she repeated her worries to him.

'It is true, Mrs Kemble. You've inherited this house and several cottages in the village, plus some shops in Swindon. There isn't a lot of money to go with them, though.'

'It'll seem like a lot to us,' Mattie said.

'And I can make the land pay better,' Jacob said, thinking aloud, lost in a dream of owning all that land. 'There's a lot I can do to earn money if everything's ours.' He frowned. 'Mr Arthur said he'd contest the will. Can he take it off us?'

'He has no grounds for doing that, I promise you. Everything was attended to properly and Miss Newington knew what she was doing.'

'But *why* did she do it?' Mattie asked. 'I hardly knew her. Why on earth would she leave everything to me?'

'In the first place, she simply wanted to be sure it couldn't fall into her cousin's hands, and sadly, she had no one else in the world, no other relatives, most of her friends dead. As to why she chose you, I can't say. But she took a great liking to you and told the doctor the last time she saw him that her will was as she wanted it.'

'Oh.'

Frank looked at his watch. 'Now, if there's nothing else you want to ask, I'll leave you to take possession of your new home and I'll come back tomorrow with a full list of the properties you own and a few more papers for you to sign.'

Chapter Seventeen

It wasn't until the lawyers had left that Mattie realised no one had been offered the refreshments which Cook had taken so much trouble with. But there had been more important things to think about. 'What do we do now, Jacob?'

'That's up to you, isn't it? This all belongs to you.'

His voice had no warmth to it, his body was stiff and she realised with a sinking heart that after his first flush of excitement, he saw the bequest as putting a wall between them. 'Please don't talk like that. We're married, so it belongs to both of us.'

'It was left to you, not me.'

'Let's go and tell Cook and the others,' she said, desperate to do something to bring them closer. Then she realised something and gasped.

'Oh! We've got servants now. We'll have to pay them wages and tell them what to do. I shan't know where to begin.'

'Maybe we'd better tell the children what's happened first – if you don't mind, that is?'

'Of course I don't. I should have thought of that myself.' She smiled, slowly beginning to realise some of the benefits. 'We can make a really good life for them now, can't we?'

A little warmth came into his eyes, but he didn't answer her question, just nodded, then studied her face intently. 'You're looking pale. You've overdone things today. Sit down and I'll bring them to you.'

As he walked out, she sank into the nearest chair, feeling as if the weight of the house was sitting on her shoulders. What was she going to do with a place as big as this? How could someone like her ever fit in here? Tears came into her eyes and she wished desperately that she had her sisters with her. Nell and Renie would have helped her cope.

She felt so strange today, unlike herself. And Jacob had looked at her distantly, as if he didn't recognise her any longer.

He came back into the drawing room with the two children.

'I didn't mean to break the plate,' Luke said at once.

'Break a plate? Were you larking around?' Jacob asked sternly.

'No. It just slipped out of my hand.'

Sarah giggled. 'He's so clumsy lately, he trips up over his own feet.'

'Shut up!' Her brother lunged for her and Jacob pulled him back.

Mattie felt sorry for the boy. 'You must be growing, Luke. The clumsiness will pass. And never mind the plate.' As silence fell, she looked at Jacob for guidance, because she couldn't seem to find the words to explain to them what had happened.

Jacob took a deep breath. 'Sit down, you two. We've got something to tell you.'

'Won't they mind if we sit on these lovely chairs?' Sarah stroked the brocade of an armchair, tracing out the pattern with a fingertip.

'That's what we have to tell you. It's Mattie's house now. Miss Newington's left it to her.'

They looked at him uncertainly.

'Everything here belongs to Mattie now, so it's her who says what you can do, where you can sit.'

'Does that mean we're going to live here?' Luke asked. When his father nodded, his scowl deepened. 'It's even further from the village than our house. I won't have any friends living nearby.'

'We'll only live here if your father wants to,' Mattie put in.

But Jacob shook his head. 'It's your house, it's for you to say.'

She could feel tears come into her eyes. 'Don't say that. It's ours now.'

The children looked anxiously from one to the other, sensing something was wrong.

She turned to Jacob, who was standing in front of the hearth as stiffly as a toy soldier. He was looking at her as if she was a stranger – and one who might not be friendly. The children were looking to him for guidance and the three of them seemed very much a family. It was she who was the outsider.

She couldn't bear it, so stood up. 'Let's tell Cook and Lyddie, then we'll go and look round the house.'

Sarah clapped her hands together. 'Goody.'

Even Luke brightened up.

'Wait here, you two,' Jacob said. 'You can look at things in the room, but don't touch.'

They left Sarah standing in front of a cabinet full of pieces of fine china, ladies in swirling skirts, a dog with its head on one side. Luke had gone to stare up at a big painting of a ship at sea.

Mattie shivered. So many possessions. And all hers now. It was too much. It was terrifying.

* * *

Although it was a warm day, they found Cook sitting by the fire, looking tired out. She turned towards them. 'We heard the cars leaving but no one rang for us. They didn't eat the refreshments. What are we going to do with all this food?'

'Mr Arthur was in a bad mood and walked out,' Jacob said. 'If the food won't keep, there are people in the village who're always hungry. We can send some down to them.'

'As long as it's not wasted,' Cook said comfortably. 'I can't abide waste.'

'Where's Lyddie? I . . . we have something to tell you.'

'She's just taken a tray across to Horace. She won't be a minute.'

'We'll wait till she comes back.'

'No use saying it twice,' Cook agreed. 'Take the weight off your feet. Do you want something to eat?'

But Jacob, usually a man with a hearty appetite, shook his head, and Mattie knew she'd be sick if she tried to force a mouthful down.

Who'd have thought that her being left a fortune would come between her and Jacob? How was she to stop that, bridge the gap that yawned between them? She couldn't bear the way he was looking at her. It was his pride that was hurting, she guessed, and what did pride matter?

She didn't know what she'd do about the

situation yet, but she'd have to do something. She wasn't going to lose the chance of them making a good life together. How pleased her mother would have been to see her rise in the world.

The difficulties had brought home to her how very fond she had grown of Jacob. She didn't just want a cool marriage, made for convenience. She wanted something warmer, the sort of marriage her mother and father had had, with laughter and cuddles and quiet happiness.

She'd thought he wanted the same but if the house could come between them, perhaps his feelings for her weren't as strong as she'd thought.

She shivered at that thought.

Lyddie came back across the yard, humming as she often did. She broke off as she saw them.

'You tell them, Jacob,' Mattie begged.

'All right. Come and sit down, Lyddie. We have something to tell you about the new owner.'

They both leant forward, eager to find out.

'It's Mattie.'

Both women gaped at him, then at her.

'Never!' said Cook. 'Well, I'll be blowed.'

'Ooh, you lucky thing,' Lyddie said, then clapped one hand to her mouth. 'I didn't mean to be cheeky, miss – I mean, ma'am.'

'You weren't,' Mattie said at once. 'You were just surprised. I was too. I don't know why she did it when she hardly knew me. We wanted to tell you that your jobs are safe.'

They showered her with thanks but she couldn't pretend to be happy, as they expected, not with Jacob taking it so hard, so she stood up. 'We're going to look round the house, all four of us. I've not even seen most of it.'

'Do you want me to show you where everything is?' Lyddie asked.

'Another time, you and me will go round together,' Mattie said. 'Just for the moment, it doesn't feel like mine. Why, I don't even know how many rooms there are or . . . or anything. So I just want to walk round and try to take it all in.'

Ben peered into the kitchen door at that moment. 'Do you still want us to stay here?' he asked Jacob.

'Yes. I think we'd better stay on our guard.' He turned to Mattie and added in that cooler tone of voice, 'If that's all right with you?'

'What do I know about that sort of thing? I'm relying on you to deal with it.' The words came out more sharply than she'd intended, but it hurt every time he deferred to her.

He nodded quietly, gravely, as if dealing with a stranger, then turned back to Ben. 'Same as before, then, lad. Oh, and the house has been left to Mattie. She's the new owner.'

Ben gaped at her, as the others had, then gave her a beaming smile. 'I'm happy for you, Mrs Kemble, for all of you.'

'Yes, well. We're still trying to take it in,' Jacob said.

Mattie found she was expected to lead the way. She was beginning to feel angry with Jacob now. Why was he treating her as if she'd done something wrong?

She went back into the big drawing room, to have a really good look at it, which she hadn't dared do at the reading of the will. It had an unused feel to it and she felt like an intruder, so moved quite quickly into the large dining room behind it. These were two wastefully huge rooms, to her who'd been used to smaller places, and they were full of heavy, dark furniture. Someone must have run a duster over the furniture, but there was still a dusty, stale smell to the dining room in particular.

The little sitting room, on the other hand, still had books with markers in them on the shelves, and an embroidery frame in one corner. This was where Miss Newington must have spent her time. Mattie fingered the embroidery, which was very pretty, full of brightly coloured flowers, wishing she knew how to make pictures like that.

They went on to the morning room, where the family had once eaten a meal with the old lady. Behind that they found another big room, this one with full bookshelves covering the walls. 'Look at that!' she gasped. 'All those books. It's like a library.'

Jacob went to finger the ones nearest with the touch of a lover, leaning closer to read their titles. 'She's let me borrow books but I've never been able to explore them properly.'

'I hate books,' Luke said, jamming his hands into his pockets.

Jacob swung round. 'Don't you ever let me hear you say such a thing again! Books are treasures, not just telling you stories but telling you about the world. I'm ashamed to hear a son of mine speak like that. Do you want to grow up ignorant?'

Luke hunched his shoulders, bottom lip jutting out in mute defiance.

Sarah was also trying to read the titles. 'There aren't any children's books, are there?' she asked in a disappointed voice.

'We could buy you some,' Mattie said.

'Not like the ones from school,' she pleaded. 'They're terrible. Children keep dying in them because they've been naughty. But my friend gets books from the library and she's let me read them. They're exciting and the children have adventures

339

and end up so happy. I wish real life was like that.'

'We'll only buy exciting ones for you and Luke,' Mattie promised recklessly. 'You can choose them yourself.'

'Adventure stories?' Luke asked. 'Really?'

'Lots of them.' She saw Jacob frowning and looked at him challengingly. 'We're going to celebrate our luck and I think it's good for children to read.'

'I agree, but I didn't want you thinking you had to spend your money on us.'

'That's so unkind,' she said in a choked voice and turned away to hide the tears welling in her eyes.

The children moved closer to one another, their eyes going anxiously from one adult to the other.

Mattie led the way out of the room, wiping her eyes quickly when she thought no one would notice. She led the way upstairs. 'Six bedrooms on this floor! Goodness. You can each choose one.' She realised she hadn't even asked Jacob if they'd be moving here now. His expression looked angry, but he had his lips pressed tightly together.

'If your father approves,' she said lamely.

'Any one we want?' Luke asked, his expression brightening still further.

'Once we've chosen ours,' Jacob said. 'Mattie?'

'I don't mind. You choose.' She saw him frown as he opened his mouth, and added sharply, 'And don't tell me it's my house. If we're all living here, it belongs to all of us.'

'Does that mean we're all rich now?' Sarah asked.

'No!'

Jacob's denial was so explosive they looked at him anxiously.

'It's Mattie who owns this house, not you. She's the one who's rich.'

Hurt at his continuing refusal to include her in the family, to show at least a little pleasure in their good fortune, she walked towards the bathroom. She smiled at the huge, claw-footed bath and indoor water closet, going over to touch the washbasin, beaming at the room. 'Isn't this wonderful? It'll be lovely to have a bath in here. I haven't dared before. Where I grew up, we had a tin bath in, filling it with kettles of hot water and emptying it with a jug afterwards.' She went to switch on the tap and within a few seconds, warm water was gushing out of it. They all had to put their fingers under it and for a moment even Jacob smiled naturally.

'Can I have a bath tonight?' Sarah asked.

'Of course you can. We all will,' Mattie promised rashly. 'Now, let's go and look at the next floor.'

Six more bedrooms. What on earth were they going to do with all these rooms?

Next came the attics. In one area the servants slept, but they didn't have a bathroom. She wondered if they were allowed to use the indoor bathroom for their baths, then realised that was up to her now.

She and Jacob had been up to this floor before, when they were finding clothes for Mattie, but she wanted the children to see everything. 'We can use more of those clothes in the trunks,' she said to Jacob. 'I can alter them for me and Sarah. I'm a good dressmaker. No use letting beautiful materials go to waste.'

Jacob nodded and went on to examine the abandoned furniture. 'Why they didn't mend these things, I don't know. It's so wasteful to throw them out like this.' He looked across the big, dusty space to where the children were looking at some old toys. 'I don't want my children growing up to think they can be wasteful.'

'They won't if we don't let them,' she said and won a quick nod from him at that. Relief coursed through her. It was like treading on eggshells talking to him at the moment.

When they got downstairs again, they sent the children outside to explore the gardens and Mattie turned to Jacob, seeing a closed-up expression on his face again. 'Don't.'

'Don't what?'

'Act as if this all belongs to me, not us.'

'It does belong to you.'

'But we're married.'

His voice was bitter. 'Maybe if you'd waited a few more days, you could have got a better husband for yourself than a struggling market gardener.'

She felt tears rise in her eyes and stretched out one hand towards him, but he brushed it aside.

'I'm sorry, Mattie. I don't mean to hurt you, but it's too much! I can't sort it all out in my mind. I need time to think, to get used to it. You have to give me time!'

And he left the house.

Didn't he realise it was too much for her as well? That she was having trouble coming to terms with it all, too? That she needed him beside her, helping her settle down to it?

She took refuge in the small sitting room, watching out of the window as he strode down the lane towards his own home. Then she bent her head, saw a tear drop on her skirt and another settle beside it and begin to soak in. But at the sound of footsteps, she hastily smeared the moisture away, fumbling for her handkerchief and pretending to blow her nose.

'There you are, ma'am,' Lyddie said. 'Cook

wants to know what to do about the extra food.'

'Can you help me make a list of the families who're short, then anything that's likely to go off can be given to them? We'll send Luke down to the village with a message and they can come up and fetch it themselves.'

'Mr Kemble will know best who to ask. You bein' a foreigner – excuse me for saying that – you won't know who to help.'

'He's . . . um . . . seeing to things at home, his old home I mean, so we'd better not wait for him.'

'You look tired, ma'am. I know you've been ill, so why don't you have a rest? Me and Luke can nip down and see him. He'll tell us who to give it to.'

'All right, Lyddie. I am tired, I must admit.'

'Shall I bring you a cup of tea before I go?'

'No, I'll come and fetch it myself later. I'm not thirsty.'

'All right.'

Mattie saw Lyddie and the children pass the window a few minutes later, chatting easily, strolling through the lovely evening sunshine.

She felt even more alone when they'd vanished from sight. A foreigner. An outsider. And now the richest woman in the village as well. None of the other women would dare try to be friends with her now.

People dreamt of being rich – and she had too – but she'd never imagined money and possessions could make you unhappy.

A little later Mattie tried to arrange for the family to eat their evening meal in the kitchen.

Cook was scandalised. 'You'll not do that while I'm here.'

'Why not?'

'Because you're the mistress now. It's not right for you to eat in here.'

'But I'm no different from what I was like this morning when we all ate our breakfast here together.'

Cook simply folded her arms and said firmly, 'Things have changed. You're the mistress. It's bound to be different.'

'I don't think I know how to be the mistress of a big place like this.'

Cook's outraged expression changed to sympathy. 'If I can help you in any way, ma'am, you've only to ask. I do see that it's a bit of a special case.'

'Thank you. Can you think why Miss Newington left it all to me? I've racked my brain and can't work it out.'

The stiffness came back. 'It's not my place to wonder what my employers are thinking. It's my place to get the meals. And talking of meals, what time will the master be back?'

'I don't know.' If she'd been her normal self, Mattie would have walked down to find out. She'd have enjoyed a stroll on such a lovely evening. But she felt utterly exhausted, so went back to sit in the armchair Miss Newington had used in the little sitting room. It was placed to watch the lane.

It suddenly occurred to her that the old lady had been lonely, too. Money hadn't made her happy, either.

It was so comfortable Mattie found herself drowsing, and since there was nothing she had to do, she let herself slide into sleep. Just this once she'd be lazy and . . .

She woke with a start when someone said her name and shook her shoulder gently.

Jacob was kneeling beside the chair, looking at her anxiously. 'Are you all right?'

'I was tired.'

'I keep forgetting how ill you've been. Don't overdo things.'

'I can't. I get tired too quickly.'

'Lyddie sent me to tell you she can serve our tea as soon as you like. Only she calls it dinner.'

Was that a trace of sarcasm in his voice? she wondered, but was too tired to pursue the matter. 'I'll just use the bathroom and be with you shortly.' She hesitated, then couldn't help asking, 'Are you feeling better about the house now?'

He avoided her eyes. 'I don't know what I'm feeling, and that's the truth. But you've got it, so I must do my best to get used to the idea.'

'I'll give it away if it upsets you that much. I don't want it to come between us.'

He looked at her in surprise. 'No need to do that. I told you: I'll get used to it. Just . . . give me time.'

And then what? she wondered.

When she came down, he was waiting for her in the hall. 'Let's have our dinner now. I can't remember you eating anything today. We don't want you fainting on us. And Luke's always hungry.'

Cook had fried up some of the fancy sandwiches, dipping them in beaten egg and milk, and they were delicious. There were scones and iced dainties to follow, little cakes so light they melted in your mouth with pretty designs in the icing on top. They'd been made for the funeral, were just as beautiful as those you saw in cake shops, not a twirl out of place. And Cook had opened a tin of peaches too, serving them with cream.

'It's a real feast!' Mattie said as the second course was brought in.

'I'll tell Cook you're pleased, shall I?' Lyddie said.

'Um . . . yes, please.'

Luke and his father did full justice to the meal, but Sarah was yawning over her plate and had to be reminded to eat a couple of times. Mattie still didn't have her normal appetite back, but managed to eat a few bits of this and that, aware of Jacob's eyes on the contents of her plate.

After the meal, Sarah asked, 'Do me and Luke have to clear the table and wash up?'

'No. Lyddie and Cook do that here.'

Luke beamed at that news.

'We'll find other jobs for you, son,' Jacob said. 'However much money Mattie has, you won't be idling around. The gardens here are a disgrace. You can help me get them in order.'

Luke scowled. 'Rich people don't do the gardening!'

'You . . . are not . . . rich.'

Mattie stood up. 'Come on, Sarah. Time for bed.' She blinked her eyes rapidly and managed not to let any tears fall at Jacob's continuing sharpness. She'd never cried easily, but lately she seemed near to tears quite often. It came of having been ill, she supposed, but knowing that didn't make it any easier to control her emotions.

Sarah stayed where she was. 'I don't like being on my own in that big bedroom.'

'You've been sleeping here on your own since Wednesday and you haven't complained before,' her father said sharply.

Mattie took her hand and led the way upstairs. 'Your father and I are only down the corridor, just like we were at your old home. And you've got your doll to keep you company. Just think, you'll be able to invite your friends from school to come and play with you here when it's rainy. It'll be fun having a big room like this.'

Lyddie popped her head round the door, then came in. 'Everything all right, ma'am?'

'Yes, thank you. Come on, Sarah. You need to use the bathroom before you go to bed.'

By that time the child was nearly asleep on her feet, but not too tired to marvel again at the inside toilet, which she seemed to consider the height of luxury. She didn't talk about taking a bath now, was far too tired.

Jacob and Luke came upstairs just as Sarah was settling into bed and she woke up enough to demand a goodnight kiss from her father.

Mattie led the way into Luke's bedroom and started straightening the bed.

Jacob immediately nudged his son. 'You help Mattie with your bed. I'll go and check on ours.'

The boy looked angry, muttering, 'It's women's work, making beds.'

'Who'll be sleeping here?' Jacob demanded. 'Who?'

Luke shuffled his feet. 'Me.'

'Then you shouldn't turn up your nose at

helping get your own bed ready. When something needs doing, especially when it's for you, you can't just leave it to others.'

Luke didn't say a word the whole time they were making the bed and Mattie wondered if the boy would ever accept her. She didn't want to take his mother's place, no one could do that, but she did want a place of her own in the family.

When she went into her own bedroom she found Jacob standing staring out of the window. She waited, hoping he'd not say anything else hurtful.

When he didn't speak, she said, 'I'll go to bed myself now, I think.'

'Before I join you, I'll go down and check that everything's all right for the night. I'm not expecting trouble, though. It's too soon, I think.'

She'd intended to wait for him but he was longer than she'd expected and in the end she stopped trying to stay awake. If he wanted to come up late to avoid talking about their problems, there was nothing she could do about it, especially now, when she was so bewildered and weary.

Chapter Eighteen

On the Sunday morning Bart and Stan went by the early train to Wootton Bassett, intending to walk out to the village. But it turned out Stan had been misinformed and it was too far for them to get there and back on foot.

'Is there a bus?'

'Not for two hours,' the station clerk said. 'Aren't you the two men who came here looking for someone the other week?'

'Yes.'

'Did you find them?'

'Not yet. But we've been told one of them is living in Shallerton Bassett.'

'Ah.' He chewed the side of his mouth, then said, 'There's not many buses out there on a Sunday, an' you'd have trouble getting back as well. My cousin could take you there in his cab. He doesn't usually turn out on Sundays, but he's a bit short of money just now. It'll cost you, though.'

'I'd be very grateful for a bit of help,' Stan said.

'I'll send a lad to fetch him.' The clerk put his fingers to his mouth and let out a piercing whistle. A lad came running, and was soon tearing down the street on his errand, richer by threepence.

It was another twenty minutes before a horse and cab clopped into view.

'Free with your money, aren't you?' Bart said sourly as the cab set off. 'She ent worth the time or the money, that one.'

'You're spending your time on her, too.'

'Only because I want to find out where my girls are. If I had my way, I'd give that Mattie a good beating, the ungrateful bitch.'

'Make sure you don't touch her this time.'

'What do you mean?'

'I don't want you hurting her again.'

'I keep telling you, she's one as needs keeping in order.'

'Just remember what I said. And anyway, that's her husband's business now.'

'Husband! He must be desperate to marry her.' With a snort of disgust, Bart slouched further down on the seat.

Stan said nothing else, just sat and endured the jolting, his thoughts on Mattie, as they had been for weeks now. He stared out of the cab window. Why anyone would want to live out in the middle of nowhere, he'd never understood, but he supposed someone had to farm the land and produce the food. He was glad it wasn't him, though. Give him the town any time.

But his thoughts kept coming back to Mattie. Who was this fellow she'd wed? Why had she broken her promise to marry him?

He didn't even know why he was doing this since she was wed and beyond him now, but for some reason he had to see the fellow she'd chosen instead of him and find out where he'd gone wrong. He didn't like to fail. And he was sorry he wasn't going to marry her. Very sorry indeed.

Mattie woke to find Jacob trying to creep quietly out of the bedroom. 'I'm awake.'

He paused near the door. 'Sorry. I wanted you to get a bit of a lie-in.'

She pushed herself into a sitting position, seeing the sunlight making bright lines along the edges of the curtains. 'On a lovely day like this? Anyway, I'm not one for lying in bed. I'd rather be getting on with things.'

'You've got servants to do that now.'

'I don't know how to deal with servants. Jacob, please . . . you have to help me!' Her voice broke on the words but it didn't bring him to her side.

His voice became gentler, though. 'I don't

know how to deal with servants, either. Tell them to carry on as usual. I've got to feed the hens. We'll have breakfast together in an hour or so and talk then. We might as well let the kids sleep in for a bit, just this once, though Luke has to get to church in time to sing in the choir.'

Jacob was out of the room before she could answer. She went through what he'd said in her mind. Was it her imagination or was he just a little less distant today? She didn't know him well enough yet to be sure. But she thought he was, prayed he was.

She went to the bathroom with a towel Lyddie had found for her, revelling in the luxury of not having to go outside, and having warm water run out of the taps. On an impulse she ran water into the bath until it covered the flowery pattern on the bottom, and sank into it with a sigh of pleasure. It was so lovely, she didn't want to get out, had to force herself. And pulling the plug, watching the water just drain away, delighted her. No need for a jug to empty this bath.

As she got dressed, she looked in the dressing table mirror and felt sorry she only had her old dresses to wear. Everything she had was shabby, except for the dress she'd got married in, which was too fancy for everyday wear, and the dark one she'd worn to the funeral. Even her Sunday best outfit was old-fashioned, and anyway, she'd left it behind in Swindon.

She'd seen ladies there wearing walking dresses with gored skirts, but she'd heard you needed about four yards of double-width material to make one of those. She could probably have made one for herself using one of the new paper patterns, but she couldn't have afforded to buy even the pattern on what her stepfather gave her, let alone the material.

He'd have seen no need to change the style of what she was wearing, the simple gathered skirts and blouses that she knew how to cut out and make.

Lyddie was in the kitchen, getting breakfast going.

'I'd have brought up a cup of tea, if you'd rung, ma'am.'

Mattie decided to be honest. 'I'm not used to being waited on. Anyway, I'd rather come down and get my own.'

'Don't let Cook hear you saying that. She doesn't like anyone meddling in her kitchen.' She studied her mistress anxiously. 'I hope you don't think I'm being cheeky telling you that.'

'Oh, Lyddie, I don't think you're cheeky at all. If you need to tell me something, just go ahead. You know far more about this house and how things should be done than I do. Let's have a cup of tea together and you can tell me how you usually spend the day, what tasks you do, in what order.'

'Well . . . Cook's a bit tired today so she's leaving the breakfasts to me – and what the eye doesn't see the heart doesn't grieve over, does it, so I will sit down for a few minutes. I could murder a cup of tea.'

When it was ready she sat down and explained how the house was run, what her duties were, mentioning the scrubbing woman from the village, who also did the washing every Monday.

'There's a room just for doing the laundry in?' Mattie asked in amazement.

'Oh, yes. It's out at the back. It has two big coppers to boil the water in and a good big mangle, and lines for drying inside as well as out, for when it's rainy. It's very well set up. Miss Newington was trying to make things more modern. She said there was no need for modern women to work like slaves.'

'What am I to do with myself if there's no housework for me to do and no washing either?' Mattie wondered aloud.

'Miss Newington used to write letters and go down to the village if anyone needed help there and sometimes Mrs Henty came up here to call on her. And Miss Newington used to do her accounts. She spent a lot of time on them.'

'I couldn't do the accounts to save my life,' Mattie said. 'I'm hoping Jacob will deal with that side of things.'

'Well, I heard Miss Newington say once he was good with figures, and he must have been to collect her rents, so I daresay he'll cope. I'm sure I don't know anything about accounts, either.' She drained the cup of tea with a happy sigh, then set it down and fiddled with its handle. 'Um . . . I don't know if it's convenient but this should be my day off. I usually leave about ten and come back about eight. My family lives on the other side of the village. My dad is a cowman for a farmer there.'

'Of course it's convenient. As long as Cook can manage. I'll tell her not to prepare anything fancy.' She remembered Miss Newington saying Lyddie came from a big family who had trouble making ends meet. 'And perhaps you could take some of the food that's left over to your family? We don't want it going to waste. We gave a lot away yesterday, but Cook made far too much.'

'She wanted to show them she could do things properly.' Lyddie beamed at her. 'Mum'll be that glad of the food. She says them young brothers of mine have hollow legs and they're always hungry. I'd better ask Cook if it's all right.'

Mattie realised she'd inadvertently made a decision without consulting the ruler of the kitchen and made a mental note not to do that again.

The children came clattering down the stairs and by the time she'd fed them, Jacob was back.

'We need to get ready for church,' he said as he finished a big plate of ham and eggs.

'I'd rather not go today, if you don't mind.' It might be cowardly but Mattie couldn't bear to face the people in the village yet, however friendly they might be, not until she'd got her own life and feelings sorted out. And she particularly didn't want to face Mrs Henty who would, she was sure, not be at all friendly. 'I'm feeling rather tired.'

'I'll tell people you're still recovering from the pneumonia and that yesterday tired you out, which is true. We'll have to let Ben go to church this morning because he's in the choir, best baritone in the village, but I can't see anything happening here today.'

'You think Mr Arthur's going to keep on causing trouble?'

'I'm not sure. I don't want to take risks, though. If you keep the windows and doors locked, you'll be all right inside the house. The rest of us can go to church in the dog cart.'

She sighed with relief as they all left, enjoying the prospect of having the house to herself.

It was good to walk quietly through the rooms and pick things up, open and close drawers. She would, she realised, be kept busy at first simply going through things in the various drawers and cupboards, finding out what she owned. Well, she'd enjoy that and it was good to know she'd have something to fill her time. If only her sisters were here to share her good fortune.

She went into the library and chose a book, but couldn't concentrate on it and dozed off.

She woke with a start, unable to remember where she was for a minute or two. To her amazement, the clock showed she'd been asleep for nearly an hour.

It was the sunshine pouring in through the windows that drew her outside. The gardens might be neglected but the flowers didn't know that and they were bursting into blossom everywhere. She'd always loved flowers. In the park you couldn't touch them but here they belonged to her, and she could touch them or pick them, do whatever she wanted. A thrill ran through her at that thought.

She stood on the steps outside the front door looking out for a few minutes, then was tempted down into the garden. She'd hear if anyone drove up the lane and could easily run back into the house for safety.

She wandered down a path, stopping to touch a flower here, a bush there. She could fully understand why Jacob loved growing things.

The cab slowed down and turned off the main road at a sign saying Shallerton Bassett.

'Aah!' Stan leant forward. 'Nearly there.'

'We'll have to ask where the big house is and

get the old lady to tell us where Mattie lives.' Bart scowled out at the rural scene. 'And I'm thirsty. I could murder a glass of beer.'

The cab drew to a halt a couple of hundred yards from the main road and the driver turned round to ask, 'Where do you want to go now? The sign says turn left for the village, but there's a big house up the hill there. Do you think that could be this Newington House you're looking for?'

Stan swung out of the cab, standing on the step and looking at the big house in the distance. Surely this Miss Newington would know where Mattie was?

He was about to tell the driver to go there when it occurred to him that it might be useful to find out the lie of the land first. 'You stay here. I need to stretch my legs. I'll walk up the hill and find out.'

'We could drive,' Bart protested.

'I want to have a look round first before I speak to anyone. You can stay here if you want.'

Bart scowled and heaved himself out of the cab. 'No, I'm coming with you.'

The driver slid down in the seat, tipping his hat over his eyes. 'If I'm asleep when you get back, give me a nudge. The baby kept us awake last night. It's nice here in the sun.'

The two men began to walk up the hill but Bart grumbled non-stop, so Stan poked him in the ribs. 'Shut up! Do you want to tell everyone we're coming? And you'll make less noise if you walk on the grass.'

'What does it matter if they see us coming?'

'I always like to have a look round in a new place. You can go back to the cab if you want.'

'I told you, I'm coming with you. You'll be too soft with her.'

'And you're too hard on people. This time we do it my way. I don't want you causing any trouble. You're not to hit her, mind. I mean that.'

For answer, Bart spat into the grass.

In church the sun shone in through the one stained glass window, casting jewel colours over the hymn book Jacob was holding. He watched his son singing in the choir, smiling at how angelic Luke looked – the only time the boy ever did. Standing next to Jacob, Sarah joined in the hymns and fiddled with her skirt when the sermon started.

He didn't try to get her to pay better attention, because Mr Henty's sermons were not only boring but also a puzzle. The man didn't seem able to make it clear what he was preaching about.

However, one word stood out in the clergyman's first statement.

'Today I shall talk about pride, a grievous sin and one we should all avoid. As it says in . . .'

The thought suddenly speared through Jacob: why was he so upset about Mattie inheriting the house? Pride, that was what it was. It was a man's job to support his family, but if one member of a family got given a lot of money, then it should be used for the benefit of them all – and that's what she'd wanted, expected.

The only thing getting in the way of that was Jacob's own pride.

As the rest of the minister's sermon flowed past him unheard, he remembered Mattie's face. He'd hurt her yesterday – and again this morning. He hadn't meant to but . . . No, honesty compelled him to admit to himself that he had known he was hurting her, but still hadn't been able to stop himself doing it.

For once, Mr Henty's sermon made its point. It was pride, Jacob admitted. He'd not wanted to be dependent on his wife. What man would? And yet he'd been happy to have her dependent on him, even though the thought of being a burden had upset her.

Mattie hadn't known what to do about the inheritance, had been shocked rigid. So had he. But he should have helped her more, not turned away from her like that.

And actually, it was a wonderful thing to inherit so much – wasn't it? For the first time he let himself enjoy the thought of what it'd mean for him and his children, what it'd mean for Mattie – and for any children he and she might have together. Their family would be secure, not dependent on other people's whims, not having to answer to men like Arthur Newington.

The sermon ended and Sarah had to tug him to his feet as everyone stood up for the final hymn: 'All Things Bright and Beautiful'.

He heard his child singing away tunefully beside him and found himself joining in, singing with all his heart, because things were bright and beautiful – or they would be once he'd set things right with Mattie.

He'd go straight home after the service and apologise for his surliness, his unkindness. Then they'd sit down together and make plans. It was going to be all right, he was sure of that now.

But after the service, people wanted to stop him to talk, to congratulate him, to ask where Mattie was, marvel at her inheriting the big house – and, once they found out she wasn't well, send their best wishes for her speedy recovery.

At one stage, as they stood in the churchyard, Luke tugged at his father's jacket and Jacob looked round quickly, while trying to listen to old Mrs Bentley.

'Can me and Sarah walk home now, Dad?'

'Yes, you run along. Tell Mattie I'll be back as soon as I can.'

He did his best to listen patiently to the old lady, and to the others who were waiting for him. He hid his frustration at this delay in speaking to Mattie. It didn't matter really. He'd be with her soon.

Stan saw Mattie in the garden and put out one hand to stop Bart, then set his forefinger to his lips to tell his friend to be quiet.

Bart nodded, a gloating expression on his face.

No time to deal with him now. Stan moved forward quietly, thankful for so much grass.

She seemed lost in thought as she wandered through a gate in a high wall. He hurried forward, wondering where that led to. But it was only another garden, this time one with paths made of crazy paving going round little flower beds. Everything looked a bit of a mess. You'd think rich people could look after things better than this.

To his fury, Bart spoke. 'So there you are, Mattie Willitt!'

She spun round, gasping, her face going white as chalk.

As Bart tried to surge forward, Stan grabbed hold of his arm and yanked him back, then shoved him aside as Mattie took off running. He ran after her, catching her as she was fumbling with another gate at the other side of the garden.

He put one hand across her mouth as she opened it to shout for help. He didn't want other folk there, needed to talk to her on his own. 'Keep quiet.'

Footsteps shuffled up towards him, heavy

breathing that he'd recognise anywhere. 'Stay back, Bart.'

'Don't let her go.'

'Leave this to me.' He looked down at Mattie, so small and dainty in between his outstretched arms. She looked terrified. 'I'm not going to hurt you,' he said, upset when she flinched as he moved one arm slightly.

She glanced to his side at her stepfather. 'I'm not Mattie Willitt. I'm married now. My husband will be back from church soon. If you touch me, he'll not be pleased.'

Bart gave his wheezing laugh. 'I'm not frightened of anyone.' He raised his clenched fists. 'Not as long as I've got these.'

'My husband's as big as you,' she said, but she shrank back from Bart.

Annoyed, Stan gave his friend a shove. 'Keep back. You've no call to threaten her like that.'

'No call! After what she's done to me?'

Stan could feel anger rising in him. 'Stay there and shut up, or I'll damned well shut you up, Bart Fuller.'

For a moment the two men eyed one another, but Bart's eyes fell first and he let his fists drop.

Stan turned back to Mattie, noticing how thin and frail she looked. 'What's happened to you? You don't look at all well. Isn't he treating you decently?'

'I've had pneumonia. I nearly died.'

'Serves you bloody right,' Bart said, saw his friend's annoyed glance and grunted.

'What did you come here for?' she asked.

Her voice wobbled as she spoke. Stan frowned, remembering rumours of how badly Bart had once beaten her. 'You've no need to be afraid of me. I'm not going to hurt you.'

'Then why are you here?'

'I want to find out . . .' He looked sideways. 'Go for a walk round the garden, Bart. I want to talk to her on my own.'

'But I—'

'You can ask her afterwards.'

After a moment's hesitation, Bart walked away. 'Five minutes,' he called as he left the walled garden.

'There's a bench over there. Come and sit down.' When she didn't move, Stan took her arm and pulled her across to it.

'What did you come here for?' she repeated.

'To ask you why.'

She didn't seem to understand.

'We were engaged, we'd got the banns being called. Why did you go back on your word like that, run away?'

'I never wanted to marry you.'

Silence, then he couldn't help asking, 'Why not? I'd have treated you well and I'm a good provider. You wouldn't have wasted the money I earned like my wife did, so we'd have got along all right. I had it all worked out.'

'I just . . . didn't want to marry you.'

'Why didn't you say so when you were asked, then? Why lead me on?'

'I wasn't asked, I was told. And I was too frightened of him to say no.'

Stan cursed himself. 'I should have done the asking myself, but he said he knew how to deal with you.'

'Threats. That's how he dealt with us. Threats and bullying and beatings. And I didn't like being sold to you. He boasted that you'd paid money for me.'

'But that was only to make things easier for you, to stop him making trouble. You know what an old miser he is.'

'I can't believe you came all this way to ask me that. Did you know I was married?'

He nodded.

'How did you find me, anyway?'

'Fanny Breedon saw you at the station the day you got married. She heard the name of the old lady who owns this house and that's how I found you. I was coming to ask the old lady where you were, didn't know you were staying here.'

Bart wandered up and down the path outside the walled garden, angry at his friend for being so soft with her. He pulled his watch out and looked at it. Two more minutes to go. He wasn't giving Stan longer, because someone might come and Bart wanted uninterrupted time with Mattie to find out where her sisters were. He'd do what he had to in order to find out, thump her if necessary, whatever Stan said.

As he was walking along the path a little girl came skipping round the corner and bumped into him. She let out a little yelp of shock.

'Watch where you're going, you stupid brat.' He gave her a quick clout over the ear.

She cried out and he shook her hard. 'Shut up, you!'

The gate was flung open and Mattie ran out. 'Sarah!'

He knew then how to get the information out of her. He scooped up the little girl in his arms. 'Stay back, Mattie, or she gets hurt.'

Luke's shoelace had broken and it took him a while to knot the ends together well enough to walk. His sister wasn't in sight, but he didn't feel like hurrying, so strolled on in the sunshine, looking at the big house.

His dad wasn't happy about Mattie inheriting it, he could tell. And Luke wasn't sure he wanted to live there, either. You didn't dare move for fear of breaking something, and it was too far from all his friends. But that bathroom was smashing. He was going to have a bath there tonight. Wait till he showed the house to his pals!

He heard Sarah give a yell and it sounded as if she'd hurt herself, so he started running. But when he got to the corner he saw her struggling against a brute of a man.

He hesitated, but knew he'd have no chance against a fellow like that, so turned and ran back the way he'd come, praying that his dad was on his way home.

Stan pulled Mattie back and stepped forward. 'Let the little girl go, Bart.'

'Not till Mattie's told me what I want to know. If she doesn't, I'll hurt the kid.'

The child started weeping loudly and he shook her again. 'Will you . . . shut up!'

He saw Stan move towards him and anger took over, as it did sometimes. 'You keep out of this or I will hurt her. It's between me and Mattie, this is.'

Stan stopped and stood there.

'What do you want to know?' Mattie asked.

'Where are they?'

'Who?'

'Your sisters, who else would I mean?'

'I don't know where they are.'

'I don't believe you.' He punched the girl's arm just to show he meant business.

Mattie took a hasty step forward. 'I don't know, honest I don't. They ran away but they didn't tell me where.'

'They'd not have run away if you'd not put it into their minds. Where did you tell them to go?' He shook the child hard.

'It wasn't up to me. Nell was going to marry Cliff and they were going wherever he could find a job. He knew better than to stay in Swindon with you around.'

'And Renie?'

'She went with them.'

'Didn't they want you?' he jeered. 'I don't blame them. You're a contrary bitch, a troublemaker, and I can't see why any fellow would want to marry you. But you'll not fool me. I know you're lying. You'd never have let them two get out of touch. You've been like a mother to them. Tell me what I want to know or this one gets hurt!'

'I can't. I don't know. Honest I don't.'

He tightened his grip on the girl, the anger boiling up in his head, clouding his vision.

Chapter Nineteen

Luke sobbed in relief as he saw his father down the lane. 'Dad, come quick. There's a big horrible man. He's got hold of our Sarah an' he's hurting her. There's another man got hold of Mattie.'

'What?'

'We have to get help, Dad. There's two of them and they're really big.'

'There isn't time. You pick up some stones and get ready to throw them. Don't let fly till you're sure of hitting your target. I'm not leaving Mattie and Sarah in some brute's power.'

They started running up the hill.

'Stay on the grass,' Jacob whispered. 'Don't make a noise. We want to take them by surprise. Where are they?'

'Just outside that garden with the wall round it.'

They got to the corner of the wall and Jacob held up one hand. He peeped round and saw Sarah in a man's grip. She was crying. Mattie was standing beside another man, looking terrified.

As he started creeping forward the man beside Mattie caught sight of him.

Jacob stopped dead, expecting the fellow holding her to yell a warning, but he didn't. Instead he turned back to the man holding Sarah and said, 'Let the little girl go, Bart. You shouldn't hurt a child.'

'Not till Mattie's told me—'

Jacob took this as a sign that for some strange reason the man holding Mattie was on his side and covered the last two yards in a run. He dragged the brute holding his daughter backwards by the collar.

Letting out a yelp of surprise, the man let go of Sarah but made a quick recovery and turned on his attacker.

The other fellow pulled Mattie back, not letting go of her, and that distracted Jacob for a minute, which let the brute get a punch in that he only half-avoided.

For the next couple of minutes it was all Jacob could do to hold his own as his opponent tried every dirty trick he could think of to get the better of him.

* * *

'He's a good fighter, Bart is,' Stan said. 'You have to give him that. No, Mattie, stay back and look after the little girl. You'll get hurt if you try to come between them.'

He let go of her and she put her arms round Sarah. 'Can't you stop him, Stan? What good does fighting ever do?'

'You'll not stop Bart now. He's in one of his rages. Anyway, I like to see a good fight.'

'You're as bad as my stepfather.'

'No, I'm damned well not!' But he continued to watch the fight and she didn't dare try to intervene, just held Sarah close.

From the corner of the garden, Luke watched in horror as the horrible man punched his dad, tried to kick his shins and then just missed gouging his eye. He wanted to help but wasn't stupid enough to get close. He hefted a stone in his hand, waiting for the opportunity. He was a good shot, best cricketer in the village. He had to make this count first time, he knew.

When the two men drew slightly apart to catch their breath, it was the perfect opportunity. Luke raised his arm and let fly with a smooth stone. The years of ball games paid off and the stone flew straight and true to hit the stranger on the temple.

He dropped to the ground without even a groan. For a moment Luke's father stood panting, wiping the sweat from his eyes with the one forearm, keeping an eye on the man on the ground as if expecting an attack from him.

But the stranger didn't move.

A new fear clutched Luke's belly. He hadn't killed the man, had he?

The man next to Mattie raised his hands in a gesture of non-aggression as Jacob turned towards him. Jacob watched him carefully, not trusting him an inch. To his relief Mattie seized her opportunity to get further away, pulling Sarah with her.

Then everyone waited, watching one another warily.

'I didn't come here to fight,' Stan said. 'I've found out what I wanted to know.' He thrust his hands deep into his pockets, watching Jacob warily.

'What were you doing here? What did you want to find out?'

'I wanted to ask Mattie something. I've asked her now. I told Bart not to attack anyone, but he sees red sometimes. Still, you were all right. You know how to handle yourself. Good fight, that. There's not many can hold their own against him.'

As Bart stirred and groaned, Luke came up to join them with a big garden fork in his hand. He jerked this towards Stan. 'If you touch my dad, I'll stab you.'

'Good lad! Always stick up for your own. But I'm not going to touch him. I've not touched anyone.'

Bart sat up warily, looking round, groaned and felt his temple, then got slowly to his feet, swaying.

Stan looked towards the house. 'I'm surprised the old lady hasn't come out to see what the trouble is.'

'She's dead,' Luke said. 'It's Mattie's house now.'

At this news Bart swung round. 'What do you mean, "It's Mattie's house"?'

'Miss Newington left it to her in the will. Mattie's rich now and we all live here.'

'I don't believe you.' Bart wiped away the blood that was streaming from a cut on his temple with a crumpled pocket handkerchief, but made no effort to attack anyone again.

'It's true.' Jacob gave Mattie a quick hug and kept her by his side, still keeping an eye on the two intruders.

Stan began to laugh suddenly. 'You've missed out there, Bart. You'd have had more than enough money for your old age if you'd not attacked your Mattie's husband.' He looked at her. 'I'd have took you without the money. Remember that.'

'I wed her before we knew she'd inherited,' Jacob said.

The two men eyed one another, the hostility between them clear to everyone else.

Bart clapped one hand to his chest, groaning. 'Bloody pain's come back.' He scowled at Mattie. 'I don't believe you about Renie and Nell. You must know where they are. Tell me!'

'I don't know. I swear it.'

'Liar! But I'll find them, see if I don't.'

'Even Cliff's family don't know where they've gone. We planned it that way to keep them safe.' She didn't add 'from you', but it was understood by all present.

After one more scowl in her direction, he started stumbling down the hill.

Stan followed him, turning after a few steps to look back at Mattie, and to her surprise what she saw in his face was longing and sadness.

She didn't speak, though, and none of them moved until the two men had disappeared from sight.

'Follow them and see where they go,' Jacob ordered his son. 'Don't let them see you, though.'

'Stan won't hurt him,' Mattie said. 'He came to see me, not to thump anyone.'

'What did he want to see you for?'

'He cares about me,' she said, unable to hide

her surprise. 'I never realised, thought he just wanted a wife for the convenience.'

'Perhaps you should have married him.'

She shuddered. 'I never could. He's too much like my stepfather.'

'They look alike, could have been father and son.' Jacob bent down to his daughter. 'You're not hurt, are you, Sarah?'

'Only a bit. I'm glad you punched that man, Dad, and I'm glad Luke hit him with a stone.'

'We should have got someone to keep an eye on the house while we were at church,' Jacob said, 'and I would have if I'd known you'd be silly enough to go outside.'

'I'm sorry. I didn't mean to cause trouble.'

'That's not what upsets me. It's the thought of you being in danger that I can't bear.'

Those words made her feel warm inside.

By the time they got into the house, Luke was running up the drive again.

Jacob stopped at the front door. 'Well?'

'They had a cab waiting. They got into it and drove away.'

'Come inside, then. Cook and Horace will be back soon. They wanted to have a cup of tea with her friend after church.'

Jacob felt a bit shy as he turned into the house. He still had to make his peace with Mattie, wasn't sure how to begin.

She'd hardly said a word to him. He looked at her and caught her staring at him. He couldn't do this in front of his children. 'We'll talk later,' he said. 'You're sure you're all right?'

She nodded, but still looked wary.

The hardest thing about having children around was a husband and wife finding time to be alone together and talk, he thought, especially hard when you were newly wed. But he wasn't going to sleep until they'd sorted this out, till he'd apologised. He owed Mattie a big apology for his churlishness, for his false pride.

They went into the kitchen to wash the cuts. Cook came back in the dog cart a short time later, exclaimed in horror at the sight of her bruised and battered master, and took charge.

She put arnica on the bruises, washed the cuts with soft rags and as Mattie saw how good she was and how much she was enjoying looking after him, she stepped back and didn't try to help.

When Cook had finished, she sent them out of her kitchen, telling them she'd bring a tea tray to the small sitting room.

'Let Luke stay with you and bring that,' Jacob said. 'You've enough to do.'

She looked fondly at the two children and nodded. 'We've not had our luncheon either. I'll feed them in here, shall I? We'll bring yours into the morning room, sir.'

'I never realised servants could order their masters around,' Mattie whispered as they went to the sitting room.

Jacob caught her hand, wincing as her fingers clung to his and inadvertently hurt his bruised knuckles.

She raised his hand to her lips and kissed it. 'Thank you for protecting us.'

'I'd a hard job with that stepfather of yours. You were right. He does fight dirty. Come and sit on the sofa with me.'

When they were seated he took her hand again. 'I got to thinking in church that I was being a fool. It was pride, Mattie, just pride that made me treat you like that. A man likes to provide for his family, only you'll be doing the providing now.'

'But I still need you. I can't possibly manage on my own. I don't know what to do with all this.' She gestured round her.

'I need you too. But not for the money, because I want you to be my wife . . . and properly. I love you, Mattie.'

She stared at him, her heart suddenly beating faster at the warm look in his eyes. 'Oh, Jacob, do you really mean that?'

'Of course I do. I'd not say it else.'

'And I love you, too.'

His smile lit up his face. He glanced over his shoulder towards the door and gave her a rueful look. 'I hardly dare kiss you in case Cook comes in and tells us off.'

She chuckled, relaxing even more, feeling happiness flood through her. 'It'd be worth a telling-off.'

His voice had thickened as he pulled her to him. 'Yes. It would.'

He kissed her gently, or at least he tried to. But the kiss didn't stay gentle, because it was Mattie and he'd been wanting her in his arms for days. And she was willing, offering her lips, clinging to him, kissing him back.

Some of the pins fell out of her hair and with a soft murmur of approval he pulled the rest out. 'Lovely hair you have, lovely skin too.'

It was the sound of giggling that pulled them out of the embrace. He turned in embarrassment to see Luke and Sarah standing at the door watching them.

Mattie flushed scarlet and buried her face in Jacob's chest.

He looked at his son first, frightened that the boy would resent his feelings for Mattie.

But Luke smiled at him and said, 'Tom told me how you'd be acting if you loved one another, kissing and all that, but I didn't think you did love one another. I don't mind you getting married again if you really love one another, though I'm never going to get married because you'll not catch me kissing a girl like that.' He shuddered eloquently.

Jacob didn't make the mistake of telling the boy off for his cheek, but said gravely, as one man to another, 'I do love her dearly, son, and I hope you will too when you get to know her.'

Luke looked at Mattie and she held her breath, desperate to win the approval of both Jacob's children. He shrugged. 'I don't mind. She's nice to Sarah and she sets a good table. I've not been hungry once since she got better.'

Jacob's voice only shook a little with amusement as he said, 'Good reasons for me to marry her, eh?' He squeezed Mattie's hand and exchanged smiles with her, then turned his attention to his daughter. 'Are you happy about Mattie being part of our family, Sarah?'

She beamed at them both. 'Oh, yes. She's nice. And she's pretty too.' She ran forward suddenly and thrust herself between them on the sofa, trying to cuddle them both at once.

Jacob looked over his daughter's head at Luke and gestured to him to join the three of them. And after a moment's hesitation Luke did that, squeezing into a corner of the sofa next to his father and smiling at them both.

'That's what I like to see,' Cook said from the

doorway. 'Families who love one another. Life's better when you've got a bit of love to help it along. Now, who's coming to help me carry the food in?'

As Jacob and Luke followed her to the kitchen, Mattie gave up the attempt to pin back her hair and let it fall to her shoulders. She was filled with joy, so much joy it felt to be sparkling all through her.

And even though she didn't know where her sisters were, she was sure now that they'd got away from Bart and that pleased her greatly. One day she'd find them again. She had to believe that.

And surely with a gentle man like Cliff, Nell and Renie would make a better life for themselves . . . just as she would with Jacob. Oh, but it was a pity they couldn't come and share in her good fortune. Maybe one day she'd be able to help them.

It was Luke who brought her out of her momentary trance. 'Come on, Mattie. I'm hungry. Aren't you?'

'You're always hungry,' Sarah said, beaming at everyone.

Mattie nodded and took her place at the table with her family, feeling as if her heart would burst with joy.

If you enjoyed *Cherry Tree Lane*
look out for *Elm Tree Road*,
the next book in the Wiltshire Girls series.